"I've had enough of playing detective for one day."

A warning flickered in the back of Sam's mind not to waste time. But then he looked into the distress darkening Brett's eyes and the warning faded. "What would you prefer to do?"

"I'd like to put on some soothing music and relax in a hot tub full of bubbles."

"Sounds good so far." Sam smiled. "And afterward?"

She returned his smile. "Afterward I'd like to go somewhere candlelit and romantic for dinner. I'd like to pretend that the police aren't hunting me and some crazy person isn't trying to kill me. And—" She lowered her gaze.

The light filling the car softened to a warm glow as Sam let his fingers dance along her neck and jaw. He lifted her face to his. "And?"

"I'd like to spend the night with you."

Dear Reader,

The word *angel* conjures up chubby cherubs or wizened old specters, not men who are virile and muscular and sinfully sexy. But you're about to enter the Denver Branch of Avenging Angels and meet some of the sexiest angels this side of heaven!

Whenever there's injustice, the Avenging Angels are on the case.

Margaret St. George brings you the first irresistible angel in *The Renegade*. Sam's a rule-breaker, real rough-and-tumble with the bad guys but oh-so-tender with the ladies!

I know you'll love Sam—and all the Avenging Angels coming your way now through May. Don't miss any of this superspecial quartet!

Regards,

Debra Matteucci
Senior Editor & Editorial Coordinator
Harlequin Books
300 East 42nd Street
New York, NY 10017

The Renegade
Margaret St. George

Harlequin Books

TORONTO • NEW YORK • LONDON
AMSTERDAM • PARIS • SYDNEY • HAMBURG
STOCKHOLM • ATHENS • TOKYO • MILAN
MADRID • WARSAW • BUDAPEST • AUCKLAND

ISBN 0-373-22358-7

THE RENEGADE

Copyright © 1996 by Margaret St. George

Printed in U.S.A.

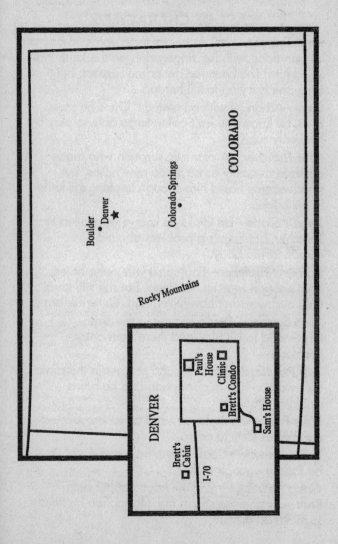

CAST OF CHARACTERS

Brett Thatcher—When her ex turns up dead on her kitchen floor, with her fingerprints on the knife that killed him, she becomes the prime suspect. But someone is trying to kill her too.

Sam—An angel with an attitude. Once he meets Brett, he knows he isn't going to be able to play by heavenly rules.

Paul Thatcher—A cosmetic surgeon who made enemies as easily as he made new noses. But which enemy hated him enough to plunge a knife in his back?

Sheriff Stone—He thinks he knows who killed Paul Thatcher, but there's a problem about a disappearing body.

Barbara Thatcher—Paul's first wife, who hates Brett enough to want her dead. But she still loves Paul and wouldn't have killed him. Or would she?

Alan Barkley—Paul's partner in the clinic threatened to kill him, and there's a money problem.

Bob Pritchard—Paul's second partner in the clinic also wanted him to disappear, and he has a drinking problem.

Billie Place—Paul's lover...and an embezzler—a dangerous lady to cross.

Karl Slivowitz—Could this unhappy client of Paul's be furious enough to kill?

Greta Rawlings—Will the housekeeper help Brett—or give the sheriff the information he needs to make an arrest?

Chapter One

"Well, damn!"

Grinding her teeth, Brett Thatcher clenched the steering wheel and hoped she didn't smack into a snowdrift before her windshield wipers could clear the mud and slush thrown up by the speeding car that zoomed past her. The driver had to be crazy to race like a maniac through one of the worst blizzards ever. Even in good weather, the road was narrow and twisting.

Squinting through the thickly falling snow, she patted the dashboard and muttered encouragement to her car. "You can do it. Don't quit on me now." The Buick was so old it no longer qualified as a vehicle; it had become an artifact. If her ex-husband, Paul, ever paid her the money he owed her, Brett promised herself a new car first thing.

Clouds of worrisome, oily smoke leaked from the engine compartment, black against the night and the blizzard. Anxious and tense, she wiped condensation off the windshield. She should have checked the weather report before she left her condo in Denver. She knew better than to trust the combination of mountain roads and November weather.

Drifts crowded the road, and shadowy firs and pines. Snow filled the ruts behind her almost as swiftly as her threadbare tires created them. "Finally!" A flood of relief eased the tightness in her shoulders as she spied the cabin looming out of a snowy curtain veiling the end of the driveway. Another thing she would do if she ever got her hands on some money was pave this lousy road.

She had almost reached the cabin when the Buick made a grinding ker-chunk sound and died. The headlights flickered once, then blinked out. Brett sighed and peered at the swirling flakes. It could have been worse. At least she could see the cabin through the darkness and flying snow.

The cabin was five miles off the highway. Aside from the car that had almost run her into a snowbank, Brett hadn't seen another set of headlights since passing through the town of Silverthorne. If the Buick had conked out earlier, she would have been stuck in the middle of nowhere with little hope for any assistance. And this was no night to be stranded, not with the temperature sinking well below zero and blowing snow cutting visibility to a few feet. Fortunately, she'd made it almost to the cabin's porch. By straining, she could glimpse the squat lines of log and glass.

Grabbing a suitcase and one of the sacks of groceries, Brett plowed toward the porch, fighting deep drifts and gusts of frigid wind that threatened to blow her off her feet.

The exertion and the altitude left her panting for breath by the time she struggled up the steps and found the key hidden over the door sill. At first the key stuck, then she discovered she didn't need it. The door was unlocked.

When Brett had phoned Greta Rawlings and asked her to give the cabin a good cleaning and turn up the thermostat, she hadn't thought it necessary to remind Mrs. Rawlings to lock the door on her way out. Apparently she should have.

Reaching inside, Brett flipped a switch and silently cheered as the porch light winked on behind her, throwing a bright beam against the storm. A second switch illuminated a table lamp beside a wing chair that faced a large rock fireplace.

Her gaze fastened gratefully on the wood stacked in the bin beside the hearth. Embers still glowed in the fireplace, and she guessed Mrs. Rawlings had made a fire earlier, but there was plenty of wood left. And more stacked on the porch.

Before bringing in the rest of her things, she rebuilt the fire, not going outside again until she was certain the flames had taken hold and were crackling cheerily.

It took three trips to the car to fetch her luggage and the rest of the groceries she had bought in Silverthorne. She set the sacks on the countertop that separated a small galley kitchen from the living room, smiling at the lime green Formica that had been popular in the early sixties. That was something else she would fix when Paul paid her the money he owed her. If he ever did. A year after calling it quits, they were still fighting about the settlement, using attorneys as weapons.

Brett warmed her hands before the fire, then inspected the cabin with a smile. She had always loved the knotty pine walls and ceiling, the rustic decor. Initially, she had considered recovering the chintz sofa and chairs, then decided the lived-in look was part of the cabin's homey charm.

That homey comfort aside, right now she was tired and tense, and her stomach rumbled. Ordinarily the drive up from Denver took little more than an hour, but today it had taken almost three hours. And she hadn't eaten since breakfast.

After inspecting the bedrooms, Brett chose the small room next to the bathroom, bypassing the large room she had shared with Paul on ski weekends. It was nice of Mrs. Rawlings to turn down the spread in the master bedroom, but there were too many memories in that room, most of them unpleasant. The marriage had been a disaster almost from the start. Though there had to have been a reason Brett had stuck with it for five years, she couldn't recall what it was. Pride, a refusal to admit a mistake, lack of confidence . . . something.

Brett frowned. When would she stop resenting Paul and rehashing the past? When would it finally be over? Paul Thatcher had been the worst thing that had happened to her. Before she found the strength to file for divorce, he had stolen her self-esteem, undermined her confidence, and made her dependent. Every time she thought of him now, anger and frustration pumped through her body.

"Stop it." After shaking her head, Brett stripped off her sweater and snow-wet jeans, then walked into the bathroom, washed her face and brushed her hair into a loose ponytail. She returned to the bedroom and donned an old flannel nightgown, her comfort nightgown, and a pair of winter slippers.

Thinking ahead to dinner, she returned to the fireplace in the living room and examined the lacy frost patterns decorating the windowpanes. Snow piled on the sills.

Suddenly, she was glad she had come. It didn't matter that the Buick was dead in a snowdrift. She had enough groceries to last several days, the air smelled like pine, and when the snow stopped, the scenery would be breathtaking. If she was marooned for a few days, so what? That's exactly what she wanted. Privacy, some time alone to think about the future, some time to work on her manuscript and decide if the project was worth finishing. She was snug and dry, dinner was only a few minutes away, and she had interesting books to read: *How to Sell Your Manuscript* and *Pediatrics, An Overview*.

Whistling under her breath, she picked up a sack of groceries and carried it around the counter. She would treat herself to shrimp lo mein and, afterward, the sinfully rich cheesecake she'd purchased at a nearly deserted Silverthorne City Market.

It had been more than a year since she had visited the cabin, but she remembered the kitchen light switch was at the end of the divider. Flipping the switch with her hip, she walked around the end of the counter, then tripped over something and fell forward against the refrigerator door, almost dropping the sack of groceries.

She did drop the groceries when she saw what she had tripped over. Legs. A man's legs.

Choking on a scream, Brett flattened herself against the refrigerator and stared down in horror.

A man was lying facedown on her kitchen floor. The handle of a butcher knife protruded from the middle of his back.

He was very dead.

WITH HER HEART SLAMMING in her chest and hardly able to breathe, Brett finally made herself step forward, kneel, then place shaking fingertips beneath the man's ear. As a former nurse, she recognized a dead person when she saw one, but she had to make sure.

This close to the body, she couldn't avoid the obvious and larger horror. The dead man in her kitchen was her ex-husband, Paul Thatcher.

"Oh, my God!"

Rocking back on her heels, not taking her eyes off Paul's still profile, Brett frantically groped behind her, found the potato chips and ripped open the bag. She pushed a handful of chips into her mouth, hoping the noise of crunching would dim the sound of her racing pulse and crashing heartbeat.

Good Lord. Paul was dead. Her shocked mind couldn't move past that thought. Why he was here, or how he had gotten here, were questions that didn't yet occur to her. All she could think about was that Paul was dead.

Toward the end of their marriage Brett had resented him, disliked him intensely. But she had never wished him dead; that kind of thinking wasn't in her nature. And it wasn't in her nature to feel relieved that her problems with Paul were now over. She stared down at him and felt . . . nothing.

Because it upset her that Paul's death didn't touch her more deeply, Brett compulsively ate another handful of potato chips.

The terrible truth was, it didn't surprise her that someone had knifed Paul in the back, not really. The bigger surprise was that it hadn't happened years ago. In fact, Paul had made jokes about the number of his enemies, as if making enemies were something to boast about.

Trembling, still in shock, Brett stood slowly and backed out of the kitchen, then dashed for the telephone. She frantically dialed 911, listened for a minute, then swore. The phone was dead.

Anxious, she shoved her hand into the potato chip bag. Some women cried when they were nervous, frightened or unsure. Brett ate. She swallowed another handful of potato chips, her mind racing. Okay, the blizzard had knocked out the phone lines. Her car was dead. She was five miles from what was sure to be a deserted highway. But there had to be something she could do.

Throwing aside the bag of chips, feeling sick inside, she jerked a parka over her nightgown, pulled on a pair of old boots, ran out into the storm, and slid behind the wheel of the Buick. After twenty minutes, she gave up. The Buick wasn't going to budge. She smacked the steering wheel with her fist, then returned to the cabin, her teeth chattering.

Shaking with cold and shock, hardly daring to glance toward the kitchen, she extended her hands to the fireplace and tried to think, oblivious to the snow caking the hem of her nightgown.

"What am I going to do?" Panic nibbled the edges of her mind, and a shudder constricted her body.

All the time she had been building the fire, carrying in groceries, changing her clothes, and thinking uncharitable thoughts about Paul, he had been lying dead in her kitchen. It was impossible, unbelievable.

Paul was dead. Murdered.

It occurred to her that she could conceivably be stuck in this cabin—for days—with Paul's dead body. Horror widened her dark eyes.

She didn't have to look into the kitchen to see him. Shock kept his image right before her eyes.

Paul lay partly on his stomach, partly on his side, stretched parallel to the countertop. The handle of the knife stuck out of his back as if the killer had intended to pin Paul's cashmere overcoat to his body.

Death had relaxed his features into the classically handsome lines that had first attracted Brett six years ago. His snow-damp hair had dried in the tangle of dark curls that she had once liked to touch. In fact, he looked almost as if he were asleep, dreaming of something that surprised him. But he wasn't merely sleeping.

The thought of stepping over and around her ex-husband's body in order to make herself something to eat was horrifying. Impossible. But eventually she'd have to eat. Feeling sick to her stomach, she rubbed her forehead. What a mess. She couldn't stay here with a dead body... but she couldn't leave, either.

Eyes brimming with tears, Brett turned toward the windows. The storm showed no signs of diminishing.

Suddenly she wondered if Paul's killer might still be out there. Maybe watching her. Galvanized by the thought, her heart pounding, she raced to lock the front door. Then she drew a deep, deep breath, edged around Paul's body, not looking at it, and checked the lock on the back door off the kitchen. Returning to the living room, she jerked the drapes shut.

"What to do... what to do."

Wringing her hands, she turned in a helpless circle in the center of the living room. A few minutes might have passed, or an hour. Brett had no idea how much time elapsed before she reached the reluctant conclusion that if she couldn't leave, Paul Thatcher had to leave. She could not face the possibility of being marooned for several days with her ex-husband's dead body in the kitchen. That scenario was too horrifying.

"But... move him? I can't, I can't," Brett groaned. About three times a year she wanted a cigarette like a drowning swimmer wanted air. If there had been a cigarette in the cabin now, she would have fallen off a five-year wagon and would have smoked it down to the filter. Instead, she ate another handful of potato chips and paced in front of the fireplace, thinking about moving Paul's body. The longer she thought about it, the more she concluded that, as repugnant as the idea was, there was no reasonable alternative. After all, it might be several days before she was able to contact anyone.

Gathering her courage, Brett walked into the kitchen, moving like an automaton. She gripped her shaking hands together and focused on a spot to the side of Paul's body. "Look, I'm...I'm sorry. But I don't know what else to do."

He couldn't hear her, of course. Paul was beyond caring what happened now. She promised herself this, but it didn't help much. And she couldn't summon the professionalism that had helped her get through upsetting situations when she was a nurse in a large hospital. This was Paul, someone she had lived with, someone she had once, a long time ago, cared about.

The idea of moving him appalled her; she couldn't picture herself doing it. But the truth was she would rather freeze outside than share the warm cabin with a dead body. Wiping at constant tears, Brett fetched a pillow from the bedroom and gently placed it beneath Paul's head. Crying so hard that she could scarcely see, she opened the door to the back porch, then, loathing every second, shaking hard, she dragged him outside.

"Oh, Paul. Damn it, Paul. Why did you let this happen to you? Why couldn't you have been—I don't know—different!"

Sweating and exhausted, she wiped her forehead and choked back a fresh onslaught of emotional weeping. No matter what had occurred between them, Paul didn't deserve to be murdered. No one did. What was he doing here, anyway? Why had he come to the cabin? Where was his Cadillac? And who had done this terrible thing?

Brett dashed the tears from her eyes and wished she were strong enough to lift him on top of the picnic table. She couldn't just leave him exposed to the blowing snow. Weeping again with frustration and upset, she fetched a coverlet they had snuggled under before things started to go sour. She covered him completely and gingerly tucked the edges around his body, trying not to look at the knife sticking out of his back. She thought she ought to say something, a prayer or a farewell or...something. But they had said too much already.

"Help will come soon," she said finally. She fervently hoped this was true. She felt a guilty reluctance to leave

him, and another minute passed before she let herself hurry
back to the warmth inside the cabin.

Amazingly, there were only a few drops of blood on the
kitchen floor. But before she finished wiping them, she
rushed to the bathroom and was sick. Finally, fatigued and
wiping at tears that she couldn't seem to stop, she put away
the groceries, trying not to step on the spot where Paul had
been sprawled. Knowing she needed to fortify herself, she
considered fixing something to eat other than the chips she
continued to grab by the handful. Opening the refrigerator, she stared unseeing at a bottle of champagne Mrs.
Rawlings had left for her.

Suddenly just the thought of food made her stomach
heave. With a grimace, she shoved the bag of chips into a
cabinet.

Instead of trying to cook, she brewed a pot of coffee, not
the kind that Paul had liked, and sat in front of the fireplace, remembering their marriage. She had known, almost from the honeymoon, that she'd made a mistake. She
wondered now if Paul had known it, too. Or had the realization arrived more slowly for him?

Toward dawn her thoughts shifted and she speculated
uneasily about who might have killed Paul. Unfortunately, he had made enemies as readily as he had made new
noses and new faces. Even his partners at the clinic disliked him. And there was Barbara, his first wife. Plus, Brett
knew of at least two enraged clients who had threatened
him. With so many enemies, there were undoubtedly others that she didn't know about.

It didn't occur to Brett that some people might consider
her Paul's number-one enemy.

DBAA, THE DENVER BRANCH of Avenging Angels, was
located on Logan Street, not far from the mansion occu-

pied by Colorado's governor. High-rise apartments and
condos gradually were replacing the single-family Victori-
ans that had graced the street for nearly a century.

The trees were coming down, too, which Samuel thought
was a shame. He liked trees, even in winter when the bare
branches lifted naked arms to the sky. First Dutch elm disease had brought down the canopy shading Logan Street;
now the old cottonwoods were giving way to tall structures
of concrete and steel.

Eventually, the charming old two-story that housed
DBAA would fall to progress. That was the way of the
mortal world. Change. A bulldozer would come, then a
soaring condominium complex, and the Avenging Angels
would have to find new headquarters. Thinking about it
saddened him.

No one was in the reception area, so he went through a
small galley kitchen to the main room, stopping to pour a
cup of coffee first. The ceiling of the main room was open
to the rafters high above, overlooked by a balcony leading
from the upstairs offices. The windows along the north wall
faced the side of the condominium next door.

Sam walked toward the French doors opening into a
small garden at the back of the building and stood gazing
outside for a moment before he nodded to Dashiell and
considered bumming a cigarette. It was that kind of morning.

"Is Angelo busy?" he asked, glancing toward the balcony and Angelo's office. The smoke from Dash's cigarette, a Camel, curled up from his mouth and drifted over
the brim of his hat. Sam smoked cigarettes on occasion, but
he didn't really like them. He preferred a pipe.

All of the Avenging Angels had picked up a mortal vice
or two, Sam thought. Working with mortals and assuming
mortal form offered constant exposure to earthly tempta-

tions. But none of the Denver-based angels reveled in mortal vices as happily or as enthusiastically as Dashiell. Sam couldn't recall the last time he'd seen Dash without a cigarette and a cup of coffee, which Dashiell referred to as java. Unlike Sam, who usually wore jeans and a sweater, Dash preferred a fedora and slouchy topcoat, which made him look like Humphrey Bogart. He reveled in his resemblance to the great Bogie.

"Angelo's talking to a spunky little enchilada named Ariel," Dashiell said, dragging on his cigarette. He spoke out of the corner of his mouth. "The kid's thinking about transferring to the Avengers."

Sam glanced toward the balcony. Child angels fascinated him as much as mortal children did. As his experience with children was limited, he never knew quite how to treat them. And it was unnerving to realize that some of the little ones had been angels longer than he had. He returned Ariel's smile, then slid a look toward Kiel, who stood in front of the windows, brooding over a club soda. Flashes of luminous fire sparked around Kiel's blond head, sending a clear signal that he preferred to be left alone with his thoughts.

"Catch you later," Sam said, leaving Dashiell and Kiel with a wave. He went upstairs to his office, checked his E-mail, returned messages, then settled in front of his computer to scroll a list of possible assignments. If Angelo didn't have something hot and breaking, they could choose their next mission. By the time he found something interesting, the kid angel had departed, and so had Kiel and Dashiell.

Sam carried a fresh cup of coffee into Angelo's office and sat down, slipping a curious glance toward the master computer. Angelo could see the universe on his monitor, but no one else could. To Sam's eyes, the screen was annoyingly blank.

"Has the Brett Thatcher case been assigned?"

"Yours if you want it," Angelo offered, glaring at Sam's coffee cup.

Angelo was a purist. If he'd had his way, no angel would ever touch mortal food or drink. Thankfully, he had no say in the matter, and thankfully the rules committee hadn't yet regulated food. Like most of the Avenging Angels, Sam considered mortal food one of the perks of the job.

Angelo, Italian from his bulging biceps to his heavy eyebrows, was a new-wave angel, supporting the myriad new rules and regs that Sam felt were choking the life and effectiveness out of the corps. Gone were the good old days of flaming swords and no-nonsense vengeance. The kick-butt days were over. Now the Avengers had to accomplish the same job hampered by a kinder, gentler, politically correct approach. It was disgusting.

"Tell me about the Thatcher case," he said, gesturing with his coffee cup, largely to annoy Angelo. He wished he'd bummed a smoke from Dash. Angelo went crazy over cigarette smoke.

Frowning, Angelo punched some computer keys and studied his blank screen. "Brett Thatcher was convicted of first-degree murder for stabbing her ex-husband, one Paul Thatcher. Thatcher was a wealthy cosmetic surgeon. His body was found in a cabin owned by Mrs. Thatcher, and her fingerprints were on the knife. She was at the cabin the night he was murdered. She gave some crazy story to the county sheriff. She had motive: a nasty divorce with lots of squabbling over the settlement. With her ex alive, she wasn't getting a cent. If he died, she stood to receive a million dollars from Thatcher's estate and another five million from stock in Dr. Thatcher's clinic. The jury convicted her in about twenty minutes.'' Angelo shrugged broad shoulders and sighed. ''The problem is . . . Brett Thatcher is innocent. She didn't kill her ex-husband.''

''So who did kill Paul Thatcher?''

Angelo folded his hands and gave Sam a long look. ''You know I can't tell you. You have to work through the client. You help the client discover the answers that will establish his or her innocence.''

If Sam had been permitted to swear, he would have scorched the air. ''Blast the new rules!'' In the old days one went directly to the offender and dealt with evil head-on. The wrongdoer was punished, the innocent victim vindicated, and the whole assignment concluded in a day or two.

He narrowed his eyes on Angelo's screen, hoping to glimpse a ghost image that would tell him who framed Brett Thatcher. The screen reflected a frustratingly blank heavenly blue.

''This isn't going to be an easy injustice to correct,'' he noted. ''How do I work through the client when the client is in prison?''

''You're always claiming that you like a challenge. . . .'' Angelo smiled and shrugged.

Sam stared at the ceiling and contemplated the problem. There was a lot that appealed to him about this case. For starters, it was an utter rank miscarriage of justice. Somewhere out there was a killer who had gotten away with murder. He hated that. Plus, there was Brett Thatcher. Sam had studied her photograph in the newspaper accounts and found himself drawn to her. The anguish in her large eyes seemed to leap out of the photo and speak directly to him.

''What are the chances that you've messed up the timing on this case?'' he asked, lowering his gaze to Angelo.

Since time was eternal to angels, earthly time had little meaning. A year, a day, it was easy to mix them up. All the

Avengers wore a watch and consulted it frequently, which was often a waste of effort since time simply did not seem especially important. The power and control that clocks exerted over mortals mystified all the angels.

Angelo bristled. "We're working on the problem, okay?" He jabbed a stubby finger at the monitor. "The time and the sequence of events is right here. There's no mistake."

"I'll take the case," Sam decided, starting to rise.

"Listen, Sam." Angelo leaned over his desk with a narrowed gaze. Sam thought he looked like an Italian frog with beautiful dark eyes. "One more ninja-type incident and you're headed for the Fifth Choir."

Sam stared. The Fifth Choir was the angel equivalent of Siberia and the salt mines. Rumor suggested punishments too terrible to think about. But no one knew for sure exactly what happened in the Fifth Choir. And no one wanted to find out.

"I explained all that." He'd gotten a trifle out of hand on his last assignment.

"Yeah, well, all I'm saying is that the rules and regs apply to you just like everyone else. You can't beat the whatever out of the bad guys. Those days are gone forever. Find another way or you're going to get your wings clipped."

"When's the last time you did any field work?" Sam demanded hotly. But it was pointless to argue with Angelo, the capo of capos of the Denver branch. Throwing off luminous sparks of frustration, Sam pulled to his feet, turned on his heel and went to work.

THE PRISON OFFICIAL gave him a puzzled look. "What was that name again?"

"Brett Thatcher," Sam repeated, striving for patience. "A capital case." He shifted his briefcase, calling attention to it. "I'm Samuel Angel, Mrs. Thatcher's new attorney. I need to consult with my client."

The official pushed back his hat and shook his head. "Sorry, pal. We've got a Marjorie Thatcher and a Lasalle Thatcher, but no Brett Thatcher." He lifted a heavy eyebrow. "How much are you charging this client that you can't find?"

Sam ground his teeth and indulged a momentary daydream about throttling Angelo. Without a word, he turned, walked out of the official's sight and disappeared.

THE COUNTY CLERK turned another page in her ledger and bit her lip. "You say it's a capital case? Thatcher?" She shook her head and peered over her glasses. "I don't have a trial scheduled for Thatcher?"

"You're positive?"

"Look for yourself." The clerk turned the ledger to face him.

Sam scanned the pages, then decided he had better leave before his anger made him transparent.

"Thank you for your help," he snapped, feeling like a fool. Gripping his briefcase, he marched out of the courthouse.

On the steps, he pushed back the cuff of his topcoat and inspected his watch while he tried to remember exactly when Paul Thatcher's murder had taken place and how that date correlated to the date and time showing on his gold wristwatch. He had no idea if his watch displayed the correct date and time. After a few minutes he gave up trying to figure it out. Angels were simply not good with numbers or with time.

"Excuse me," he said, stopping a harried-looking man carrying a briefcase like his. "What day is today?"

"November 14," the man called, hurrying past him.

Sam's eyebrows lifted. Blast. Paul Thatcher's murder had occurred two days ago. Angelo's records were at least six months off the mark. Brett Thatcher not only had not been convicted, she probably hadn't yet been arrested.

Immediately Sam's spirits lifted. It would be much easier to obey the new rules and regs and work through his client if his client was at large instead of locked behind bars. Excellent.

He'd try the murder scene next, check to see if Brett Thatcher was still at the cabin. He was so confident that his assignment was finally about to begin that he materialized a Mercedes, a lawyer-type car, and gave himself the pleasure of driving from Denver to Mrs. Thatcher's cabin in the mountains. If his instincts were correct, that was where he would find his client.

Since driving was one of the mortal pleasures he most relished, Sam applied himself to whipping around mountain curves and didn't anticipate the obvious until he'd been driving for nearly an hour. Brett Thatcher hadn't been arrested yet, but she was about to be. In fact, the lady was probably enjoying her last hours of freedom. If he remembered correctly, the county sheriff and his men had started checking outlying cabins to see if anyone needed assistance after the blizzard, and that's when Brett Thatcher had been discovered with a dead body on her porch.

Sam frowned at the clear, cold sky and stepped on the gas pedal. The storm had ended last night. The sheriff and his men were on the move.

Thirty-five minutes later, the big Mercedes spun into the snowy driveway leading to Brett Thatcher's cabin. Parked near the porch was an unoccupied white Wagoneer with the sheriff's star on the side.

Sam hit the brake and concentrated, listening to the conversation occurring inside the living room.

"I know it sounds cold and heartless," he heard Brett Thatcher explaining in a shaky voice, "but I didn't know what else to do or how long I'd be stuck here, so I—I dragged his body outside to the back porch."

There was an incredulous pause, then the sheriff said, "Let me get this straight. You found your ex-husband's murdered body in your kitchen, then you dragged him outside? In the blizzard?"

"Yes," Brett answered slowly, speaking in a tone that suggested she understood her reaction would sound strange to a law officer.

"Well," the sheriff said after another pause. Sam could imagine him staring at Brett Thatcher and checking his belt to make sure he had his cuffs. "Let's see this dead body."

Blast. Sam deeply regretted that he couldn't rush in with flashing wings and a flaming sword. All he had under the new rules were his wits and a few puny miracles.

His wits told him that Brett Thatcher was mere minutes from being arrested for a murder she hadn't committed, unless Sam did something to buy her a little time. And they were going to need some time to discover who did kill Paul Thatcher.

Fired with the angel equivalent of adrenaline, Sam leaped from the Mercedes and instantly appeared on Brett's back porch. He looked down at Paul Thatcher's snow-covered body with an expression of distaste. It wasn't his place to judge this man, but from what he knew about Thatcher, Sam didn't think many people were going to mourn his death.

He lifted the body, then ran toward the forest of pine and aspen. There would be a dozen hiding places in the trees. Concealing Thatcher's body was not an elegant solution to the immediate problem, but it would save Brett Thatcher from being detained and arrested before the day was over.

"He's right there," Brett said, opening the back door and pointing. Since she couldn't bring herself to glance at Paul's body or the knife sticking out of his back, she looked across the railing at the sunlight sparkling on the snowdrifts.

"Right where?" The sheriff stepped onto the porch and looked around."

"He's right…" Brett let the screen door slam behind her. She stared openmouthed at a depression in the snow on the porch. "He was right there!" Incredulous, she moved to the edge and peered over the railing at a mound of undisturbed snow, then scanned the picnic table and bent to peer beneath it. "I don't understand this," she whispered. "I swear he was right here. It just isn't possible…and yet he's gone!" She blinked up at the sheriff. "I must be going crazy. This can't happen."

The sheriff helped her to her feet. "Maybe you imagined the whole thing." His expression combined relief and indulgence. "You were alone here during the worst storm so far this year. Wouldn't surprise me if you got a case of the willies."

"I didn't imagine this! I swear to you, Paul was dead on my kitchen floor, there was a *knife* sticking out of his back! Someone—the killer—must have moved him!"

"Mrs. Thatcher, there aren't any footprints out there. There isn't a mark on the snow."

"Well, maybe the killer moved Paul before it stopped snowing." She pushed a shaking hand through her hair. "Except I checked on him this morning and he was still there. And it wasn't snowing then."

Sam hurried around the corner of the cabin and bounded up the steps of the back porch. He thrust a hand toward the sheriff. "Hi, I'm Samuel Angel, Mrs. Thatcher's attorney."

Brett jumped and turned wide eyes in his direction. "Who?" she asked, staring blankly while Sam and the sheriff shook hands.

The key to whisking her away from the sheriff was to keep her from talking too much, from saying any more than she already had.

"You aren't my attorney! I've never seen you before."

It wasn't going to be easy.

Chapter Two

"The firm who represented you during your divorce sent me," Sam said smoothly. A gray area existed concerning the rule that prohibited lying. Some degree of impersonation was usually necessary when working a case; acting a role was not considered lying.

"Oh." For a moment she continued to look puzzled, then she twisted her hands together, drew a deep breath of cold air, and lifted those lovely anxious eyes that had made such an impact on Sam when he examined them in the newspaper photos. "I can't say I'm not glad to see you. I need help. I found Paul's body—"

"We'll discuss it later," Sam interrupted, speaking in a soothing tone, aware the sheriff was listening. "Right now, it's important that we return to Denver immediately."

"It is?" Raising a hand, she shielded her eyes from the sunlight. Bewilderment puckered her brow.

"Immediately," he repeated firmly, studying her.

At once Sam decided the newspaper photos had not done her justice. Even disheveled and upset, Brett Thatcher was a lovely woman.

Warm brown tendrils dripped out of a loose ponytail to frame an oval face, pale now, but a face of arresting beauty. When he gazed into Brett Thatcher's deep eyes, Sam was reminded of caramel candy, rimmed by a darker brown circle. At the moment, her emotional state made her eyes seem too large for the delicate lines of her face and throat. As ludicrous as it sounded, those appealing large eyes almost made him overlook her slim nose, classic cheekbones, and a rosy mouth shaped like a valentine. She wore a baggy sweater over faded jeans, but this was a woman who didn't need anything fancy or formfitting to be memorable. Regardless of what she wore, few men would gaze into Brett Thatcher's eyes and then forget her.

Experiencing an odd desire to touch this mortal woman, and telling himself he did so only as a gesture of reassurance, Sam placed his hands on her shoulders. A tremble reverberated beneath his palms, revealing how frightened and nervous she was. "We're going to work this out," he promised, speaking in a low, soothing voice. "The best thing you can do now is follow my instructions. Will you do that?"

Leaning to one side, she flicked an anxious glance toward the sheriff, who watched them with interest and curiosity. Then she raised those melting caramel eyes. "You don't know the whole story, Mr. Angel. I found a dead body! *Paul's* body. And then—this is unbelievable—he just . . . he just disappeared!" She threw out her hands and her trembling increased. "I didn't imagine any of this! No matter how it sounds, every word is true! It was—"

He cut her off again, pressing her shoulders in an attempt to signal silence. "We'll talk about all of it, I promise. I want to hear what happened. But right now we're going to go inside. I want you to get whatever you need, then we'll leave. Do you understand?"

She didn't. Her frown reflected bewilderment and frustration. But she was beginning to grasp that Sam didn't want her to talk about her ex-husband or finding his body.

Nodding slowly, she cast another uncomfortable glance toward the sheriff, then she opened the screen door and hurried into the cabin.

Turning, Sam contemplated Sheriff Stone. Had Sam not interfered, the sheriff would have been leading Brett Thatcher to his car about now, suggesting that they discuss the body on her porch at his office. Before nightfall, she would have been under arrest.

"You don't object to Mrs. Thatcher leaving the county, do you, sheriff?" Sam inquired pleasantly. "I assume you have her Denver address."

The shoulders of the sheriff's uniform shifted in a shrug, and he thumbed back his Stetson. "This gets curiouser and curiouser. Mind telling me what's going on here?"

"Mrs. Thatcher is very upset."

"I can see that." The sheriff crossed the porch to the depression in the snow where Paul Thatcher's body had lain for two days. "It does sort of look like a man might have been lying there...." He lifted his head. "And it raises a red flag when an attorney shows up at a very convenient moment...but as far as I can see, nothing happened here except a woman got spooked by the storm and let her imagination run away with her." He looked again at the depression in the snow. "Still...it's a strange story. Very strange."

Sam opened the screen door, inviting the sheriff inside. "I know you have questions. So do I." The sheriff looked around the porch again, then stepped past Sam and entered the cabin, turning into the kitchen. They both studied the floor.

Sam opened the cabinet beneath the sink and noticed a couple of bloody paper towels in the wastebasket. There was also a tiny scarlet crescent on the floor. If the sheriff saw any of this, he wouldn't allow Brett to leave. Sam quickly closed the cabinet door.

"Looking for clues?" he asked.

The sheriff rocked back on his heels and studied Sam's expression. "Clues. Right. Don't tell me you believe this cock-and-bull story."

"I'm not sure what to think. I haven't had a chance to talk to my client."

The sheriff peered into the refrigerator, noticing the bottle of champagne pushed to the back of the box. "You know, it strikes me that it would be a good idea to give Mr. Thatcher a phone call," he said, closing the refrigerator door. "It might make Mrs. Thatcher feel better to learn that he's alive and well."

"That's an excellent idea." Sam watched Sheriff Stone walk toward the telephone in the living room. Phone service had been restored, but Sam took care of that with a thought, disabling the lines. The sheriff picked up the receiver, then muttered a curse.

"It's still out of service."

Brett Thatcher entered the cabin's small living room from the hallway, carrying a suitcase and a coat over her arm. She had smoothed her hair and added a dab of pink lipstick. Sam couldn't help staring, wondering if she knew how lovely she was. Even the sheriff, who probably thought she was half nuts, gazed at her with admiration.

"Look," she said uneasily, examining Sam, "I don't really know you, and I'm having second—"

"It's important that we focus on getting you back to Denver," Sam interrupted. "That's what matters right now." More specifically, getting her away from the sheriff and the scene of the crime was what mattered.

A flash of anger darkened Brett Thatcher's gaze. "I keep trying to tell you that a murder happened here! Not in Denver, right here! I think we should—"

"I understand," Sam interrupted, then turned to the sheriff. "I believe it would reassure Mrs. Thatcher if we treat the cabin as a crime scene. Just in case."

"Damn it, both of you! This *is* a crime scene!"

Tilting his head back, the sheriff examined the ceiling as if looking at rafters was preferable to dealing with a crazy woman. "There's no body, no sign of foul play. But if this is indeed a crime scene," he remarked with an expression of disgust, "it's been contaminated." Lowering his head, he stared at Brett.

"I tried not to touch anything that I didn't have to," she interjected defensively. "The cabin is pretty much as I found it. Except that Paul's body is—"

"I believe we all agree that we shouldn't contaminate the scene any further," Sam said hastily, leading them both toward the cabin's front door. "So we'll lock up behind us—" he waited while Brett and the sheriff stepped outside "—and we'll give the key to the sheriff." He looked at Brett. "How many keys to the cabin are there?"

She hesitated, then pointed to the door sill. "As far as I know, that's the only one. Paul may have had a key, but I don't think so. It wasn't necessary, as we've always hidden the key up there." Her shoulders moved in a helpless little shrug. "I really don't know who might have a key. Sometimes Paul lent the cabin to his friends for a skiing weekend. He might have given them an extra key."

Sam retrieved the key from above the sill. "So, there's no telling how many people might have had a key or knew about the hiding place," he said before he handed the key to the sheriff. "If I were searching for a key, that's the first place I'd look."

"I get your point," Sheriff Stone said with a pained expression. He rocked back on his heels. "You're selling pretty hard for a man with nothing to sell." He swung a narrowed gaze from Sam to Brett. "First, Mrs. Thatcher insists she found a man murdered on her floor. Then it turns out the murdered man just happens to be her ex-husband. But there's no body. Apparently the body vanished into thin air. Then her attorney shows up and insists nothing is amiss, but manages to suggest that we may have a crime scene here. All this while he's doing his damnedest to whisk the lady away." The sheriff stared at them. "Makes a person think something very peculiar is going on."

"Really?" Sam edged Brett a little closer toward the Mercedes and raised an eyebrow. "Like what?"

"Damned if I know. But if I had the slightest reason to hold your client, I think I'd do it."

Brett backed up a step and gasped. "Me? I didn't do anything! I just—"

Sam interrupted her again. "As you pointed out, sheriff, we don't know what happened here. So far, the only thing we have to go on is Mrs. Thatcher's story, which as you pointed out yourself doesn't make a lot of sense at this point."

"You got that right. But you can bet your Mercedes that I plan to look into this."

"You do that sheriff." Gripping Brett's elbow, Sam guided her swiftly to the car and opened the door for her. The sheriff stood on the porch of the cabin, rocking back on the heels of his boots and watching as Sam eased around Brett's Buick, then backed down the driveway.

Sam didn't relax until they had rounded a curve and the sheriff was lost to sight. That's when he realized Brett was hunched against the door, arms folded over her chest, staring at him with an angry expression.

"Do you ever let anyone finish a sentence?" she asked coldly. "I'm so frustrated, I could scream."

Sam shared her frustration. "You kept trying to convince the sheriff that a murder had taken place in your cabin."

"A murder *did* take place!"

"I know. But believe me, trying to convince the sheriff was not a good idea."

Her eyebrows soared and her stare intensified. "If you know about the murder—and there's no way that you could—then why wouldn't you let me tell my story to Sheriff Stone? Someone *killed* my ex-husband!"

Sam turned his head from the road to give her an exasperated look. "Mrs. Thatcher, suppose you had succeeded in convincing the sheriff that your ex-husband was murdered in your kitchen. Now, who do you think the sheriff would immediately tag as the prime suspect?"

She straightened and her lovely caramel-colored eyes widened. "That's crazy. I didn't kill Paul!"

"I know that. But would the sheriff? Consider. Thatcher turns up dead in your cabin, killed by a knife with your fingerprints on it, and there's no sign that anyone else was present. The two of you have been fighting for a year, and you come into a lot of money at his death." Sam frowned at the snowy road twisting down toward the highway. "Motive and opportunity spell suspect."

She twitched and sucked in a breath. "My fingerprints can't be on the murder weapon. I haven't touched that knife in six months!"

"Count on it. Your fingerprints are still on the handle."

She maintained an uneasy silence until they reached the ramp leading up to I-70. "Listen, what did you mean about

me coming into a lot of money at Paul's death?'' When
Sam informed her about the money she would inherit from
Paul's estate and the stock in his clinic, she fell against the
seat and covered her eyes with a hand. "Paul didn't get
around to changing his will. Is that what you're telling
me?"

"You didn't know?"

Her ponytail swung when she shook her head. "I swear
to you, I didn't know about the money until this minute.
It's true that we've been fighting over the divorce settlement, but that situation was about to be resolved. Or so
Paul led me to expect. Believe me, Mr. Angel, I didn't kill
Paul! I didn't like him, that's also true. I've been upset and
angry at him. But I didn't kill him!"

Brett Thatcher was no dummy. Shock and her own innocence had insulated her from considering the situation
from the law's viewpoint. But now that Sam had drawn her
a picture, she saw at once that she was going to be the prime
suspect.

"Good Lord," she murmured, staring at a range of
snowy mountain peaks through the windshield. "You're
right. When Paul's body turns up, the sheriff is going to
remember that I said I found him in my—" No way was
Sheriff Stone going to forget Brett's story. She turned a pale
face to Sam. "Mr. Angel—"

"Sam, please."

"Sam, if what you're saying is true, then I'm in big
trouble, aren't I?"

"Yes."

The air around him seemed heavier, pressing against
Sam's chest, his skin. It was always this way when he
moved outside of the known and stepped into the unknown. Angels did not, could not, alter history. But a
loophole existed within the rule. Sometimes history itself

went awry. In such cases, the flawed history could be changed, and restored to its intended track. That's where the Avenging Angels came in.

Stepping into the uncharted waters of the loophole to restructure history was the element Sam liked best about his job. He relished the exhilaration of living as mortals did, not knowing what the next minute might bring. And he liked the uncertainty of the outcome. Right now, since Sam had entered the picture, Angelo's computer would be showing a range of possible results, any one of which could be the final outcome. Once Sam had done his job, history's loophole would close and the client's life would continue to unfold along one of the possible lifelines now appearing on Angelo's computer. Sam liked knowing his actions turned his clients' lives down a different but better path.

Most of all, he enjoyed experiencing an earthly existence during his travels in the loophole. He could feel the pressure of the air around him as he stepped into a place unoccupied a minute before, could feel an electrifying sense of uncertainty that was both nerve-racking and exciting. The uncertainty as to what would happen next was, in his opinion, a defining mortal quality and one of the best perks of the job. While in the loophole, anything could happen. The possibilities were endlessly fascinating.

Until Brett Thatcher interrupted his reverie, he hadn't realized they had driven almost thirty miles in silence.

"I wonder," she said in a thin, peculiar voice, "if you'd mind stopping in Georgetown. My mouth is so dry... I'd really like a cup of coffee. Could we do that, please?"

When he glanced at her, curious about the strange tightness in her tone, she was sitting rigidly forward, staring out the windshield. Her hands were clenched in her lap.

He swept a glance across the snowy slopes, trying to see what occupied her attention. The sky was clear and cold, the pine forests frosted with white. He watched an alpine wind whip a tail of snow off a distant peak, exalted over the sight of a hawk wheeling in the sky. Lowering his gaze, he inspected the rooftops of Georgetown dotting the steep slope of a narrow valley.

"We don't need to waste time stopping. There's a thermos of coffee near your feet," Sam said, making it so by thinking it.

In the good old days he had manifested armies of chariots and horses, had stormed citadels and walled cities. Justice had been swift and awesome in those days. Now he was called on the carpet for a little ninja-type work, reduced to producing a thermos of coffee instead of creating something really impressive. The diminished aspects of the job obliterated the good feelings of a minute ago. He was definitely conflicted about his job, no doubt about it.

"Oh," Brett said softly, inspecting the thermos with an unhappy expression. "I don't know how I overlooked this before."

"Is something wrong?"

"Oh, no, nothing's wrong, not at all," she said, running the words together. Bending so he couldn't see her face, she reached for the thermos. When she poured coffee into the lid, her hands shook so badly that she spilled dark droplets on the leather seat, then wiped at them with the tail of her oversized shirt.

But there was a whole lot wrong. Brett was, in fact, thinking herself into a state of genuine fear. Turning her face to the window, she bit her lip and watched the off ramp to Georgetown appear, rush by, then recede into the distance.

As the town slipped away behind them, so did her hastily conceived plan to escape from Sam Angel.

Gripping the thermos lid and wondering if the coffee might be poisoned, she stared at the highway and frantically tried to think of some way to signal the other cars, to let them know that she needed help and they should find a phone and call the police on her behalf.

She closed her eyes and rubbed her forehead. Okay. Suppose her rescue fantasy came true. What would she tell the police if she had the chance?

"Listen, officer, this man *knows* my ex-husband was murdered in my cabin, and he *knows* my fingerprints are on the murder weapon, but he *knows* I didn't do it. He told me so. But the only way he could *know* this is if *he's* the murderer. So arrest him and save me."

She slid a look toward Sam's profile and swallowed hard. The fantasy policeman would make a few phone calls and discover there was no murdered body at the cabin. Ergo, there was no murder and no murderer.

Ergo? Brett winced. She had never used that word in her entire life. Truly, she was losing her mind. Closing her eyes, she held her face over the steam rising from the coffee and rubbed one of her temples.

But how could Sam Angel *know* about Paul? And he did know, Brett had no doubt. There wasn't a nuance of uncertainty in his voice or manner. And the way he had shown up on her back porch...as if he'd been lurking in the woods watching her, maybe since the moment she had discovered Paul's body. And his certainty about the fingerprints on the knife being hers...how could he know that unless he'd planned it that way?

The more she thought about Sam knowing things he couldn't possibly know, the more panicked and certain she became that Sam Angel had killed Paul and he intended to frame her for the murder. Or maybe he planned to kill her, too?

"I don't think I want any coffee, after all," she murmured. Even to her, her voice sounded squeaky and weird. She would have crawled over a field of ground glass for a handful of potato chips to steady her nerves. But she wasn't going to swallow poisoned coffee. She wasn't going to make it easy for him.

The thing that galled her most was the realization of how stupid she had been. She didn't know this man, she had never seen him or heard his name before, yet she had trotted out to his car and driven off with him. She had let him sweep aside one tiny moment of sensible hesitation.

Disgust thinned her lips. How could she have done such a stupid and dangerous thing?

Part of the reason, she decided, sliding a sideways glance toward him, was that Sam Angel didn't look like a murderer. In fact, she couldn't think of anyone who looked less like a bad guy. But now that she thought about it, most murderers didn't look like murderers. Most of them looked like average, ordinary people.

Sam Angel didn't look like an average, ordinary person, either, she realized with a tiny shock of surprise. Pushing all distractions from her mind, Brett shifted on the car seat to look at him, really look at him.

Good heavens. This man was absolutely gorgeous. When Sam Angel had first appeared on the back porch, Brett had dimly registered that he was good-looking, but she'd been too shocked by Paul's missing body to pay much attention or to notice what a fabulous man he really was.

She did now. She stared openly, absorbing every detail.

His hair was white blond, stylishly coiffed, worn on the longish side. She thought she identified a few gray strands at his temples, but it was hard to tell since his blond hair was so light to begin with.

Next, she examined his profile. His nose was thin and high bridged, the sort of nose that seemed obligatory for statues of Greek gods. He had a great nose, actually, the kind of nose that Paul's patients begged Paul to create. Sam's nose suggested character and strength. No way could that nose belong to a murderer. Surely not.

Frowning, Brett moved to an examination of his mouth. Her heart rolled in her chest. He had a fantastic mouth, wide and perfectly shaped. The contour lines were prominent and well defined, marking lips that were neither too full nor too thin. She had a sudden idea that those lips could whisper poetry or twist in anger with equal facility. But, oddly, she couldn't picture those lips telling lies. On the other hand, Brett reminded herself that she was not a great judge of character. She had married Paul, hadn't she?

Next, she lowered her glance to Sam Angel's jaw. Aha. Finally she identified a sign of something less than masculine perfection. His jawline screamed stubbornness. Hinted rebellion. The clean, hard sweep of line and bone stated that this was a determined man who would go down fighting rather than admit defeat. This man would never give up, never surrender.

Finally, Brett considered his clothing. He wore a very lawyerly three-piece charcoal suit with a conservative navy tie and crisp white shirt. The suit was superbly tailored. She had an uneasy suspicion that the tailoring was designed to disguise a hard, muscular body. There were hints in the way the soft woolen material pulled over his thighs and occasionally tugged across broad shoulders. It occurred to her that three-piece suits were not Sam Angel's uniform of choice. She sensed that he was the type who preferred jeans and a pullover, certainly something casual that offered hard muscles more freedom to move.

When he turned his head to glance at her, Brett sucked in a breath and smothered a gasp. Now she had an unobstructed view of his eyes, and his eyes were so luminously blue that she was utterly amazed that she hadn't noticed previously. There wasn't a speck of additional color, just blue. Blue like the heavens, blue like the Mediterranean, a clear crystal blue like melting ice made from the purest distilled water. Except there was nothing chill or cold in his gaze.

Brett met his steady gaze and felt a rush of warmth and reassurance shoot through her body. No man with eyes like his, compassionate eyes, sympathetic and sexy eyes, could be a murderer. Sam Angel could be a bigamist. He could be a man who seduced women out of their panty hose and their fortunes. Or he could be a model or a film star. But no way could a man with such beautiful, luminous eyes be a killer.

Or was she simply the most naive woman ever to hop into a car with a complete stranger?

Brett moistened her lips, then whispered, "Who are you? Really."

"Well, I'll be…you're thinking that…blast!" He stared at her for so long that she worried he would drift off the highway and they would crash. The road was dry and clear, but there was an impressive drop-off a few feet beyond the guardrail. "You're afraid of me!"

"I don't believe that you're one of my divorce attorneys as you claimed. They couldn't have sent you to Silverthorne, because no one at the firm knew I'd be at the cabin." Brett clasped her hands tightly and gathered her courage. "Finally, there's no way that you could know that

Paul is really dead or know that I didn't kill him, unless . . ."

"Unless?" He sounded amazed.

Worse, he had not looked at the road for a full minute. The Mercedes seemed to be driving itself, taking the mountain curves as smoothly as if Sam were paying attention, which he was not.

"Please," Brett begged, wetting her lips in mounting fear. "Look at the damned road, will you? You're going to kill us."

He frowned at the highway for less than a minute, then turned to stare at her again. The amazement had faded from his gaze, and now his eyes reminded her of blue daggers. "Unless what?" He was angry enough to make her state the accusation aloud.

"Unless you're the one who killed Paul," Brett whispered.

There. She'd done it. She'd signed her death warrant. After a lifetime of being a reasonably bright woman, she had turned stupid. Like an idiot, she thought it was a good idea to accuse a man with whom she was trapped of being a murderer. Her brain cells had turned to mush.

"Blast!"

He looked thunderstruck. And he was such a skilled actor, affected such an innocent demeanor, that more appalling words rolled off of Brett's tongue. Her heart flew around in her chest, her mouth felt like it was stuffed with cotton, and she was scared enough to think about jumping out of the speeding Mercedes, but instead more words came, making the situation worse.

"You moved Paul's body, didn't you?"

He glared at her and hesitated. Then he said the one word that Brett expected, but absolutely did not want to hear.

"Yes."

"I thought so," she whispered in a choking voice. "It had to be you. There was no one else. Oh, God."

Now he knew that she knew. And she was as good as dead. She couldn't believe that she had played this so dumb.

"You're going to kill me, too, aren't you?" Now that she had tipped him to the fact that she knew he was the murderer, she'd left him few choices.

"What?"

He had to get rid of her. But maybe that's what he had intended to do from the beginning.

The last thing Brett saw before fear overwhelmed her and she fainted was a mirage. It seemed to her that Sam Angel grew larger. She could have sworn that a halo of angry, brilliant light blazed and flashed around his handsome white blond head. The air seemed to thicken and shimmer.

She made a gurgling sound, then slumped to the floor of the car.

Chapter Three

Sam's anger evaporated the instant Brett slid to the car floor in a sprawled pile. He stared at her in dismay, not sure what to do. Guardian Angels were better at handling this kind of thing, but when an Avenging Angel came on duty, the Guardians took a leave of absence. Generally, Sam was glad the Guardians split because, as a group, he considered them sissies. They sat around sick rooms, fretted over broken hearts, tried to prevent accidents . . . all of it largely passive. They weren't action angels.

But he wished a Guardian were present now. Sam wasn't especially skilled at handling mortal women in the throes of acting like mortal women. He had no idea what to do with a fainting female. Moreover, he was absolutely stunned that Brett actually seemed to think he could be a murderer. Such a catastrophe had never occurred before. He was so firmly entrenched on the side of good, justice and decency that he hadn't even supposed he *could* be mistaken for one of the cretins on the other side.

"Blast!"

After braking the Mercedes on the verge of the road, he stared down at Brett Thatcher's crumpled form and frowned. She believed that he was a killer. He simply could not get over it. The accusation was amazing. Offensive, outrageous, and more than a little ungrateful.

Often he could do his job, right the wrongs, restore justice, and succeed without having to reveal his true identity. That was a perfect run.

But he saw at once that this case was not going to be a perfect run. It was, in fact, going to get sticky. He was going to have to reveal his identity, and that meant all sorts of problems, because for the most part people didn't believe in angels. They *wanted* to believe, some honestly thought they did believe, but the truth was, it scared the living heck out of mortals when they actually encountered an angel.

Either they denied the experience, or they inflated it, or they laid huge expectations on the poor angel, or they decided the angel was really a lunatic mortal who should be locked away. Plus, few humans understood the angel hierarchy, which was confusing in any case, but they didn't grasp the difference between a Guardian and an Avenger, or a Cherub and a Ministering angel.

Sam realized he was procrastinating. He had to do something about the woman on the floor of the car.

Leaning over the console that separated the seats, he gave her head a tentative pat. "Mrs. Thatcher? Brett?"

She moaned, blinked up at him, then gasped and fell back in a pile on the floor mat.

Blast. Emotion made him fizz and flash like a fireworks display, and being mistaken for a killer had definitely made him emotional. Touching her hair had proven to be a strangely emotional experience, too. The bottom line: he'd probably frightened her badly. Taking a minute, Sam composed his thoughts and assumed a firmer grasp on his mortal form. When he felt as solid, as steady, as heavily flesh and bone as he was going to get, he tried again.

"Brett?"

Gradually she came around. She blinked again, gave her head a shake, then looked up at him dizzily. Her eyes widened to the size of halos.

"Wait! Don't faint again. I'm not going to hurt you."

"Did you kill Paul?" she whispered. Her face was as white as a choir robe and her eyes remained huge.

"Of course not! I swear to you, I am absolutely not a killer."

Extending his hand, he helped her onto the car seat. She permitted the assistance reluctantly, then snatched her fingers away as quickly as she could. She flattened herself against the car door, looking from Sam to the cars whizzing past on the interstate.

"Then how do you know so much about Paul's murder?"

He looked at her, arms wrapped around herself, her eyes disbelieving, suspicious, accusing. He sighed heavily. Here they went. There was no avoiding it. He was going to have to tell her.

"Do you believe in angels?"

"I beg your pardon?" She stared at him as if he'd suddenly started babbling nonsense. He'd seen that look before. The truth was going to make dealing with her a thousand times more difficult.

"Angels exist. And we do take an active interest in mortal affairs." He drew a deep breath, feeling her incredulous stare and her disbelief like a weight pressing against his chest. "I'm here to prevent a miscarriage of justice. To make certain that Paul's killer is caught and punished."

A long, uncomfortable silence ensued. Finally, she raised an eyebrow and said, "Look, whoever you are, I wasn't born yesterday. I don't know what you're trying to pull here, but no way am I going to believe that you're an angel."

"Not just an angel, an Avenging Angel." He couldn't help it, a note of pride deepened his tone. He didn't want her to mistake him for one of the wienie Guardians.

"I don't know why you're suddenly talking about angels, but I'll tell you flat out, it's a big leap from suspecting you might have killed Paul to believing you're an angel. So forget it."

When she grabbed the door handle and would have jumped outside into the flow of traffic, Sam saw how it was going to go. The hard way.

"Look, I'm not crazy, not deluded, not dangerous to you." She wasn't paying attention to what he was saying; she was jerking at the door handle, making choking noises of fear and frustration when it wouldn't open. Her fear utterly appalled Sam.

"Brett, please, listen to me." She gave up trying to open the car door and turned toward him, pressing her body into the metal and upholstery of the door. He'd never seen eyes that enormous.

"Please. I'm on your side. I'm here to *help* you." This situation was so unique, so horrifying, that he wasn't sure how to handle it. When he gazed at the fear in her eyes, his mind went dark with shock.

"You claim you're an angel," she said in a choking voice that he wouldn't have heard if he had been a true mortal. "You have to be crazy."

His instinct was to pat her or stroke her, somehow to soothe her. But she would have jumped out of her skin if he'd extended his hand. Or fainted again. And to tell the truth, which he was constrained to do, at least most of the time, touching her earlier had made him feel peculiar, restless inside and tingly.

"I know you're finding this difficult to believe, many people do. But just listen for a moment."

"Please unlock the car door."

"Just listen, okay?"

Speaking in a low, soothing tone, he gave her a crash course on angel lore, focusing on the Avenging Angels. He even mentioned Angelo and his master computer, and finally he explained how he had run across her case. The minute he had asked her to give him stretched into forty-five minutes. He kept talking until he sensed that her curiosity was gradually outdistancing her fear.

"Wait a minute," she interrupted, frowning. Sam didn't know if she believed anything he was saying, but he'd piqued her interest to the point that she didn't appear quite as terrified. A little color had returned to her cheeks. "You claim that you read in the newspaper that I'd been sent to prison for murdering Paul?"

"If I hadn't stepped in when I did, Sheriff Stone would have arrested you by now. Eventually you would have gone to prison. Yes."

"But, according to you, I *did* get arrested and go to prison. You claim you read about it after the fact." Confusion swirled in her gaze. "How can you know what happened before it happened? Even more important, how can you step in and change what has already happened?"

This part was tricky to explain.

"I'm an angel," he stated gently, watching her carefully to see if that explained everything. But of course it didn't.

So he talked about destiny being a result of personal choices, but sometimes things went awry and injustices occurred that shouldn't have happened, in which case a loophole opened and that's where he came in. Sam talked for another twenty minutes, at the end of which, he peered at her. "It's an interruption in time and history, you could say. A loophole opens and a wrong future can be corrected. Now do you understand?"

"You've jumped into my history before it happens to keep it from happening incorrectly," Brett said in a low, bewildered voice. She looked so confused and vulnerable that he wanted to embrace her and pat her back. "Is that the crux of it?"

"Yes!" Delighted, he smiled. Maybe this was going to work out well, after all.

For an instant she seemed taken aback by his smile, then she swallowed and said, "If I understand this, you want me to believe that you're sort of an angel private eye, is that it?"

That comment stung. But unfortunately, it was basically true. That's what the corps had been reduced to. "You could say that," he admitted, irritated afresh by the changes from above. The governing council had pulled the Avenger's teeth. A private eye, indeed. Yet that, blast it, was what he had sunk to.

"I hope this question won't offend you, but...are you seeing a doctor?" she inquired after a minute of silence. "Are you taking medication?"

They were wasting time, sitting on the side of the road talking about things that should never have been a subject of conversation in the first place. But, as always, time and drastic measures were required to convince mortals of a reality that existed right in front of their eyes. This always surprised Sam. It seemed to him that if he were in desperate straits and someone came along who wanted to help, he would gratefully accept that help without subjecting the Good Samaritan to a relentless grilling followed by insulting statements of outright disbelief. But that wasn't how it worked.

"How do you think I moved Paul's body without leaving any tracks in the snow?" he asked, striving for patience.

Her face went white again. "I can't imagine."

"I'll show you. Let's step outside." When her eyes lit, he made a sound of exasperation. "Forget about trying to wave down a car. For the purposes of this demonstration, we are invisible. Plus, you don't need help. *I'm* your help, if you'll just accept it." Naturally, she didn't listen to him.

The minute she slid out of the Mercedes, she dashed to the edge of the road and tried to flag down one of the passing cars. The drivers whizzed past without a flicker of comprehension that a beautiful woman was waving and shouting on the side of the road. Sam waited until she finally accepted that no one was going to stop. She turned toward him with a dazed expression.

"Are you satisfied?" he asked irritably. It annoyed him that mortals were so hard to convince. They ought to be wildly grateful and willing to accept someone who was doing his darnedest to help their sorry selves.

"We can't be invisible. That isn't possible," she murmured, wetting her lips and looking at him.

He would have loved to appear to her in full angel regalia. Wings and radiant light would have wiped the disbelief from her eyes. But it would also have frightened the daylights out of her. He needed a demonstration strong enough to make her believe, but mild enough that she wouldn't be badly frightened.

"Come over here and watch this."

Still feeling appalled by the necessity of a demonstration, he stepped over the guardrail onto a six-foot expanse of clean, undisturbed snow. After hesitating, he heard her approach the rail.

"All right, now, pay attention."

He walked up and down the unmarked snow, then turned to face her. She stood with her hands thrust deep in the pockets of her red parka. Sunlight slid along the swinging cascade of her ponytail.

"See? No footprints. Only an angel can do that because we are weightless. When I moved Paul's body to buy us some time and save you from being arrested, I left no telltale footprints in the snow. The fact is, I couldn't leave footprints if I wanted to."

She studied the unmarked snow, then raised her chin and stared at him a minute before she stepped over the guardrail and walked into the snow herself. Frowning, she looked over her shoulder at the slushy prints she left. A puzzled look tugged her brow.

"All right, how did you do that?"

"Watch."

Feeling like an idiot, Sam jumped up and down, he stamped his feet, he tried to kick at a low drift. He could try from now until Judgment Day, and he wouldn't leave a mark on the snow. Or sand, or dirt, or whatever the surface happened to be.

For the first time since he'd met her, a tiny smile appeared on her lips. He didn't blame her. He had to look ridiculous, a grown man in a three-piece suit jumping up and down like a cartoon character, stamping around like he was trying to put out the flames of hell. Flushing, he straightened his tie and walked toward her.

"Convinced?"

"I don't know," she said uncomfortably, gazing up at him. She frowned and pushed back a strand of hair that had fallen out of her ponytail. Her gaze shifted to the unmarked snow. "But I have to admit . . . I can't explain how you did that. It's an impressive trick. Amazing, really. And very undignified," she added with the ghost of a grin.

He laughed, then smiled at her, admiring the effort she was making to cope. First she'd stumbled over a murdered body, then had to deal with it, then the body disappeared, and now here he came, telling her that he was an angel. From her point of view, it had to be one shock followed by another followed by something she would consider incredible and nearly impossible to believe.

"Something strange is happening here," she admitted as they climbed back over the guardrail and walked toward the Mercedes. She kept three feet between them. "But I'm not sure that— Is Sam your real name?"

"Samuel," he said, watching her cast a wistful glance toward the cars on the highway. "They honestly do not see us," he said quietly.

"We're invisible," she said in a flat voice.

"If you can accept the lack of footprints..."

She watched the cars zip past them, tried waving again, then, without looking at him, she lowered her head and returned to the car. She gave him a long, speculative gaze above the roof of the car before she opened the door then slid gingerly inside as if her body were acting against her mind's instructions.

"Most angels' names end in *el,*" Sam said, mostly to take her mind off her failure to flag down a passing motorist. "Not all, but most." There were rules even for names, he thought with disgust. After making a pretense of checking the traffic, he pulled the car onto the highway.

"You look like a normal person," she commented after several minutes of silence, studying his profile. She was trying to make up her mind whether to believe him or not. Every cell in her brain resisted belief, he knew that. But his demonstration on the snow and the possibility that they had indeed been invisible had shaken her. "Look, don't angels have wings and a halo?"

"There's some disagreement on that point," he admitted. "Centuries ago, artists began depicting angels with wings to symbolize flight. That's how they explained an angel's ability to appear and disappear." He turned a frown toward her. "But we're not birds, for heaven's sake. We don't *need* wings to get around." She returned his stare and he sighed. "When we want to make a quick impression, most of us appear in wings so the mortal won't question who he's dealing with. And some angels *like* manifesting in wings." He tugged his collar, remembering a few incidents in his own past. Wings were impressive as heck, useful when you wanted instant attention or couldn't appear in mortal form for whatever reason.

The car swept around a curve, and they glimpsed Denver sprawling across the snowy plains beyond the foothills.

"I'm not saying that I'm convinced," Brett remarked, following a lengthy silence. "In fact, I feel foolish merely admitting the possibility, but let's assume for a minute that you really are an angel, okay?"

"Let's," Sam answered dryly.

"Why me?" She turned her head and gazed at him with huge eyes. A flush of uncomfortable pink brightened her pale cheeks. "I'm not really religious, Sam. I mean, I believe in God—" she waved her hands and her color deepened "—but I don't attend church regularly. I swear on occasion, I've done things in my life that I'm not proud of, things you'd probably consider sins. And I've—"

"Hold it." He lifted a hand and tried to swallow a rush of acute discomfort. Mortals' sins usually sounded like a lot of fun, at least the minor ones did, and like most angels, he was fascinated by the temptations mortals were subjected to. But Brett's sins, or what she thought were sins, were really none of his business. The rules were crystal clear on this point. "There's no need to confess every mistake you've ever made. I'm not here to judge you, that isn't my job. I'm here to save you from a gross injustice."

"But why me and not someone like…I don't know…like Mother Teresa?"

"Mother Teresa is not a murder suspect." Which didn't really answer her question. "Look, you don't have to be saintly, and you don't have to have led a perfect and blameless life to merit help. Okay? The criterion for the Avengers is injustice. Unless someone—me—intervenes, you're going to spend your life in prison for a crime you didn't commit." He resisted another urge to pat her hands. "Just accept that I'm here to help you."

Naturally, he couldn't help wondering what "sins" she had committed. Sliding her a look of curiosity, he tried to imagine Brett Thatcher doing something really bad. He couldn't. There was an appealing wholesomeness about her that simply didn't suggest any terrible character flaws. Her sins, he suspected, were small ones.

"Okay. Let's, just for the moment, let's say you are an angel and you have intervened in my case."

Sam rolled his eyes. "What's it going to take to convince you that I am who I say I am, and that I'm here to help you?"

"What happens next? Do you arrest whoever murdered Paul?"

"I wish it were that easy," he said fervently.

She stared at him. "Well? Who *did* murder Paul?"

This was embarrassing. "I don't know."

Brett threw out her hands, and her eyes flared with suspicion. "Uh-huh." She crossed her arms over her chest. "Let's see if I understand this correctly. You're an angel sent here to save me and make sure I don't go to prison for murdering Paul. You don't leave footprints and you can make both of us invisible…but you don't know who the murderer is. Is that right? It seems to me that someone who can make themselves invisible and who claims to be an angel, someone who says they can create a loophole in time and history, should have no trouble arriving on the scene knowing who the killer is!"

"Look," Sam said, taking his eyes off the road, "there have been some rule changes, okay? Believe me, I don't like operating in the dark, either, but we're stuck. I have to work through you and other mortals." He ground his perfect teeth. "I wish I could say, So-and-so did it and you're off the hook. But that isn't how the process operates. We have to lay a groundwork that the authorities will accept. We have to prove your case in a way that does not depend on divine intervention. Trial attorneys would ridicule divine intervention right out of court! Much as I hate to admit this, there's sound logic behind the rule about doing this the mortal way. It wouldn't be good enough for an angel to simply announce, So-and-so did it. Look at the trouble I'm having just convincing you! We have to build a body of evidence and proof."

"Right." Her stare burned into him.

Irritation swelled his shoulders. "It isn't like we don't have a couple of advantages on our side. I *can* perform small miracles. They haven't taken that away yet."

"Frankly, the ability to walk on snow without leaving prints strikes me as a miracle that can't be much in demand. And I only have your word for it that you and I were invisible. So, what else can you do?"

"I'm not a performing seal, Mrs. Thatcher, I don't have to audition or run through a routine of cute miracles!"

"Huh!"

Her disbelief and sarcasm provoked angry sparks in his eyes. "Leaving no footprints helped get you away from the sheriff and the cabin. Footprints would have led the sheriff straight to Thatcher's body. That's no small thing. And it isn't a magic trick," he said hotly. "Have you ever seen it done before? No, you haven't!"

That gave her something to think about, he was pleased to notice.

"But it isn't a miracle, either," he admitted after a moment. "In some circles, it's considered a limitation, actually."

"Listen, Sam," she said, narrowing her eyes, "I don't know how we got off on this angel thing. Is this some kind of gullibility test?"

"Can we move beyond this issue?" Sam inquired, annoyed. "I'm an angel, okay? I'm here to help you. End of story."

"Well I'm sorry, but I haven't met any angels before. It's hard to accept. And it seems to me that angels ought to be sweet tempered. Which you don't especially seem to be. And angels ought to know things ordinary people don't know. Like who the real murderer is. How do you expect anyone to believe this?"

"Blast!"

She rubbed her forehead and leaned forward to look at the buffalo grazing through the snow on the left side of the highway. The buffalo herd wasn't far from the outskirts of Denver. "I can't believe we've digressed so far from the real problem. I could be in a lot of trouble. I ought to be thinking about what to do next. And I don't have a clue."

She shook her head as if to clear it. "All right, Sam, I don't know who or what you are, or why you appeared at the cabin when you did, or how you know so much about Paul's murder...but I no longer think you killed Paul. We're square on that point. I appreciate the ride back to Denver, and it's been an...interesting conversation. Now, if you wouldn't mind dropping me off at my condominium, I'd appreciate it."

Frustrated, Sam felt like swelling into a really impressive size, felt like manifesting a pair of gigantic pearly wings and calling up one of the Cherub choirs. He wanted a luminous fiery sword and chains around his waist. It irritated him no end that she only half believed him. If he hadn't known how badly it would frighten her, he would have put on a demonstration that *nobody* could ignore or disbelieve. He didn't ask himself why Brett Thatcher's opinion mattered so much, it just did.

He spoke through clenched teeth. "I'll take you to your condo if that's what you really want. But where do you think the police will start looking for you once Thatcher's body is found? Are you ready to be arrested? Before we've uncovered a scrap of evidence?"

She was suddenly angry, too. "No one's looking for me. I tried like hell to convince the sheriff that Paul was dead, but he wasn't buying it. Besides, I'm *innocent!*" Sliding him a sidelong glance, she studied his face for a reaction to "hell."

Sam kept his face expressionless. "We're in the loophole now, so I can't predict when Thatcher's body will be found. But when it is, the police are going to come looking for you. We have from now until then to discover who murdered your ex-husband, because once you're arrested, Brett, the police are going to stop looking for the real killer."

"Keep your eyes on the road. You are absolutely the most careless, most nerve-racking driver I've even seen!"

"We're not going to have an accident. This car can drive itself." He glared at her. "I think we should go to the safe house. We can stay there while we work out a plan and begin our investigation."

When his words registered, her eyebrows soared toward her hairline. "Your place or mine? You're kidding, right? You want me to stay at your place?"

"We'll stop by your condo so you can pick up anything that might be helpful," Sam said, thinking out loud. "Any paperwork relating to your ex-husband, your address book, any financial and tax records left over from your marriage, that kind of thing."

"Forget it, Sam, I'm not staying at your place. But I would like to hear why a so-called angel needs an apartment. Or is it a house?" Arms crossed on her chest, she stared at him. "You had me going there for a while, I admit it. I really was starting to wonder if maybe..." Making a sound of disgust, she turned her face to the window.

Sam stopped the Mercedes at the bottom of the ramp leading off of I-70, and rested his forearm on the steering wheel. "It doesn't matter if you believe I'm an angel, or if you want to think I'm nuts or a crime-chasing attorney hustling business or a private eye handing you a bill of goods. But believe this..." He paused and waited until she looked at him, then he stared deeply into her beautiful eyes. "I'm committed to helping you. And I'm here for the duration. I'm on the case whether you and I work together or whether I work alone. Nothing you say, no amount of sarcasm, is going to change that."

She blinked then lowered her head and looked at her hands. "Look, I'm sorry. I just..."

"I think it would be easier and more efficient if we worked together, and I think it would be safer for you if you stayed at the safe house, but if that isn't comfortable for you, it isn't a requirement. It isn't even a requirement that you be free and not in prison. I'll prove your innocence regardless. How much involvement you choose is entirely up to you, Brett."

She watched him return his attention to the road and point the Mercedes toward Littleton, a suburb southwest of Denver. In about fifteen minutes they would pull up in front of her condo. She had to decide what she was going to do.

"A safe house," she murmured, trying to consider the concept seriously. An alarming thought occurred to her. "Are you suggesting that *I* could be in danger?"

"At this point, I don't know. But it's certainly worth considering. *Someone* let you go to prison for a crime that he or she committed. That outcome has been interrupted and diverted. There's no way to predict how the killer will react this time around."

Brett released a breath. "You can't possibly know how bizarre that sounds."

The crazy thing was, he spoke so seriously and with such conviction that she found herself nodding and going along with what he said.

Nibbling a thumbnail, wishing she had something to eat, Brett tried to decide what was her best course of action. She didn't have to rely on this man, who might be crazy. There were other people who would help her.

She could phone…who? Who did she know who would be willing to accept her word about all that had happened, and who would help her prove her innocence? Because Sam was right. Sooner or later Paul's body would be discovered, and then Brett was going to be in trouble up to her eyebrows. Sam's point about motive and opportunity had made an impact. The police weren't going to look much further than her. So who could she call on for help?

Her mind rifled through a list of friends and acquaintances, the roster smaller since her divorce. She couldn't think of anyone who might be genuinely helpful or whom she wanted to involve in this mess.

When the car stopped, she frowned at Sam's profile. "Look, I don't doubt your sincerity in wanting to help." He was utterly convincing on that point. "And the truth is—" this admission came hard "—I don't have too many people I can turn to right now. But if you *are* an angel, then you must know how hard it is for people like me to believe in you, and if you *aren't* an angel, then you must be crazy." She strove for a weak smile. "It puts me in something of a dilemma."

It was odd that her hope for vindication and help would narrow to a stranger who claimed to be an angel. But she didn't know anyone else who had any experience with murder, and Sam insisted that he did. And she didn't know anyone else who would really believe that Paul's body had vanished, nor could she guess how many of her acquaintances would honestly believe in her innocence. That was a sobering realization. Brett could think of at least three friends who had made jokes that Brett ought to kill Paul instead of divorcing him. Maybe they would think she'd taken their suggestions.

Anxious and indecisive, she stared hard at Sam Angel and rubbed moist palms across the knees of her jeans. "I wish I knew if I could trust you."

"You can trust this," he said quietly, looking steadily into her eyes. "I want to help you."

Because looking into his clear, warm eyes swept away all her doubts, and because she wasn't sure if that was wise, Brett shifted her glance to the front of her condo as the Mercedes glided to a smooth stop at the curb.

She remembered the day she had bought the condo, and how happy she had felt that she finally owned a small home of her own and was making her way in the world. After she married Paul, Paul had advised her to sell the unit, but Brett had resisted his arguments. After growing up in a series of foster homes, having a place that was hers, all hers, mattered at a visceral level. And after the divorce she'd been thankful to have somewhere to go.

Sliding out of the car, she thrust her hands in the pockets of the parka and looked toward the windows of her unit on the third floor. A puzzled frown drew her brow. She could have sworn that she had left the drapes open so her plants would catch the morning sun, but obviously she hadn't. The drapes were drawn tight.

"Well?" Sam said at her elbow. "Have you decided? Do you want to stay here or go to the safe house?"

"I don't know yet." She hesitated, eyeing him. "I think we should talk some more."

Sam tilted his head and looked up, his gaze steadying on the windows of her unit. "Something's wrong."

Brett sighed and glanced at the storm clouds rolling over the mountain peaks to the west. "If one more thing goes wrong, I'm going to fall apart." She moved forward, suddenly eager to be in her own home, surrounded by familiar things. What she wanted most right now was to hide out for a couple of days until her equilibrium was restored and she could figure out what to do next.

Sam placed a hand on her arm, and she felt a tingle of warmth travel to her shoulder and body. He continued to stare up at the windows of her unit, a frown twisting his eyebrows into slender S shapes.

"The danger is past . . . but something . . ."

Brett examined his expression and felt her heart lurch, then she pulled away from his hand and ran toward the entrance.

Chapter Four

Brett rushed inside the lobby elevator the instant the doors opened, narrowly averting a collision with one of her neighbors. Mr. Glassy gripped her forearms to steady Brett and himself, flicked a glance toward Sam, then stepped out of the elevator.

"That was some noisy party you had Saturday night." He glared back at Brett from beneath the folds of a blue stocking cap. "What were you doing, anyway? Throwing furniture at the walls?"

"I beg your pardon?"

"You're lucky no one called the police!"

"I wasn't here Saturday night," Brett said.

Mr. Glassy pointed a finger. "Next time, I will call the police. You just keep that in mind, young lady."

Brett gave Sam an uneasy look as the elevator doors hissed shut. "What do you suppose that was all about?"

"I don't know, but I think I'd better check it out. Excuse me a minute."

And he vanished.

Brett blinked, rubbed her eyes and blinked again. She spun around in the elevator, her heart pounding out of control. "Sam? Sam?"

When the door opened, she was leaning against the elevator wall, eyes closed, moaning softly. "Believe me," she whispered when she saw him, "that was a more convincing demonstration than the snow and footprints thing." Sam stood in the corridor, waiting for her, his face grim.

"Prepare yourself," he warned as Brett slowly walked forward, staring hard at him.

"Who are you?" she murmured when she could speak. Her mind was reeling, stunned. This man could vanish at will. It was unbelievable. White-faced and awed, she continued to stare at him as if this were the first time she was seeing him. Maybe it was.

"Brett, we don't have time for this. You know who I am." Taking her arm, he assisted her down the corridor as if she were an invalid. Right now, she felt like one. "Your home has been vandalized."

Brett peered up at his handsome face, studying the sculpted lines. "Right now, I'm half scared of you, and half grateful that you're here." She couldn't take her eyes off of him. And she wondered if all angels were this great-looking, this unnerving. "You're amazing, really amazing."

They stopped in front of her door and Sam clasped her shoulders, peering intently into her eyes. It seemed to Brett that a thrilling warmth radiated from his palms, spreading through her body like warm molasses. "We have to decide if we should call the police."

"The police," she repeated, unable to concentrate. She was still struggling to wrap her mind around the realization that he was who he claimed to be. Plus, it occurred to her that a woman could drown in the ocean blue of Sam's steady eyes, could be lulled by the hypnotic rumble of his deep voice. He intrigued her, astonished her, fascinated her.

She couldn't push her thoughts past the wonder of it; an angel was gripping her by the shoulders. A real, honest-to-God angel. After his vanishing act, she no longer doubted. An angel had appeared to help her.

"I'm so sorry," she whispered. "I hope I didn't offend you by anything I said. It's just—"

"This could go either way," Sam commented, thinking out loud. "Your neighbors apparently believe you were here Saturday night when someone murdered Paul eighty miles away. That might buy us some extra time. On the other hand, they didn't actually see you. And the Summit County sheriff knows you were at the cabin because you told him you were...."

Despite the cloud of white blond hair, there were no lines on his face. She hadn't noticed that before. It was part of his striking appeal, the white blond hair coupled to a youthful face. "You look like an ordinary person. Who could guess that you're actually—" she murmured helplessly. "Well, not ordinary, exactly, I didn't mean that like it sounded, but—"

Sam gave her a gentle shake and gazed into her wide, awed eyes. Then he sighed and opened her door. "Sometimes a picture is worth a thousand words. Not an original thought, but..."

Clasping her shoulders, he turned her to face inside her condominium. For an instant the scene didn't register, her mind was still concentrated on the amazement of standing beside an angel, and she was frantically trying to remember everything he had told her about angels, information she had only half listened to.

Then suddenly her vision cleared and she saw what Sam wanted her to see. She gasped and her hands flew to her mouth. "Oh, my God!"

Mr. Glassy had not exaggerated. It looked as if a hurricane had torn through her condo, hurling down lamps and cushions, books and papers. One of the sofa side tables was broken. It did indeed appear that the drawers from her desk had been flung against the wall. The devastation was incredible.

Brett sagged against the doorjamb, unable to speak. Whoever had done this had been filled with fury. Not merely content to trash her place, he or she had also smashed her aquarium.

"Oh!" Picking her way across strewn cushions and broken lamps, Brett knelt beside her dead angel fish, blinking hard. Who would do this? Glass was everywhere; the carpet was still wet under her feet. Killing her fish seemed gratuitous, so unnecessary. So vicious.

Standing, shaking, as a tremor began in her toes and swept upward, Brett surveyed the awesome disarray. There was nothing that hadn't been disturbed in some manner. Pictures were jerked from the walls, books tumbled out of the shelves. Even the kitchen drawers hung open, those that hadn't been pulled out and dumped on the floor.

Moving in numbed silence, Brett walked through each room in her small unit. Her bedroom was totally trashed, the top mattress pulled nearly off the bed. Her closet looked as if a bomb had exploded inside, tossing clothing and hangers every which way. Broken medicine and makeup bottles littered her bathroom floor.

"What kind of person does something like this?" she whispered.

Returning to the living room, she knelt and stretched a trembling hand toward a pile of papers, magazines and picture frames. Carefully, she brushed broken glass away from a photograph, moaning softly when she saw the glass had scratched the faces within the bent frame.

"This was the last photo taken before my family..."

They had been so happy the day this photograph was taken, anticipating a ski trip to Vail. She gazed at her father's arm around her mother's waist, at her mother's upturned face. She wished her mother had faced the camera, but she liked to think that her mother had turned at that instant to tell Brett's father that she loved him.

Her father had a hand on ten-year-old Brett's shoulder; her mother had a hand on twelve-year-old Marcie's shoulder. Both girls proudly displayed the new skis they had received for Christmas.

Brett closed her eyes and impulsively pressed the scarred photo against her chest. She and Marcie had been thrilled to have their own skis. They had marked X's on the kitchen calendar, counting off the days until the much-awaited ski vacation.

When she examined the photo again, looked at the deep scratches that now scarred the faces of her parents, rage exploded in her heart. Rage and helplessness and a bone-deep sense of violation.

Choking on tears, she stood and turned blindly into Sam's arms, beating her fists on his chest.

"I hate whoever did this! I hate him!" Hot tears released in a flood, great giant sobs that shook her whole body.

The guilt from long ago swept over her. The rescue team had found Brett immediately after the avalanche, but they hadn't found the rest of her family in time to save their lives. As an adult, she had learned that survivors of a catastrophe often experienced guilt, but she hadn't known that at ten years old. She had floundered, hating herself for years because she had survived and her family had not.

If she had known and understood the guilt, or if she'd had some kind of counseling after the accident, maybe she wouldn't have been such a problem for the good people in one foster home after another. Maybe she would have felt more secure as an adult. Maybe she wouldn't have reached maturity driven by a deep need to create a family of her own.

Sam's strong arms enclosed her within a circle of warmth and sympathy. "Shh. It's all right. These are just things, and things can be replaced."

"It's *not* all right!" Eyes streaming tears, she waved the photograph. "Look! My most precious possession is ruined!" But when the photograph moved past her face, she saw that the scratches had vanished. Sucking in a breath, she stared at the picture, then lifted her head. "You fixed it, didn't you? Thank you," she whispered, her eyes moist.

For a long instant she and Sam gazed into each other's eyes. Eventually Brett realized that she was standing in the arms of an angel and having sudden and very earthly thoughts, more earthly thoughts than she had experienced in years. Confusion dispatched a rush of pink to her cheeks. It didn't seem appropriate to be thinking that Sam had the sexiest mouth and eyes that she had ever seen, the hardest body. Hastily, she stepped backward, slipping on a shard of broken glass before she caught her balance. She set the photograph of her family in its place of honor on the mantel above the fireplace, then she leaned against the fireplace bricks and rubbed her temples.

"Sam, I can't think. I'm frightened and overwhelmed. What do we do now?"

He gazed at the destruction and frowned. "I'd suggest you take a quick look around to see what's missing. Then let's get out of here."

"Right," she said, grateful for direction. "Shall we phone the police about this?"

He hesitated. "We can always phone them later...."

"Fine."

Too much had happened in the last few days, and vandalism of her condo was the last straw. Her mind retreated to a far corner and refused to deal with this latest assault. Twenty minutes later, moving like a robot, she returned to the kitchen and accepted the cup of strong, hot coffee that Sam handed her.

"I can't be absolutely sure," she said after tasting the coffee, "but as far as I can tell, nothing is missing. My jewelry is here." Tossed all over the bedroom, but nothing had been stolen. "I had some money hidden in the closet. He found it, but he didn't steal it. I don't understand this."

Opening a cabinet door, she withdrew a bag of pretzels. "Want some?" Sam was drinking coffee, but she didn't know if he ate human food. She did know that she was nervous enough to eat the whole bag of pretzels by herself.

"What? No thanks." Holding his coffee cup midway between his waist and his lips, Sam gazed past the kitchen divider into the living room. "I'd guess that whoever did this was searching for something specific."

He'd removed his suit jacket and pulled his tie loose. Brett noticed the muscles shifting beneath his rolled-up sleeves.

"Do you work out? Do you have to shave like real men do?" she asked, the blurted questions coming out of nowhere. "I didn't mean 'real' men," she apologized quickly, "I mean, you're real enough. I meant, I don't know, human men, okay?"

"I beg your pardon?"

She bit her lip and felt the heat rise in her cheeks. "I'm sorry. Nothing. What were you saying?"

"Brett, did you take something with you to the cabin? Something valuable? Something someone else might want?"

"The only things of value are here," she said truthfully, waving a hand at the litter and destruction around them. It would take days to clean up the mess and sort things out. "If someone was looking for something, I have no idea what it might have been."

"We'll figure it out," he replied absently, thinking about something else.

Suddenly Brett knew she couldn't stay here. The sense of violation was too powerful, too frightening. Someone had gained entry to her home, had poked through her private things, had killed her fish. Someone had read her personal letters, examined her bills, had tossed her life around the room as if it were insignificant. A deep shudder convulsed her shoulders.

"If that offer of a safe house still stands," she said in a small voice, "I think I'd like to take you up on it."

"Maybe we're approaching the problem from the wrong direction," Sam speculated, studying her face. "Maybe you're the target. Maybe Thatcher's murder was set up to frame you."

Brett's eyes widened and she swallowed a gasp. "No," she said finally, rejecting the terrifying idea, "that can't be. I don't have any enemies."

But someone had entered her home. Someone hated her enough to destroy her belongings. And in another time, another history, someone had let her go to prison for a murder she hadn't committed.

BRETT WAS TOO UPSET, too distracted, to pay much attention to where Sam was taking her. Lost in her own spinning thoughts, she had only a distant impression that they headed west, toward the foothills, and she recalled passing a few isolated homes, one of which already had wrapped

Christmas lights around two large spruce trees flanking a country porch.

"Where are we?" she asked, rousing herself from the lethargy that had overtaken her after they left her condo.

Sam turned off the pavement onto a graveled road, but the days were November-short and darkness cloaked the surrounding area. Brett couldn't see anything beyond the pines.

"We're near Roxborough Park," Sam replied.

Brett nodded. Roxborough lay well beyond the next closest suburb. The area was gradually growing, but there were still isolated stretches, rocky canyons that sliced into the foothills, stands of pine and spruce. Five-acre lots and larger ones were common here. It was a good area for people who liked country living and who valued privacy.

"The safe house is protected by means I'd rather not discuss," Sam added with a slight smile. The dashboard lights made his hair look like a white cloud flowing back from his face. "You'll be secure here."

He braked the Mercedes before a one-story house with a soaring roofline, and Brett leaned forward to peer through the windshield. Instantly, motion-sensitive lights winked on, washing the front of the house in strong light. She had an impression of stone and glass and wood, natural materials that seemed to grow out of the setting.

"Somehow I'd expected something more along the lines of a fortress," she murmured.

Instead, the house was beautiful. The kind of house that Brett had always imagined her family would have lived in if they had survived the avalanche. The tight knot in her chest relaxed a little, and she drew a deep breath for the first time in hours.

"The door's unlocked," Sam called from the back of the car. He opened the trunk and removed her suitcase.

"Unlocked?" Her eyebrows lifted in alarm.

"It's all right," Sam promised, walking past her toward a covered porch. His utter conviction eased her apprehension enough that Brett followed him inside.

"Oh!" Surprise halted her steps at the entrance to the living room, that and a rush of pleasure. If someone had asked her to design her dream house, this would have been the result.

The entire back of the house was glass, windows and more windows arching up to meet the exposed beams of a vaulted ceiling. A spacious living room flowed into the kitchen, which opened to a breakfast and dining room. The interior was finished in softly glowing aspen paneling, complimenting a towering moss rock fireplace. The furniture mixed old and new in a pleasing eclectic blend, the colors vibrant but not overwhelming. There was a slightly cluttered aspect that made the house seem homey and lived-in, as if someone had passed through the rooms minutes earlier, dropping a book on this table, leaving an afghan on the end of that sofa.

"I love this house!" Brett said softly.

She had a feeling that she had come home. The impression was so strong that she felt as if she knew the titles of the books crowding the bookcase, knew which albums would be in the case beside the CD system. She knew which kitchen drawer had been chosen for the silverware, and which cabinet contained the pots and pans. She even sensed what the bedrooms and baths would look like.

"Sam, this is very strange." Even the artwork on the walls were pieces she might have selected. "I feel like I must have been here before, but I know I haven't."

He grinned and set her suitcase in the hallway leading to the bedrooms. "You won't understand this, Brett, but this is your house." His smile widened at her puzzled expression. "The house is different each time I've been here. It becomes whatever will make my client feel most safe and secure and comfortable."

She stared at him. "Am I dreaming all of this? Am I dreaming you? And this house?"

"It would probably be easier to accept if I told you that you were dreaming, but you're not," he said gently, letting his fingertips brush her cheek. When he dropped his hand, he flexed his fingers as if the touch of her skin had left a tingle. "Do you feel like talking awhile? Or are you exhausted?"

The question seemed so ridiculous that Brett almost laughed. "I'm exhausted, confused, angry, frightened . . . all that and more. I feel as if I've been plucked out of a sane world and set down in a strange place where absolutely nothing makes sense." Her face paled. "Paul is dead, my home has been vandalized, and you're an angel. I'm scared and in trouble up to my hairline, and I think I may be losing my mind. Is that the answer you were looking for?"

He smiled down at her. "All that aside . . . are you up to working a little. Talking about Paul?"

She considered, then shrugged. Eventually, she had to face Paul's death and deal with it in light of her own peril. "I doubt the things I'm feeling are going to change, so we might as well get started. Whatever you say. You're the boss."

"No, Brett. We're in this together."

She gazed into his blue, blue eyes, drawing strength from the calm warmth she saw there. When quick tears appeared between her lashes, she made herself turn toward the kitchen. She was so damned grateful that Sam was here, and that she wasn't alone. She had been alone for so much of her life.

"Let me see if I can find us something to eat, then we'll talk. Is the house stocked with food?" She halted and looked back at him, enjoying the sight of his face and body, thinking him impossibly handsome. "Do angels eat?"

"Angels love mortal food. You can't imagine how tiresome a steady diet of nectar and manna can get."

Her eyes widened. "There's really such a thing as manna from heaven?"

He rolled his eyes and grinned. "That was a joke."

"A joke?" she repeated stupidly. "Oh." Obviously, she had a lot to learn about angels.

"Look, whatever's there will be fine. Can I help you put something together?" Taking off his jacket, he tossed it over the back of a chair, then pulled off his tie and opened his collar.

"Can you make a salad?" She couldn't believe she was having this conversation with an angel. It was too insignificant. It seemed they should be talking about something deep and philosophical, something profound and life altering. Not things as prosaic as whether she liked tomatoes in her salad or whether he preferred ranch or Italian dressing. And he looked so normal moving around the kitchen tearing lettuce and chopping cucumbers.

While Brett grilled a couple of small steaks on the Jenn-Air, she peeked at Sam as he made a fire in the living room fireplace, then set TV trays in front of the flames. He whistled under his breath as he performed these simple chores, and no one watching would have suspected he was anything other than an especially good-looking, ordinary man. Brett shook her head and tried not to dwell on it.

When they were settled in comfortable chairs before the fire, cutting into their steaks, Sam asked, "How did you meet Thatcher?"

Brett lowered her fork. "I accompanied a friend to Paul's clinic. She was scheduled for rhinoplasty. That's a nose job," she added, wondering if he knew about such things. "My friend was a patient of Alan Barkley's, one of Paul's partners, but Paul was there." She paused, remembering how charming he had been. "I ran into him again about ten days later, at a gallery opening. And again a week later at the hospital where I worked."

"You were a nurse, right?"

Brett nodded. "Pediatrics, mostly. I loved nursing. I only quit because Paul objected to a working wife. Anyway, after running into Paul at the hospital, we started seeing each other by design rather than by accident." She contemplated the flames leaping in the fireplace. "Most of my friends were married, some already had babies. That's what I wanted more than anything, a family of my own." She frowned down at her plate. "I think I would have convinced myself that I was in love with whoever I met at that particular time. I was lonely and more than ready to get married."

"Did you love Thatcher?" Sam asked in an even tone.

"I thought I did. At least in the beginning." A sigh lifted her chest. "Paul could be charming when he wanted to be. He was sophisticated, successful…everyone kept telling me what a great catch he was." She let a silence develop. Remembering. "I wanted Paul to be Mr. Right so badly that I refused to see the difference between the public Paul and the private, real Paul. The real Paul was petty, ruthlessly ambitious, manipulative, and his tongue was like a scalpel. He could cut to the bone with a few well-chosen words." After a minute, she added in a whisper. "He had an instinct for recognizing weak spots in the people around him."

Sam drowned his steak in A.1. sauce. "Thatcher had been married before, hadn't he?"

Brett nodded and sighed. "Barbara is convinced that I broke up her marriage. But I didn't meet Paul until months after his divorce." She hesitated. "I've always felt sorry for Barbara. I think she was a good wife to Paul. She doted on him. If you saw her, you would swear she was, oh, maybe thirty-five, a good fifteen years younger than she is. But to Paul, she was old. She was five years older than he was, and he didn't like that."

Brett leaned back in her chair and watched the flames leaping in the hearth. "I think Paul wanted a perpetually young wife, a walking advertisement for his clinic, maybe, or an ornament to prove his virility and desirability. Barbara is a beautiful woman, but she's no longer young." A silence developed, followed by a soft sigh. "I was twenty-four when we married. Paul was almost forty."

"Did he operate on you?" Sam asked, eyebrows rising.

"Did you think I was born with Elizabeth Taylor's nose?" Brett asked with a humorless laugh. "Paul reshaped my nose the first year we were married. If I had agreed, he would have given me a cheek implant, a breast augmentation, and heaven knows what else. But I realized early on that unless I stopped it, there wouldn't be an end. He'd be 'fixing' and reshaping me until I wasn't me anymore."

"Is that how Barbara felt? That Paul had reshaped her into someone else?"

"I don't know. Barbara and I ran into each other occasionally, but our relationship wasn't cordial. Certainly we never talked about anything personal."

Moving her TV tray aside, Brett approached the fireplace and extended her hands. "Things weren't good between us before, but when I refused additional cosmetic surgery... that's when our marriage took a real nosedive.''

"You're a beautiful woman," Sam said quietly, watching her. "You were right to refuse any alterations."

"Thank you," Brett said, feeling a shadow of pink appear on her cheeks. She drew a breath and continued the story, wanting to get it over with. "There were other problems. Paul didn't want me to work. Said it looked bad, as if he couldn't support me." She rubbed her forehead. "That was difficult, giving up nursing. And then he didn't like my friends. So, I gave up my profession and people who mattered to me because I wanted a family, and because I couldn't admit that I'd made a bad mistake by marrying Paul.

"The biggest heartache was discovering that Paul absolutely did not want children, not ever." She leaned against the fireplace and looked into the flames. "When I finally accepted that Paul wasn't going to change his opinion about having a family, that's when I found an attorney and began divorce proceedings." She glanced at Sam then back to the fire. "I'll be thirty in June. If I'm ever going to start a family..."

Now she was back where she had begun. Alone, and with no immediate prospect of remarriage or the children she wanted. Sometimes it seemed that she would never replace the family she had lost so long ago.

"Brett?"

"Sorry, I was daydreaming." She picked up the discussion about Paul. "I don't mean to give the impression that Paul is solely to blame for our bad marriage," she continued, trying to be absolutely truthful. "In the beginning, I was too much of an approval seeker to risk confronting him on the large issues, but I fought him on a smaller basis. He didn't like me popping into the clinic unannounced, so I did it frequently. He didn't like to discuss problem patients or operations that went awry, so I made a point of finding out about them." She watched Sam blot his lips with a napkin. "I crossed Paul in a hundred ways. It sounds petty and small and it was. We were both trying to hurt and annoy each other. I didn't like myself very much at the end."

"Who do you think killed Paul?"

Absently, she pulled the rubber band from her ponytail and shook out a tumble of dark, shoulder-length hair. "I thought about that while I was alone in the cabin with Paul's body out on the porch." She restrained a shudder. "But I honestly don't have any idea. Eventually Paul alienated everyone around him. He made enemies easily." A slight shrug lifted her shoulders. "The killer could be any one of a number of people."

Mentioning the cabin and those awful hours before the sheriff appeared sparked a sudden memory. "Sam, did I tell you about the car that almost ran me off the road when I was driving to the cabin?"

Interest flickered in his eyes and he set aside his TV tray. "Tell me." When she finished, he nodded thoughtfully. "Did you see the driver?"

She tugged a hand through her loose hair. "I wish I had, but I didn't."

"What color was the car? Was it large? Small?"

Frustration tightened her shoulders. "It was dark outside and blowing snow. I have an impression that it was a large car, heavy, but I couldn't swear to it. I just don't know for certain. I was concentrating on keeping my car out of the ditch." Here was their only clue, and she couldn't remember anything about it. Damn!

"I didn't realize this until now, but immediately after the car passed, I started thinking about Paul. Maybe something about the car reminded me of him. Maybe it was a Cadillac. Or maybe not." She lifted eyes filled with frustration. "I just don't remember. I didn't see the car well enough."

As if he'd read her mind and knew the sense of futility she was experiencing, Sam walked to where she stood in front of the fire. He pressed her hand. "We're just getting started," he assured her.

Brett looked down at the solid warm hand enclosing hers. His fingers were long and tapered, more the fingers of a doctor or a piano player than a fighter. If he was a fighter, that is; she really didn't know much about angels. But she liked his hands. His nails were nicely shaped, his palm square. The warmth of his skin tingled against hers, radiating up her arm and reminding her of how cold it was outside.

Although it startled Brett to realize she was attracted to him, she supposed it wasn't really surprising. Sam was her champion, the one person in the world who could say with utter conviction that he *knew* she hadn't murdered her ex-husband. The one person who was trying to help her. Plus, he was stunningly handsome, and the most unusual man she had ever met.

But an attraction was the last thing she wanted, a complication she absolutely did not need. This had to be the ultimate example of a relationship with no future. The thought made her smile and step away from him.

"I think you should get some sleep," Sam commented, studying her face. "You're swaying on your feet, you're so exhausted."

"You're right," she agreed. "I hardly slept at all while I was at the cabin. I'll just clean up these dishes, then I'll—"

He caught her when she stumbled, lifting her in his arms as if she were weightless. "You're going to bed now."

She was too tired to argue. And it felt so good, so safe, to relax in his arms. Letting go for the first time in days, Brett rested her head on his shoulder while he carried her down the corridor and into a master bedroom that was exactly as she had imagined it would be.

The room was large, yet cozy and snug at the same time, decorated in complementing tones of blue and cream. When Sam placed her on the king-size bed, she looked around with a dreamy smile of delight, then kicked out of her boots and fell back on a mound of pillows.

"Oh," she said suddenly, sitting up. "Paul's car! He must have driven up from Denver, but where is his car?" Another thought occurred. "Maybe that *was* Paul's car that passed me. But the killer was driving it!"

"I'll check it out," Sam murmured, pulling the spread and blankets up to her chin. "Go to sleep now."

She should get up and put on her nightgown, but the pillows seemed to pull her deeper into their softness. "Sam? Will you be staying here, too?" she murmured, hardly able to keep her eyes open.

"Do you want me to?" he asked, sounding pleased and surprised.

"I think so."

"I'll be here when you wake up," he promised when he noticed that she was struggling to remain awake until he reassured her.

He was reaching to turn off the lights when Brett made one final effort to speak before sleep claimed her.

"Sam?"

"Yes?"

"Thank you. Thank you for...everything. I'm sorry I doubted you. I said some things that—"

"Shh."

The last thing she remembered was his hand on her forehead, then she went out like a light.

Chapter Five

Sam returned to the living room, where he picked up the dishes and put away the TV trays before he settled in front of the fire with a snifter of brandy.

Although they hadn't made any progress toward solving the mystery of Thatcher's murder or the vandalism at Brett's condo, he was pleased overall with how the day had gone. Brett had not been arrested, they had gained a little time, and she was accepting his reality better than Sam had expected.

What surprised him, he thought, frowning into the flames dancing in the fireplace, was his response to her. He always experienced sympathy and compassion for the victims of injustice, but something more was happening here. Something subtle but definite.

In the last hours, Brett Thatcher had changed from being an assignment into being a cause. He was going to rescue this woman if it took from now until eternity because...because...

His frown deepened. Something about her touched him on a level that hadn't stirred in a long, long time. Part of it was her unique beauty. She presented an odd blend of unconscious sensuality and wholesome innocence. It was as if the world had touched her lightly, although he knew this was not true. Brett Thatcher had experienced tragedy in her life. She had not walked an easy path.

He had researched her background, of course. He knew about the deaths of her parents and sister, knew about the series of foster parents who hadn't known how to handle a lonely, guilt-ridden and withdrawn little girl. He could guess how she had struggled to cope with what would have seemed like one rejection after another as she was passed through the foster care system.

Then came the painful teenage years when she had not recognized the budding beauty she was becoming. Then the years of fighting to finance her way through college and nursing school.

When he had read her background file, two things had leaped out at Sam. Brett Thatcher's deep loneliness, and her profound love of children.

The inner strength and stubborn determination shining through the recap of her background formed a large part of his attraction to her. An example of her fortitude could be found in the recent upsetting days she had endured. Despite her protests, she was coping with all that had happened to her. Brett Thatcher possessed the spirit of a natural fighter, and he admired that quality.

He also liked her house. Sam understood that the ever-changing safe house spoke volumes about his clients. And he had seen some strange layouts in his time. Once he had driven up to a moat encircling a stone castle. He had seen fortresses and cottages, mansions and caves, and everything in between.

Brett's house was not large, but neither was it cramped. The rooms were well proportioned, the ambience warm and welcoming, airy and open. There were books on every subject and fresh flowers, and furniture that invited one to relax and be comfortable. The house was practical, sensible and as lovely as she was.

What tugged his heart were the children's rooms. Children were part of Brett's psyche, a deeply imbedded desire. Her brief comments about discovering that Paul Thatcher would never agree to have children had concealed a universe of emotion. The discovery must have utterly devastated her as Brett Thatcher was meant to be surrounded by children.

Sam sipped his brandy and an unconscious sigh lifted his chest.

Earthbound angels such as the Avengers could enjoy sexual congress with a mortal, although it drove Angelo crazy to hear about it. But angels could not sire children. Such a hybrid mixture as mortal and angel was not part of the divine plan. Consequently, most angels venerated parenthood and the mystery of conception. In truth, most angels experienced a little jealousy toward a mortal's ability to procreate.

Sam jerked from his reverie with a start. What on earth was he doing? He hadn't thought about sex or children or fixated on a particular woman in . . . he couldn't remember when.

Annoyed, he drained the last of the brandy, then stood and reached for his jacket. He had more important things to do than regret that he would never live in a house with a nursery or sire a child or experience the radiant and enduring love of a woman like Brett Thatcher.

Muttering, he stepped outside into the clear, icy night and thrust his hands deep into his pockets. The cold air smelled of pine and wood smoke.

It smelled the same when he materialized outside Brett's cabin, nearly eighty miles from where she lay sleeping. He didn't worry about her. The safe house was invisible to all but another angel. If he could just shake loose the memory of large caramel eyes, he might actually accomplish something.

Concentrating, he peered through the silent darkness surrounding the cabin. Nothing had been disturbed since they left it. By opening his senses, Sam could feel a residue of dark fury, of sudden and passionate hatred. The echo of strong emotions swirled in his mind; dark bass notes preceding a murderous rage followed by the lighter top notes of Brett's arrival.

He glanced toward the woods where Paul's body awaited discovery, frowned, then scanned the driveway, looking for a snow-covered lump the size of a Cadillac. But the only car in the driveway was Brett's old Buick. There was no sign of Paul's car.

Had Thatcher arrived here with someone else? Had they driven from Denver together? Or had Paul met his killer nearby and then shared a ride to the cabin? Sam already knew that Paul's car was not in his Denver garage since he'd checked that possibility before coming here.

Invisible to a mortal's eye and invulnerable to the cold, he moved swiftly along the five-mile stretch of road between the cabin and Highway 9. Undoubtedly, the sheriff would have noticed an abandoned car, but Sam was not one to leave details to chance.

Once he assured himself that Paul Thatcher's car would not be found easily, the real work began. He would have to check every car in Summit County, searching for a dark Cadillac bearing vanity plates that read GOD. The license plate offended him. Dr. Paul Thatcher truly had been an arrogant son of a . . . gun.

Shortly before dawn he found Thatcher's car nosed over the bank of a shallow drop-off. Passing snow plows had created a small mountain of snow along the sides of the road, blocking the Cadillac from sight. It would be a while before it was discovered.

The windshield was shattered, and the interior was littered with empty beer cans. A condom lay on the floor of the back seat.

BRETT WOKE SLOWLY and with pleasure, gazing at bright winter sunshine falling through tall windows. This room was everything she would want a bedroom to be. A gas fireplace snuggled in one corner. Sliding glass doors opened to a pine-and-aspen enclosed deck. When she entered the bathroom she discovered a Jacuzzi tub surrounded by plants, plus a shower. In the medicine cabinet above double sinks she found a toothbrush and her favorite toothpaste alongside a makeup bag containing the cosmetics she usually used.

It wasn't until she stepped into the shower that her dream bubble burst, and the events of the last few days returned in a flood. Groaning softly, she sagged against the shower tiles and let the water cascade over her.

This was not her house. Nothing was right in her world. If Sam hadn't appeared, she would be in jail right now, facing an unthinkable future. For all she knew, that could still happen.

Hurrying, she toweled dry, then rushed to the closet, not surprised to find that she didn't need to open the suitcase she had brought from the cabin. Her clothing had magically appeared inside the closet. She peered at racks of garments that should have been at her condo but were here, instead. And she decided that nothing could surprise her at this point.

After dressing in brown slacks and boots, and a sweater that highlighted the green flecks in her eyes, she applied mascara and pink lipstick, then fluffed her hair, letting it fall loose around her shoulders. She hesitated, then spritzed a little perfume on her wrists, avoiding her eyes in the mirror and not asking herself why she was so concerned about her appearance.

In short order she discovered that she'd been wrong about there being no more surprises. As she walked down the hallway, she glanced into doorways that she had been too tired to explore last night, stopping abruptly before one of them. A soft sound closed her throat and sudden moisture sprang to her eyes.

This was a small, bright room, flooded with morning light that appeared to chase the teddy bears dancing across the wallpaper. A real teddy bear smiled at her through the wooden slats of a crib. It was a lovely room, perfect in every way. All it lacked was an infant to love it.

And all Brett lacked was an infant to love. The reminder opened a hole in her heart. Aching inside, listening to the tick of her biological clock, she quietly closed the door to the nursery.

"Good morning," Sam said when she entered the kitchen.

"Hi." Going directly to the coffeepot, she poured a cup, then looked at him as the first sip sent a welcome jolt of caffeine through her system.

This morning her angel wore jeans, boots and a loose blue sweater. The sun streaming through the kitchen window shimmered around him, creating an illusion that he was lit from within. He was an absolutely stunning man. White blond-haired, blue-eyed, lean and tall. He was a great advertisement for heaven.

Brett tilted her head and met his eyes. "Ah, there's something I keep wondering . . . this is going to sound kind of . . ." Awkwardness heated her cheeks. "But I wanted to ask if you . . ."

"If I've met God?" he finished for her, smiling. "It's a common question."

"Well . . . yes. Have you?"

His deep voice was gentle when he answered. "There are things—mysteries—that I'm not permitted to discuss."

"I'm not allowed to ask you questions?" She took a seat at the kitchen table and gazed up at him.

He leaned against the countertop near the sink and smiled. "I can guess some of the things you want to ask, and I'll answer what I can. First, yes, I was once a mortal. Most of the Avenging Angels were. Having experienced mortality, we better understand the concept of injustice. However, most angels were never mortal."

"But you were," she said, staring at him and wanting to know who he had been and when he had lived, and where, and if he had loved.

"My earthly life was brief and very long ago. I don't recall much about it except that it ended badly. My family and I were victims of a petty tyrant's revenge." He shrugged. "I was in my mid-twenties when I left this plane. The time period was harsh and brutal—there was nothing remarkable or memorable about my mortal life."

"What did you do for a living? Were you married? Did you have children?"

"I managed my father's estate. I acquired some renown as a jouster, I believe." He smiled at her expression. "I was betrothed, but made the transition before the marriage occurred. It was all very long ago."

"What happened to you when you, ah, left this plane?"

Tilting his head and still smiling, he wagged a finger at her, and Brett felt her cheeks turn pink. "I think you can guess that I'm not permitted to answer that question," he said gently.

"Can you tell me more about being an Avenging Angel?"

Something new appeared in his eyes. "One of the difficulties is being so closely bound to mortals and mortal problems. Too closely bound, in the opinions of some, since our proximity occasionally leads us to fall prey to many of the same temptations and attitudes that plague humankind."

"Really?" Fascinated, Brett stared at him. "What kind of temptations?"

He shrugged again, unconsciously calling attention to wide shoulders and an elegant stance. "I have a friend who smokes cigarettes. We lost a skilled avenger to drugs, another to alcohol. Some of us have resorted to episodes of violence. Some have formed attachments to mortal women."

They gazed at each other, and suddenly the simple act of sharing morning coffee in a winter-bright kitchen seemed extraordinarily intimate.

Sam straightened abruptly and turned away from her toward the coffeepot. He took his time refilling his cup.

"I found Thatcher's car," he announced.

Brett cleared her throat. "Where is it?" After she heard about the condition of the Cadillac, she said, "Paul was not a beer drinker. My guess is that he wasn't driving when the car crashed."

"I don't think so, either," Sam agreed.

"On the face of it, what you've described sounds like teenagers taking a joyride."

Sam sat down at the table across from her, nodding. "That's my guess, too. As a working theory, let's suppose that Thatcher met someone in Silverthorne, perhaps for dinner, and afterward they drove to the cabin in Thatcher's car. Something happens and Thatcher gets murdered.

The killer drives the Cadillac back to his own car, parks it and leaves the keys in the ignition, hoping someone will steal it. Someone does, probably teenagers, and the car gets wrecked.''

Brett poured more coffee, then returned to the table. ''Why do you think Paul and someone had dinner before going to the cabin?''

''It doesn't seem logical that Thatcher and the killer each drove eighty miles to meet at a cabin he no longer owned. It makes more sense to me that he and his killer went somewhere else first, it doesn't have to be out for dinner, then drove together to the cabin almost as an after-thought.'' He hesitated. ''Is there any possibility that Thatcher knew you would be at the cabin? Could he, and someone else, have gone there to talk to you?''

Brett frowned and looked into her cup. ''If Paul wanted to talk to me, he would have phoned my condo to make an appointment. We were far beyond unscheduled meetings. But he didn't call last weekend.''

Sam gazed into space, concentrating. ''Plus, he must have left for the mountains hours before you did. So that idea doesn't work. Who knew that you were going to the cabin?''

Brett thought a minute. ''Greta Rawlings, the house-keeper. I phoned her midweek and asked if she would stop by and clean the place.''

''Mrs. Rawlings lives in Silverthorne?''

Brett nodded. ''And I dropped by the clinic last week. I might have mentioned the cabin to the receptionist. Billie and I have known each other for years.''

''Why did you go to the clinic? Was it to see Thatcher?''

''Absolutely not! Billie and I were going to lunch.''

"So, you could have mentioned your plans to Billie, and she could have mentioned to Paul that you were going to the cabin?"

"She could have," Brett agreed, "but I doubt that she did. I trust Billie. She knows how things stand between Paul and me."

"Is there anyone else who knew?"

"I told a couple of friends that I would be gone for a while. But, Sam, neither of them know where the cabin is, and they didn't know Paul."

He studied her, bright sunshine emphasizing the strong angles of his face. "Why did you decide to go to the cabin?"

Brett shrugged and cupped her hands around her coffee cup. "I wanted some time alone, away from distractions, to think about my future. I need to decide what I'm going to do with the rest of my life." In a habitual gesture, she pushed a wave of hair away from her forehead. "I want to return to nursing, but I'd have to take some refresher classes. I took the registration forms with me, intending to fill them out. And I've also always been interested in writing. In fact, I'm working on a manuscript. I'd hoped to do a little editing on it while I was at the cabin." She released a sigh. "I suppose I saw my time at the cabin as a chance to catch up on some things I've been putting off, a chance to relax and think about what happens next. Before I could think about anything, I found Paul's body."

Sam nodded, his eyes on her mouth. "On another subject...have you thought any further about your condominium being vandalized? Who might have done it and what they might have been searching for?"

Brett shook her head. "I'd like to think it was just a random act."

"Brett...do you really believe that?"

"No," she admitted reluctantly, looking away from the intensity in his gaze. A small tremor of apprehension traveled up her spine. "I might be able to convince myself it was a random thing if something had been stolen, but nothing was."

She couldn't help wondering what would have happened if she had been home when the intruder arrived. Would her presence have deflected his entry? Or had he hoped that she would be there?

Reacting to a sudden tremor, she pushed her coffee cup away and wrapped her arms around her waist before she lifted her head. "So what do we do now?"

"How about breakfast? I make French toast that melts in your mouth."

Brett stared, then burst into laughter. When she caught her breath, she wiped her eyes and smiled. "I suspect that meeting you is going to be one of the highlights of my life. I'll never feel the same about angels again."

"About that French toast . . ." he said, grinning.

"I'd love some. I tend to eat when I'm nervous. By the time this is over, I'll weigh a hundred extra pounds." She stood to set the table, then looked at him. "Sam? We're going to solve Paul's murder, aren't we? I'm not going to spend my life in prison . . . ?" She thought about the sun-washed nursery down the hall and again felt a hole open inside her chest. "I guess I'm asking if, ah, angels are always successful?"

He touched his fingertips to her cheek and gazed into her eyes. "I've had a few failures, but not many. We'll find the answers. After breakfast, we'll drive to Paul's house and have a look around. We'll start there. Then we'll stop by the clinic and ask a few questions."

"But what if—" She bit off the question. There was no point borrowing hypothetical trouble. She would take it one step at a time and try not to worry herself into a frenzy.

Meanwhile, she was with Sam, her angel, her champion. And being with him was beginning to feel more comfortable, yet more electric, with every passing minute.

Still, she would have felt better if he hadn't mentioned having had a few failures.

THE SKY WAS COLD but bright. Sunshine sparkled on the snow as if the drifts had been strewn with sequins. It wasn't until they entered the outskirts of town that the snow bordering the highway turned gray and slushy.

"Do you know where Paul lives?" Brett asked. Immediately she felt foolish. Of course he knew. But she babbled on, anyway, because thinking about entering Paul's home made her nervous. "When we were married, Paul and I lived in Cherry Hills. It was a huge house with a live-in housekeeper. Much too large for two people." She had disliked that house intensely, especially after Paul made it crystal clear that they would never fill the rooms with children.

"After the divorce, I moved back to my condominium. I was glad I hadn't sold it as Paul had advised." She looked straight ahead through the windshield. "Paul sold the house in Cherry Hills and bought a very upscale renovation in the Capital Hill area. Near the Denver Country Club." Biting her lip, she swung toward Sam. "Look, do we have to go inside the house?"

Even though he'd told her the Mercedes could drive itself, it made Brett's nerves jump when Sam looked away from the road.

"I don't know how much time we have before Paul's body is discovered. But once it is, you'll be arrested shortly thereafter.'' Sympathy warmed his gaze, and a flicker of something else that Brett would have interpreted as sexy and speculative in any other man. ''I'm sorry, but we don't have time to be delicate.''

Brett nodded and pushed shaking hands beneath her thighs. They didn't speak again until Sam guided the Mercedes to a stop along the slushy curb of a narrow, tree-lined street. Although spaced closely together, the houses were large, impressive, and most had been extensively renovated within the last decade. In the days of the silver barons, this had been Denver's elite area. It was headed that way again.

Brett peered out the window at Paul's house, a boxy two-story built in the early 1900s. She had an impression of stucco and glass, European balconies and climbing vines that would be lush and charming in summer. The wrought iron fence enclosing the property was so like Paul, a warning that one could approach this far but no farther.

She jumped when Sam touched her shoulder.

''I'll go inside and open the front door for you,'' he said in a conversational tone. They might have been discussing the cloudless sky and frigid temperature instead of planning to break and enter. His gaze followed the tumble of warm brown hair that curled on her shoulders. ''I'd suggest you raise the hood of your parka. And don't touch anything while we're inside.''

''Maybe there's a housekeeper....''

Sam shook his head. ''I'd sense it if anyone were inside.''

Suddenly Brett wondered who would handle Paul's final affairs? Who would arrange his funeral service? Who would clean out his closets and dispose of the thousand-dollar suits? Who would decide what happened to his art collection and his antiques?

Probably his sister who lived back east somewhere, a sister Paul had never liked and hadn't spoken to in fifteen years.

"It's sad," she murmured.

But Sam had already gone. One minute he was sitting beside her; the next instant, he was simply... gone.

Wondering if she would ever get used to his abrupt disappearances, Brett waited until her heartbeat settled, then she pulled the hood of her parka over her head and adjusted the edges to conceal her features.

The wrought iron gate squealed when she pushed it open, and she cast a quick, furtive glance up and down the sidewalk. At the far end of the block, a man waited at the corner for the light to change; a car passed in the street behind her, its tires spraying mud and slush across the side of Sam's Mercedes.

Hastily, Brett closed the gate behind her and hurried up the wide steps of a stone-floored veranda. Before she could raise a hand to knock, the door opened and she swallowed hard, then slipped inside the foyer.

"My heart's beating like a trip-hammer," she confessed. "I hate this."

Sam gave her a quick touch of assurance, pressing her shoulder. "We'll walk through the house. If you feel inclined to open a drawer or touch anything...don't. Tell me, and I'll do it."

"Let me guess. You don't leave fingerprints, either. Right?"

"Right." His smile was distracted and failed to reach his eyes.

Brett drew a deep breath, then looked around her. The foyer was large enough to accommodate several pieces of furniture, and she expected to see the table and mirror that had been in their foyer in Cherry Hills. But the space was empty.

"Exactly what are we searching for?" she inquired, pushing her hands into the pockets of her parka. She spoke in a nervous whisper, half expecting someone to jump out of a door and arrest them on the spot for trespassing.

"You'll know better than I if there's anything unusual or out of place. We're looking for anything that might suggest a state of mind or another person or—"

"I get the picture," Brett interrupted. She could think of four million places she would rather be than standing in Paul's dim, silent house. "Let's get this over with."

Stepping forward, trying to walk quietly, she moved through double French doors into an enormous living room. The draperies were drawn, but enough light filtered through that she noticed an ornately appointed fireplace and the carved molding that defined the base of a high ceiling.

Brett stopped short and frowned, scanning the few pieces of furniture that seemed adrift on an ocean of pale blue carpet.

"That's very odd."

"What is?"

"The lack of furniture. And artwork." Stepping farther into the room, she puzzled over the empty room and bare walls. "Paul owns an extremely valuable art collection. And he's very proud of his antiques. He insisted on a prenuptial agreement stating that I would never make any claim on his art or antiques. He was happier than I'd ever seen him when he learned I intended to honor the agreement and didn't want his art or his furniture."

The empty room was unnerving. The small, mismatched arrangement of unremarkable furniture made her think of squatters camping out in a vacant house.

"Does Thatcher keep his artwork in a vault some-where?"

"No. That's what's so peculiar about this bare room. Paul liked to impress people. And he genuinely enjoyed his collection. He liked to display it." Her bewilderment deep-ened. "I would have expected this room to be elegantly and completely furnished, the walls crowded with wonderful paintings."

Sam stood with his back to the fireplace, watching her in the dim light. "Perhaps a theft?"

Brett shook her head. "I don't think so. There are no hangers or marks on the wall to indicate that anything was ever hung in this room."

The mystery deepened as they continued their inspec-tion. There was not a stick of furniture in the beautifully wallpapered and mirrored dining room. It appeared that Paul ate at the kitchen table, from a set which could have been purchased at a garage sale.

Brett stared at the table and chairs in amazement. Paul didn't eat, he dined. She absolutely could not imagine Paul "dining" at this scarred kitchen set.

Neither was there any furniture in the library, and only one shelf contained a few of Paul's prized first editions, carefully braced by a pile of popular novels instead of the expensive bookends Brett remembered. The other shelves were empty.

"This is very strange," she murmured as they climbed to the upper story. She glanced at the stair railing. "And ev-erything is dusty. But Paul certainly would have a house-keeper."

Six bedrooms and two baths opened off the upper hall-way. Like the rooms downstairs, these rooms were also puzzlingly empty except for the master bedroom at the end of the corridor.

Brett stopped in the doorway. "Finally. This room looks more like I would expect."

An antique bed adapted to accommodate a king-size mattress was positioned against a wall beautifully papered in flocked silk. It faced a bank of windows situated to gather the morning light. The master bedroom was completely furnished, though sparsely, with valuable antiques. But here too the walls were bare of the art Paul had treasured. Gone was the small Matisse sketch that had been his first purchase and which he had told her had hung in his bedroom for ten years. He had joked that the sketch had outlasted one wife and would probably outlast several more.

Brett entered the bedroom gingerly, feeling like an intruder, and stepped to the bed.

"I'm surprised the bed is made. I never knew Paul to make a bed." She followed the scent of his after-shave to the door of the master bathroom and glanced inside. The scent was stronger here, making her feel slightly sick.

Then she saw the jar of cotton balls, and a cosmetics bag.

She stared a minute before she noticed a woman's silk bathrobe hanging beside the shower stall next to Paul's imported terry-cloth wrapper.

"Sam?" she whispered. "Would you mind opening the closet door?"

He complied at once and stepped back so Brett could enter a large walk-in closet. Eyes widening, she gazed at a row of women's clothing, then inspected a line of pumps and the sweaters neatly folded on the shelves separating the closet into two halves.

Feeling betrayed, Brett stumbled out of the closet and sat on the edge of the bed, staring at the floor.

Sam studied her with a frown. "You've been divorced for almost a year, and you were separated for six months before that."

When she understood his mistake, she waved a listless hand. "It isn't that he was seeing someone, I don't care about that." She raised her head. "It's who he's been seeing. I recognize one of the sweaters because I gave it to her. It's hand knitted. One of a kind. Paul's been living with Billie Place, the receptionist at the clinic."

"Is that a surprise?"

Brett pushed back the hood of her parka and ran a hand through her hair. She wished she had something to eat.

"A *big* surprise. A shock, actually. I believed Billie and I were friends. We have lunch once a month or so. Occasionally we go out to dinner, take in a movie. I wanted to keep in touch because I like Billie and because she's been helping with my manuscript." A hint of bitterness made her voice sound ragged. "I thought she was being sympathetic when she asked about the difficulties over the settlement. I never dreamed..." She waved a hand toward the closet. "I guess I know now how Paul's lawyers always seemed to be one step ahead of mine. Billie must have told Paul everything I confided in her."

"Let's go downstairs. We'll take a look at Thatcher's office," Sam suggested gently, extending a hand.

Brett let him pull her to her feet. "I can't get over it. Billie and Paul. The thing is, he didn't like her. At least that's what he told me. He always said there was something sneaky about Billie that he didn't trust." Sam placed his hand against the small of her back and guided her out of the bedroom into the dusty corridor. "Plus, Billie just isn't the type of woman I would have thought Paul would be interested in."

"Why not?" Sam asked, stepping back to allow her to precede him down the staircase.

"Billie is pretty, but she's not—" Brett stopped, realizing how immodest the comment would sound. A flush of pink flared on her cheeks. "And she's in her late thirties. Age and image was such a factor with Paul. I'd have expected him to choose someone much younger." She glanced into the empty rooms they passed on the way to Paul's study. "I don't understand any of this, Sam."

She recognized Paul's desk. He'd bought it in Europe when he was married to Barbara. But a small TV had replaced the wide-screen television that she remembered, and the credenza that matched the desk was missing.

"I don't feel right about going through Paul's desk," she said, looking up at Sam's stern expression. But she would have loved to examine the files in the locked file cabinet. Paul didn't keep certain files at the clinic. The files of patients whose operations had gone awry were kept here, at home. There weren't many, but those were the files Brett longed to inspect.

Ignoring her remark, Sam opened a desk drawer, examined the contents, then opened another drawer containing correspondence.

Brett glared at him and jammed twitching fingers deeper into her pockets. "Is this really necessary?" she asked after a minute. "I'm really not comfortable about—"

"Have you ever heard of Sansmith Development?" Sam asked, glancing through the loose pages thrust inside a file folder.

"Sansmith? No. Why?" Despite herself, Brett edged closer. Finally she abandoned the high road and sank to the low road of curiosity, interested in whatever Sam had found.

"Look, but don't touch," he warned. Turning the folder to face her, he spread out several pages. "This appears to be a loosely organized ledger of some kind."

Brett peered over his arm, standing close enough to feel the warm radiance of his body. For an instant, Sam's closeness made her head reel, then she forced her thoughts to steady on the pages.

"Those are large figures," she commented, puzzled.

The handwriting was Paul's, but sloppier than she recalled, written as if he were angry. Dates ran down one side of the pages, beginning shortly before Brett filed for divorce. The dates were followed by dollar figures. Ten thousand, fifty thousand, eighteen thousand, and so on. A running total appeared to be scribbled in the margins.

"What is the starting figure?" she asked.

Sam ruffled the pages. "It looks like five million. The entries reduce the figure. Let's see . . . here it is. The list of ledger entries reduces the figure to a million and change."

A soft gasp closed Brett's throat. "Five million! Paul had money, but not *that* kind of money!"

Neither of them assumed the handwritten ledger reflected monies paid to Paul. The empty house suggested otherwise.

"Was Paul making payments of some kind to this Sansmith Development?" Brett wondered out loud. "Did he have to sell his antiques and artwork?" Something had happened to Paul's treasured belongings, that was certain. And Paul would not have parted willingly with his artwork or antiques.

Sam replaced the papers in the file. "Sansmith is the name on the folder. But this could record money received." Neither of them believed it. "But I'd guess he's keeping a record of monies paid out."

"We need to talk to Billie Place," Brett decided. And it wasn't going to be easy. Although she wanted to give Billie the benefit of the doubt, it seemed obvious that Billie had repeated Brett's confidences to Paul. A friend's betrayal was never easy to deal with. If, that is, Billie had really been a friend. Now Brett wondered.

Sam nodded and the movement captivated her. She could have sworn that part of the light in the dim room radiated from him, although he didn't seem to be aware of it. He seemed to be concentrating, utilizing senses that Brett didn't possess.

"There's anger here," he said softly, as if talking to himself. "Anger and frustration. Ambition. Deceit."

Suddenly Brett wondered what it would be like to kiss him. What would she feel? And what would he feel? Would it be the same?

Ducking her head so he wouldn't see the sudden color climbing from her throat, Brett jerked her hood back over her hair.

"Please, Sam. Can we get out of here? It's so... quiet." The dim stillness, and the knowledge that Paul would never return to these rooms, made the hair prickle on the back of her neck.

Almost running, she strode rapidly to the foyer. "I'll wait for you by the car," she called over her shoulder.

"I'll only be a minute."

Outside, she paused on the veranda to draw a deep, chilled breath. She withdrew balled hands from her pockets and shook the tightness from her fingers before she started down the stone steps.

At the bottom of the steps Brett halted, frowned and looked around, peering through a thick tangle of winter-bare shrubbery that partially blocked the view to the street.

Someone was watching her. She could sense it, could feel a concentrated flow of fury as if she stood in a dark beam.

Panicked, she spun toward the street and released a quick breath of relief when she saw Sam waiting beside the Mercedes. But her relief was short-lived. His body was tense, and he glared intently toward the house looming on Brett's right.

She rushed toward the curb, letting the wrought iron gate bang shut behind her. "Someone—" she began breathlessly.

"I know. I think it's coming from that direction, but I can't pin it down." He hesitated. "Wherever he is, he's withdrawing."

Brett leaned against the car before she opened the door. Her heart was still racing. "What? No X ray vision?"

Sam slid behind the wheel, but he didn't immediately reach for the ignition. He stretched a long arm across the seat backs and examined her face.

"The vandalism, this incident…this is a situation I didn't anticipate." His steady thoughtful look unnerved her.

"Don't say that, Sam. Aren't angels supposed to know everything?"

"I wish we did."

Brett peered anxiously at the houses crowding the block, looking for shadowy movement. "I do, too. Someone was watching me and it didn't feel good."

"I know this much—you're in danger."

Chapter Six

"We didn't actually see anyone," Brett said over a cup of *caffé latte*. "But someone was there, watching us. Me."

Raising her head, she studied the patrons in the small coffee shop. No one appeared to be paying any attention to them, but she still felt like someone was staring, still felt creepy inside. The sensation of hatred had been so powerful that a residue of frightening intensity lingered.

"The question is," Sam said, thinking out loud, "was he waiting for Thatcher? Or does he know Thatcher is dead, and he was waiting for you?"

"Are you sure it was a male?"

"Actually, no."

The fragrant warmth in the coffee shop had felt good when they first entered, but now the heat began to feel stifling. Brett slipped out of her parka and tugged at the collar of her sweater. The heat, Sam's nearness, the incident at Paul's house . . . everything conspired to keep her emotions in turmoil.

"Whoever it was, he couldn't have been waiting for me. There's no way anyone could guess that I'd go to Paul's house this morning."

Sam gazed at her across the small table. "The killer might."

Suddenly she felt cold again. How on earth had all this happened? How had Brett Thatcher, ordinary person, gotten involved in a murder? What had she done to generate the malevolence that she'd felt so strongly in front of Paul's house?

A sip of hot coffee made her feel better, but not by much. Shaking her head, Brett gazed into Sam's eyes with an expression of bewilderment. "This whole situation feels so weird. One day a person is living their life, concerned with ordinary things, and the next day the same person is smack in the middle of a murder case and scared half to death. How did this happen?"

"That's what we're trying to find out," Sam said gently. Reaching across the table, he covered her hand with his. His warmth felt good, easing the chill in her bones. "I know the process seems slow to you, but finding answers involves a lot of plodding legwork, a lot of questions. That's how it's done. And that's what we're going to do."

Sudden anger flared in her eyes. "What's the good of having an angel on my side? Tell me that, Sam. If we have to deal with this through ordinary means, then how is an angel better than—" she threw out her hands "—than hiring a private detective?"

A pained look clouded his gaze, but he answered patiently. "In some regards there's little or no difference. A private detective—or the police, for that matter—start with questions. Look, Brett, I wish I could promise you a quick resolution. I wish I could summon some kind of mystical intervention that would make all of this go away for you. But I can't." Frustration tightened his jaw. "I have to start at the same place a mortal would, and use the same resources available to a mortal. Otherwise, any case we build won't hold up in court. And that's the bottom line. You must be exonerated, and the real killer must be punished."

The anger left Brett as quickly as it had come. Her shoulders deflated, and she pushed a weary hand through her hair. "I'm sorry I flared up at you," she apologized in a low voice. "I don't know what's going to happen, and I'm frightened."

"Justifiably so."

She gave him a wobbly smile. "That's not what you're supposed to say. I'd feel a lot better if you told me that you're going to use some angel magic and get me out of this mess."

She pushed aside the plate that had contained the cinnamon roll she had just eaten, and looked at Sam's roll. "Are you going to eat that?"

"Take it," he said, returning her smile.

"Thanks." She recalled the legendary stories about prison food and, with a sigh, bit into the roll.

Sam's smile widened as he watched her eat. "I'm afraid we can't rely on angel magic, as you called it."

His answer startled Brett in that his expression underscored the temporary nature of their association. Oddly, despite their short acquaintance, she had begun to feel as if she had known Sam for years. The feeling didn't make much sense, but it was very real. She knew the things about him that mattered.

She knew she could trust Sam. She knew he was firmly on her side. Being with him made her feel safe. She knew he was a complex man, which made him interesting, a man with a keen and insightful intelligence. She suspected he was a free spirit, certainly he appeared to chafe under the restraints of imposed authority.

And when she gazed into the clear blue of his eyes and saw his warmth and compassion reflected there, her heart sensed this was a man she could deeply love. This was the man she had been waiting for all of her lonely life.

The thought shocked her. And depressed her. Sam wasn't a man. Sam was an Avenging Angel. To him, she was merely another victim whom he was pledged to rescue from gross injustice.

Ducking her head, she blinked rapidly. "Sorry," she whispered, in case he noticed the moisture in her eyes. "My emotions are right on the surface. Running away with me."

"Do you mind if I smoke?"

The question surprised her so greatly that the threat of tears receded. "You smoke?"

"I like a pipe occasionally." He sounded a tiny bit defensive. "It helps me relax and think."

It was the same excuse that Brett had used when she was a smoker. "Go ahead. If the coffee shop doesn't mind, neither do I." She watched him pack tobacco into the pipe and fool with it while she ate the rest of his cinnamon roll. Amusement twinkled in her eyes. "Whoever it is who worries that you Avengers are tempted by mortal vices is right to worry," she teased.

He puffed, exhaled a stream of fragrant, cherry-scented smoke, then smiled. "I could have worse vices."

She gazed into his eyes and felt a tingle skitter over her skin. The pipe took nothing away from the power of his presence. He still looked like a man who was half seeking a fight. As handsome as Sam was, there was a coiled tension about him, a sense of high energy held in check.

"Would you like another coffee?"

"No, thanks." Brett shook her head and blinked. It was crazy to be sitting here fantasizing over an angel, for heaven's sake. Their association would be brief, there could be no ongoing friendship. A relationship was utterly out of the question.

The realization made her feel sad, as if she had suffered a sudden loss. Sam was everything she had wanted Paul to be. Strong, charming, attentive, trustworthy, sexy as hell…

She had to stop thinking like this.

"So. What happens next?" she asked, trying not to dwell on Sam's wide, firm mouth, and the way his lips seemed to kiss the stem of the pipe. And she told herself that she had to forget what he had said earlier about angels forming attachments to mortal women. But she wished she had asked how such attachments developed and what the angel and the woman did about their attraction.

"I think we'll pay a visit to Paul's clinic. Can you tell me what the setup is?"

This was safe ground. Something Brett could talk about without triggering emotions that only upset and confused her.

"Paul opened the clinic about fifteen years ago. It was an immediate success. A money machine, he said." Lowering her head, she pressed her fingertip against the crumbs on her plate, then touched her finger to her tongue. "Predictably, Paul didn't get along with his original partners. He bought them out. But the clientele was too large for one doctor to handle, so about eight years ago, Paul invited Alan Barkley and Bob Pritchard in as partners."

"Did he get along with Barkley and Pritchard?"

"Initially he must have. But eventually Paul managed to alienate nearly everyone he knew." Brett paused. "Last year Alan and Bob made Paul a buyout offer, but Paul refused to sell his share of the partnership. He was outraged. Accused Alan and Bob of trying to steal his clinic. Since then, relations between the partners have been strained, to put it mildly."

"Strained enough that one of them might have killed him?"

Brett frowned toward a glass case displaying burlap bags of coffee beans. "I can't imagine doctors being murderers," she said finally. "Alan has a quick temper, but...and Bob said some threatening things when Paul refused to sell out. Still..." She shrugged. "I really can't picture either of them killing Paul."

"With Paul dead, they get what they wanted. The clinic." He studied her face. "After they buy out the stock you'll inherit."

Brett nodded reluctantly. "That's true." She thought about it a minute. "And there's a key-man insurance policy on each partner. The policy on Paul will pay Alan and Bob several million dollars to buy out my stock."

"So Dr. Barkley and Dr. Pritchard can get control of the clinic without it costing them a dime personally. The insurance covers the buyout."

"When you put it that way, it sounds like a sweetheart deal."

"It sounds like a motive," Sam said.

They looked at each other. Then Sam stood and tapped out his pipe. He dropped some change on the table. "Let's pay a visit to the clinic."

"And Billie Place," Brett added grimly.

THE THATCHER CLINIC was located at a good address in southeast Denver, but the address was not so fashionable as to pose a threat to clients. No woman wanted to risk being seen by friends or acquaintances as she hurried inside for a little cosmetic nipping and tucking.

Keeping this truism in mind, the clinic was designed to ensure the utmost in privacy. Underground parking concealed parked cars from street traffic. Two elevators whisked clients up two stories to the receptionist's area and individual waiting rooms provided for the comfort and privacy of celebrities and socialites, each flatteringly lit and tastefully furnished. Each had a second door opening to a corridor that led to the doctor's offices and examining rooms.

The actual surgery was performed on the third floor, which was outfitted as a minihospital. Four patient rooms resembled hotel suites more than hospital rooms. There was also a third, very private, elevator, which whisked a client directly to the parking garage. Presumably, a client could engage the services of the clinic with little or no risk of running into anyone but Billie Place, the receptionist, and his or her doctor. One of the sacred hallmarks of the Thatcher Clinic was discretion.

Sam parked the Mercedes in the underground lot facing the two elevators that led up to the clinic.

"I think we'll have better luck if I go in alone."

"Not on your life," Brett promptly objected. "I want to talk to Billie."

Sam had only to glance at those flashing eyes to know she wouldn't be dissuaded. He suppressed a sigh. Working with a client could be a help or a hindrance. Sometimes a little of both.

"All right," he reluctantly agreed. "Our objective is to discover whatever we can. It would be helpful to know where Billie and the good doctors were Saturday night." He opened the car door. "We'll go in separately. We don't know each other."

"Right," Brett said, sliding out of the car. But Sam was already gone; she was speaking to thin air. Throwing up her hands, she rolled her eyes, then zipped her parka and headed toward the elevators. There might be similarities between working with a detective and an angel, but the differences were profound.

SAM STOOD IN FRONT of Billie Place's oak desk. She glanced up from her IBM computer and the billing information she was inputting. Frowning, she gazed around the small, empty receptionist area, sensing Sam's presence but unable to see him.

She was much as Brett had described: blond, thirtyish and attractive in a sharp-featured way. A subtle slyness in her expression suggested that Billie Place was a woman who liked secrets. It would please her to know which socialite had augmented breasts, and which political figure had purchased a new nose.

Leaving Miss Place to Brett, Sam entered the corridor beyond the receptionist area and walked through a door into Dr. Alan Barkley's office. Barkley was explaining the difference between an upper and lower face-lift to an intense-looking woman of indeterminate age.

Sam listened for a minute, studying Dr. Barkley. Alan Barkley was in his early forties, handsome, beginning to gray at the temples. The quick temper Brett had mentioned flared in a brief flash of annoyance as his patient asked a question Barkley had undoubtedly heard a hundred times before. When he answered, it was clear that he made an effort to suppress his impatience.

While listening to the good doctor, Sam inspected the diplomas mounted on an expensively paneled wall, glanced at the books behind glassed-in shelves. When he saw Barkley's appointment book on the edge of his desk, he opened it to Saturday.

But first he had to freeze Dr. Barkley and his client. He called it freezing, because that's how it looked from his perspective, but that isn't what happened.

What Sam did was tinker with time. He slowed time for Dr. Barkley and his client, and speeded his own time. The effect was that he could move objects in the room without

Barkley or his client noticing. If they saw anything, it would be a shadow of a blur, a suggestion of movement that was gone before it fully registered.

Standing beside Alan Barkley, whose gesture occurred so slowly that no movement was apparent even to Sam, Sam lifted the doctor's appointment book and opened the pages.

There was an entry for last Saturday morning at ten o'clock: Golf... lucky 4. The rest of the page was blank, although something had been marked out in the five o'clock slot. Even if the golf game had not been canceled because of the weather, Barkley would have had time to play eighteen holes and still easily meet Paul Thatcher in Silverthorne later that evening.

Sam tried to read what lay beneath the marked-out section, hoping to find Paul Thatcher's name. But the block was so heavy, he couldn't make out the name beneath. The impression was that Barkley had canceled an appointment for Saturday night. Which left him with no obvious alibi.

Sam replaced the appointment book near Barkley's elbow, then examined the photograph on his desk. The picture showed Barkley standing on the deck of a boat with one proud hand on a giant marlin. There were no family photos of a wife and kiddies.

After correcting the time distortion, Sam entered Dr. Bob Pritchard's office. As Pritchard wasn't present, it was a simple matter to go through his desk. In short order Sam discovered that Bob Pritchard appeared to be experiencing serious financial difficulties. Among others, he had recently bounced checks to two ex-wives. But none of the stubs in his checkbook reflected a payment to an outfit called Sansmith Development.

Next Sam checked Pritchard's appointment book. Pritchard kept two books, one for business appointments, one for social engagements. He was a busy fellow, Sam discovered, and judging from the names appearing in his social calendar, popular with the ladies. Last week, he'd had dinner with three different women. Idly Sam wondered how Pritchard could afford the expensive restaurants.

For Saturday night, Pritchard had penciled in his social calendar: Windell Fund-raiser—Betty at 6:30. It would be an easy alibi to check.

After Sam had inspected everything except the patient files in the drawers along the west wall, he instantly appeared in the operating theater upstairs and watched as Dr. Bob Pritchard performed liposuction on the thighs of a client. The sight was shocking: it appeared to be a brutal assault on the poor unconscious patient.

One of the nurses made a joke about fat, and Dr. Pritchard looked up from his patient's draped torso. "Now, Lydia," he said in an admonishing tone that suggested they'd had this conversation before, "you know I don't permit jokes in here."

"She's out cold."

"We don't know what the sleeping mind hears and retains on an unconscious level. It's better to err on the side of blandness."

Sam liked Pritchard's philosophy, and admired his concern for his patient. He hoped Pritchard's alibi held up, and decided he would be very disappointed if Dr. Pritchard turned out to be the murderer.

After watching the operation for another minute, he flashed downstairs into Paul Thatcher's office.

Thatcher had furnished his sunny corner office in antiques and rich wall hangings. The room was impressive. No one stepping into Thatcher's office could doubt that the doctor's fee would be steep. It was also apparent that some of the furnishings were missing. Indented marks on the carpet suggested heavy furniture had once sat there. And dark squares on the wallpaper spoke of missing paintings.

But it was Paul Thatcher's appointment book that yielded the clinic's first bit of hard evidence. In the column for Saturday, Thatcher had noted: Dinner with B.— Silverthorne, 6:00 p.m.

Unfortunately, the name that jumped to mind was Brett's. It was no wonder the D.A.'s office had experienced so little trouble convicting her. All the evidence so far appeared to implicate Brett, or could be presented to seem that it did.

But it occurred to Sam that "B." could refer to just about everyone connected with Paul Thatcher. Billie Place, Alan Barkley, Bob Pritchard and Barbara Thatcher. Of course, none of *their* fingerprints were on the murder weapon, and none of them owned the cabin where Paul had been killed.

Frowning, he studied the other entries in Paul Thatcher's appointment book, and tuned in on Brett's conversation with Billie Place.

WHEN BRETT STEPPED OUT of the elevator, she glanced around the small reception area as she always did, taking pleasure in the decor she had chosen. Decorating the reception area and the private waiting rooms had been the one thing she had done during her marriage that Paul had approved of.

The carpet and walls were a soothing, trust-inspiring dove gray. A classic sofa and side chairs blended rich tones of burgundy and cream. The wall hangings that Brett had chosen were good, but not overly stimulating. A sculpted head of Nefertiti rested on a pedestal near a lush, hanging fern.

Brett's glance finally came to rest on Billie Place, and she studied Billie from a fresh perspective. Now she noticed what she had overlooked during recent lunches and occasional evening outings.

Billie had a new nose. With a twinge of amusement and sadness, Brett remembered that Paul always began a new relationship by giving his favored lady a new nose. She also noticed that Billie was wearing her hair more stylishly; she'd had her dark hair streaked and lightened around her face. All the signs of a new man were evident, the new hairdo, lacquered nails, and, if Brett wasn't mistaken, Billie had lost a few pounds.

When Billie looked up from her desk something flashed behind her eyes—surprise? dismay?—then she smiled. "Brett! I didn't expect—" And then she noticed Brett's grim expression and her smile faded abruptly.

"I know about you and Paul," Brett said quietly. She tried to keep any tone of accusation out of her voice, but she couldn't help herself. The accusation was there.

Billie folded her hands on top of her desk, and her face set in a defiant expression. "So?" she asked finally, raising her chin.

"I confided in you, Billie. You let me believe we were friends. And all the time you were pumping me for information, and then telling Paul everything I revealed." She felt betrayed and foolish.

Billie had the grace to look uncomfortable. But she shrugged it off and lifted her chin another notch. "Haven't you heard? All's fair in love and war."

No apology. Okay, so that was how it was going to be. "Did you tell Paul that I was going to the cabin last weekend?"

"I knew it! You met him there, didn't you." Something ugly and jealous glittered in Billie's eyes.

Brett's chest tightened. Billie believed Paul had gone to Silverthorne to meet her. The case against her got stronger and stronger. She touched her fingertips to her forehead and briefly closed her eyes. "You told Paul I was going to the cabin."

"Believe it or not, Paul and I have more interesting things to talk about than you!" Billie's face hardened, and watching her, Brett realized they had never been friends. "You walked out on *him,* remember? Maybe you didn't appreciate the life he gave you, but others do appreciate a little luxury! So butt out, Brett. Leave us alone!"

"Of all people, you should know that I'm not interested in Paul." The sadness of losing someone she had considered a friend darkened her eyes. "I thought you didn't like Paul. You said he was arrogant and hard to work for. You said he treated women like servants."

Billie's tight smile was as hard as the red lacquer coating her false nails. "So, maybe I was wrong. Or maybe I decided the trade-off was worth it. Whichever, it's none of your business."

Brett knew Billie hadn't had an easy life. It wasn't a great stretch to accept that Billie would overlook a lot of male flaws for a chance at a more comfortable life. But Brett didn't understand Paul's side of it.

Paul had claimed he disliked Billie Place. A year ago he had wanted to fire her, but Barkley and Pritchard had outvoted him. Moreover, Paul had been attracted to beautiful young women whom he could drape over his arm like an ornament. Billie was attractive, even more so with her new nose, but she was not a showstopper and she was not young. She didn't possess the hint of patrician ancestors in her profile or her manner that Paul had preferred, first in Barbara and later in Brett.

"Billie, I truly don't care if you're seeing Paul. If that's what you want, fine. But I am worried about him. What's going on? Why did he sell his paintings and antiques? And who or what is Sansmith Development?"

Billie's eyes widened, then her expression snapped shut. "I have a couple of questions for you, too. *Did* you meet Paul at the cabin this weekend? And where the hell is he now?" She waved her hand over a stack of pink message slips. "He didn't show up for his appointments yesterday or today. And he hasn't been home since—" She bit off the sentence. "Where is he?"

"Billie, why would I know where Paul is?"

"Well . . . do you?"

Brett hesitated. Billie sounded genuinely annoyed. But maybe she was a skilled actress. Certainly Brett had never suspected Billie was prying information out of her during those lunches and occasional dinners. And Billie had known where Paul was going on Saturday night. She could have followed him to the cabin. Maybe she had been jealous enough to—

"Where were you Saturday night?" Brett asked in a low, intense voice.

"That is none of your business!"

They stared at each other over Billie's desktop.

"Paul did not go to the Silverthorne cabin to meet me. That's the truth, Billie. And I don't know where he is now."

That was also the truth. She had an idea where Paul's body was, but she didn't know for sure.

Billie's eyes narrowed. "I don't believe you," she said flatly. "Paul didn't know that I knew you were going to the cabin. He said he had an appointment in Silverthorne. But I know he drove up there to meet you! Why else would he go out in a blizzard like that?" Jealous venom propelled the words like tiny explosions.

Brett raised a shaking hand to her forehead. "I can't believe you think there was still something between Paul and me. Paul wouldn't cross the street to talk to me, let alone drive through a blizzard. And I wouldn't want him to."

Billie stood behind her desk, her mouth twisting. "Are you kidding? Paul would have taken you back this fast," she snapped her fingers, "if he thought that would stop you from trying to rape him financially! You're trying to bleed him dry, trying to ruin him!"

Shock drained the color from Brett's face. "That isn't true," she whispered. "I only wanted what he agreed to in the divorce settlement! Not a penny more."

"He would have driven through a blizzard twice as bad if you dangled the right bait, if he thought you were willing to sign off his assets! Is that what you told him? Is that how you got him up to the cabin? Or do you want him back?" Her face pinched in an ugly expression. "Maybe you regret giving up the cushy life and the big house and all the perks that came with being Mrs. Paul Thatcher!"

"Don't push your ambitions on me, Billie. I don't want anything to do with Paul. I don't regret divorcing him, I wasn't trying to ruin him financially, and I did not meet him at the cabin!"

"I've got a flash for you, Brett. Things have changed!" Billie leaned forward over her desk, her cheeks mottled with anger. "Paul is mine now, and believe me, he isn't getting out of this relationship! I've made sure of that. And you aren't going to get any money, settlement agreement be damned! He's going to get out of his present problems, and when he does, he's going to build me a house that will make the house you had in Cherry Hills look like a shack! I'm warning you. Get out of our lives and leave us alone or you'll regret it!"

Brett stepped backward, moving away from the fury drawing Billie's expression. She almost collided with Alan Barkley.

"Billie, when is my next—Brett! What are you doing here?" Alan's handsome features contracted in a frown. He didn't appear any happier to see her than Billie had.

"I was just leaving," Brett murmured. She'd had enough. Clearly she had just flunked Sleuthing 101. What she wanted to do now was cut and run.

"Are you still working on that manuscript?"

Brett sighed, then threw an accusing glance toward Billie. Here was another betrayal. The manuscript she was writing was not exactly a secret, but only a few people knew about it. She hadn't known that Alan Barkley was one of them. "Yes."

Alan Barkley drew himself up. "Then you aren't welcome here." Heavy eyebrows crashed together above his stare. "If you publish anything even vaguely slanderous, I'll sue you from here to kingdom come! I mean it, Brett. Don't come snooping around here again!"

"Get out," Billie blurted, speaking between her teeth.

Brett spun on her heels and blindly rushed toward the elevators.

SAM WAS WAITING BESIDE the Mercedes. He watched her emerge from the underground elevator and hurry toward him, dodging puddles of melting snow.

She stopped and looked up at him with large, mute eyes. "It was terrible."

"I heard." He opened the door for her, then walked around to the driver's side and gunned the car out of the underground lot. They both breathed a little easier when the Mercedes emerged into the cold, crisp daylight and sped away from the clinic.

Brett leaned her head against the back rest and closed her eyes. "Did you learn anything?" After she heard about the notation in Paul's appointment book, she released a disheartened sigh. "Oh, great. Billie will swear on a stack of Bibles that 'B.' refers to me. Score another point for the prosecution."

"There are a lot of 'B.'s in this case," Sam reminded her, speaking with a confidence he didn't entirely feel. "So far only Pritchard has an alibi for Saturday night. And we don't know yet if his alibi will stand up to scrutiny. We don't know where Barkley or Billie were Saturday night."

"We can hardly expect that Billie would admit that she followed Paul to the cabin and killed him. Or that we'd be lucky enough to discover Barkley made a note in his appointment book saying, 'Don't forget to kill Paul on Saturday night.'" She made a sound that emerged somewhere between a laugh and a gasp. "Maybe we're wasting our time, Sam. Maybe we should let the police handle this."

Sam's mouth tightened as he wound the car through traffic. "That kind of thinking will get you a life sentence in prison."

Nibbling a fingernail, Brett turned her head to stare out the window. "I thought Billie and I were friends. I keep wondering what else I was wrong about." When Sam remained tactfully silent, she gave herself a shake and straightened in the car seat, pushing back a wave of hair. "Look, I'm sorry. I'm not a quitter and I want to see this through. It's just that I'm not good at playing detective, and we don't seem to be getting anywhere."

"Not so," Sam objected crisply. "We've learned a lot today. And we're getting a close-up look at the prosecutor's case. We're discovering what we're up against."

"Frankly, the prosecutor's case looks pretty convincing and pretty damned scary from where I sit." Brett made a face. "Hell, if I were on that jury, I think I'd convict me, too!"

They looked at each other, then both of them laughed. After all the grimness, the laughter felt good and eased the tension both were feeling.

"Let's not call a vote quite yet, Madam Foreman," Sam said, still smiling. "We haven't heard from the defense."

Brett's smile wavered. "The defense doesn't have much of a case so far. I don't think it's going to cut it to just say, 'I can't prove it, but I didn't do it, Your Honor.'" She touched his sleeve. "Sorry about the swearing."

Sam felt the warmth and pressure of her fingertips through his overcoat and sweater. He couldn't remember the last time he had been this aware of a woman. The light perfume she wore remained with him even when they were apart. He was beginning to recognize her expressions and understand what subtle changes signaled. And his thoughts kept returning to that thrilling moment in her vandalized apartment when he had held her in his arms. She had fit so perfectly. Her warmth and softness and her reality had seared him.

She drew a deep breath. "What's next, Sherlock?"

"I'd say we've identified the players," Sam said, struggling to focus his thoughts on the case instead of her fascinating eyes.

"We haven't talked to Barbara yet. I'm dreading that interview. To put it mildly, Barbara and I are not friends."

"We'll get to her. She's on our list. But I think it's time we ran a background check on our suspects."

"How do we do that?" she asked, shifting to look at him.

"I'll do it at my office." When her eyebrows lifted, he offered a word of explanation. "We're still playing by the rules. My computer won't give me any insider information, nothing the police can't find." Blast it. Privately Sam agreed with Brett's earlier assessment. There ought to be more advantages to having an angel in your corner. But the new rules and regs effectively reduced him to mortal status. He suffered the same handicaps and frustrations.

"I'll drive you back to the Roxborough house, then I'll go to the office," he said.

Brett twisted on the seat, shining those wonderful eyes on him. "I'd like to see your office. Can I tag along? Sam, never mind what I said earlier. I want to be part of the investigation. It's my life that's on the line."

Sam considered, then he shrugged and his eyes flashed rebellion. What she was saying was correct. It was her life they were fighting for, and her future that hung in the balance. In his opinion, she did indeed have the right to participate in all facets of the investigation.

"We're on our way," he said, swinging the car toward downtown.

Chapter Seven

Fuzzy gray mud and slush coated the snow melting along the sidewalk leading to the small porch fronting the Logan Street Avenging Angel's office. Sam held the door for Brett, then paused in the galley kitchen to pick up a couple of doughnuts and glasses of Perrier since Brett said she couldn't drink another cup of coffee. She nibbled at the chocolate doughnut as she looked around, her eyes large with curiosity.

"This doesn't look like an office. It's more like someone's house."

"I think it used to be an artist's studio years ago," Sam said.

They entered the main room, and Brett moved along the walls, inspecting the mounted swords and paintings commemorating memorable events from the distant past. The good old days.

She didn't see Dashiell enter from the copy room, or see Kiel turn aside from the library shelves; nor did she hear the angels speak to Sam.

"That's one good-looking tomato," Dash remarked with a grin and wink. Leaning in the doorway, he pushed back his Bogart hat and lit a fresh cigarette, ogling Brett. Then he studied Sam and his grin widened. "You don't look like you've lost your mind. What do you think, Kiel? He has to be nuts, but does he look it?''

Kiel shook his handsome head and shrugged. "Sam, old friend, you have to know that bringing a client here is like waving a red flag at the Italian bull.'' He nodded toward Angelo's office on the balcony above them. "You're just begging to be sent to the Fifth Choir. Just begging for it, Sam.''

Sam scowled. "It's an idiotic rule. Brett's input will be helpful on the background checks.''

"So it's Brett, is it?'' Dash wiggled an eyebrow at Kiel. "Not the client, not Mrs. Thatcher, but Brett. Could it be that our pal Sam has succumbed to the temptations of the flesh?''

A flush of heat warmed Sam's throat. There were distinct disadvantages to the rule against lying. He wanted to deny Dash's suggestion, but the blasted rules interfered. He glared at the angelic grins flashing back at him. "Yeah, well just wait until it happens to you,'' he muttered.

"Did you say something?'' Brett asked, turning toward him.

She looked so wholesome and vulnerable with her large dark eyes and the tendrils of silky hair curling near cold-rosy cheeks. For the most part her parka concealed her breasts and the sweet curve of her waist, but Sam could picture both in his mind. And the fragrance of her soap and perfume lingered in his senses. He was definitely experiencing earthly urges.

"My office is upstairs,'' he said gruffly, steadfastly refusing to watch Dash and Kiel roll their eyes.

Instead, he watched Brett walk toward the stairs, observed the unconsciously sexy roll of her hips. The longer he knew her, the more desirable she became in his eyes.

"This place seems so...empty," Brett said over her shoulder as she started up the staircase. "I guess I expected more activity. Are there other Avengers?"

"None worth mentioning," Sam said, glaring back at Dash and Kiel. They laughed and gave him snappy salutes.

"Good luck," Dash called, speaking out of the side of his mouth. The great Bogart could have been talking.

"You don't mind if we hang around, do you?" Kiel asked, smiling. "We wouldn't miss this for anything."

Sam's jaw stiffened. Ignoring them, he touched Brett's elbow and directed her into his office. She halted inside the door and gazed around with a nod of appreciation.

"Nice," she commented.

Sam tried to see his office through her eyes. The framed commendations wouldn't mean much to her as they were written in Latin. But she would like the plants on the windowsill, and the faded, homey carpet in wine-colored tones of rose and champagne. Most of the books in his bookcase wouldn't be familiar to her, either, but she would appreciate that he loved reading as much as she did.

"The fireplace doesn't work. Hasn't for about forty years," he remarked, absurdly pleased by her approving expression.

"I like the painting above the mantel."

"That's St. Michael. The big boss," he explained with a smile.

Tilting her head, Brett studied him with a quizzical look. "Sometimes I forget who you are. I wouldn't have believed that could happen, but it does." She studied the painting of St. Michael, then cleared her throat with a self-conscious sound. "You have an entire mysterious life that I can't know anything about."

Their eyes met and held, and throughout that long moment Sam felt a stab of deep regret that he was not a mortal, that this was not a beginning for them, that he would have to leave her soon. He wished that she could understand his life and be part of it, wished that he could fully understand her life and be part of it.

Her eyes drew him, and he took a step toward her, dropping his gaze to her lips, then he stopped abruptly.

What in the name of heaven was he about to do? Shock flooded his system, and a sizzling sound buzzed in his ears. If he hadn't come to his senses, he would have pulled her to him and kissed her. He wanted to kiss her. He had wanted to cover her lips with his and drink the sweet taste of her almost from the first moment he had met her.

"Blast," he whispered, staring into her eyes.

She gazed at him with a longing that matched his. And he didn't doubt that the confusion and surprise he saw in her gaze was reflected in his own. Pink flooded her cheeks, and she gripped her hands together in sudden tension as if she understood that he had come within a whisper of kissing her.

"Is that your computer?" she asked, turning toward his desk. Then she gave him a helpless shrug as if conceding the question was idiotic, merely a diversion to take them beyond an awkward moment.

Sam cleared his throat. "Give me a minute to boot up, then we'll get to work." Trying to pretend that his heart wasn't marching at double time, Sam sat in front of his desk and flipped on the unit and his printer.

"What can I do to help?" Brett pulled a side chair next to the desk, near enough that he inhaled the light fragrance of the scent she wore, and beneath it the natural sweetness of her skin.

He stared at his monitor and struggled to collect his thoughts. "Okay. Let's begin with the obvious. Do any of the principals in the case have a criminal record that you're aware of?'' He punched some buttons and hacked into the FBI's VICAP system. If anything could focus his mind, it was the FBI's roster of violent criminals.

"Nothing major, at least that I'm aware of," Brett said after he'd explained what he was doing on the computer.

"We'll run the names, just in case." But the FBI had no record of the Thatcher suspects ever committing a violent crime.

"Can you get into local files?" Brett asked, moving closer and watching his screen. "I think Billie Place may have had a run-in with the law a few years ago. And try Dr. Barkley and Dr. Pritchard on the local network."

After fiddling with menus and passwords, Sam leaned back in his chair, studying the monitor. "We've scored a small hit. Billie Place was arrested for shoplifting eight years ago."

Brett nodded. "I think that's what I'm remembering. Billie or Paul must have told me about it. The shoplifting incident happened before Billie went to work for the clinic."

"Look at this." Sam pointed to the screen. "Six years ago Billie was arrested for embezzling from a bank she worked for. But the bank didn't prosecute. They dropped all charges, presumably to avoid unpleasant publicity."

"Embezzlement?" Brett's eyes widened. "I didn't know about that. I wonder if the doctors know. I can't imagine they would have hired her, or that they'd keep her employed if they knew. Billie does all the invoicing, and she handles the bank deposits."

Sam punched the computer keys. "Check this. Dr. Alan Barkley has been arrested twice on drunk driving charges. Both times the charge was bargained down to a lesser offense. And Dr. Bob Pritchard was arrested in 1993 for drunk and disorderly. Seems he tore up a bar one night."

"In 1993? That must have been right after his second divorce."

"Could be," Sam agreed, checking the information on the screen. He typed in Barbara Thatcher's name. "Nothing but a ticket for driving on an expired license," he said after a minute. Next he tried Paul Thatcher. "This is probably not important, but we'll check it out, anyway. Thatcher got into a fistfight with an antique dealer in the Cherry Creek area. The police were called, but no arrest was made."

"You're kidding! Paul? In a fistfight?" Brett leaned forward to peer at the screen. "Brawling wasn't his style." She thought for a minute. "Can you access banking and financial records?"

Sam was about to explain that he could access any information that the police could when Angelo swept into the room in full regalia. Shining wings soared above his glossy head, the tips brushing the ceiling. He wore a flowing white robe belted with the silver cord that designated his rank. Furious sparks flashed around his head and he glowed like a halogen lamp.

"You," he thundered, jabbing a finger at Sam, "are in deep trouble. Reference rule number fourteen, page twenty-two in your manual! Clients are *never* permitted to enter the offices of the Avengers! That is *never,* as in *not ever!*"

Sam stood slowly and faced his boss. "There are several incomprehensible rules of which that particular bit of nonsense is a prime example." In a reflex action of which he was only dimly aware, he too swelled and manifested tall, iridescent wings. His jeans and sweater vanished, replaced by a white robe and the maroon-colored cord of a warrior. An angry radiant glow expanded and pulsed around his head, the flashing and sparking equal to that which fizzed around Angelo's hair.

Brett's mouth dropped open. Speechless, she stared at his sudden transformation, then sagged limply against her chair.

Angelo's voice boomed so loudly that the plants fluttered on the windowsill. "It is not your place to decide if a rule is acceptable or not! Your duty is to obey!"

Sam's chest swelled with the anger and resentment he had been carrying for a century. "It is my duty to vindicate my client! It is my duty to avenge wrongdoing and correct injustice! If one of the egregious new rules impedes those goals, I see it as my duty to ignore that rule! My primary responsibility is to my client!"

"Sam?" Brett's voice emerged in an awed croak. "Ah...who are you talking to?" Wide-eyed and too apprehensive to move, she gripped the edges of her chair and cautiously peered around the room. When she looked at him again, she seemed transfixed by his wings.

"Ignore a rule?" Angelo sputtered. His voice reverberated like thunder. "Ignore a rule?" His hand shot forward in a fiery blur and he pointed a shaking finger at Sam. "This incident will go into your file, Samuel. A file bulging with transgressions, I might add. We'll discuss your punishment when this case is concluded, and there *will* be a punishment. In the meantime, remove your client from the premises at once! At once, do you hear?"

Angelo vanished in a furious burst of radiant orange and gold, leaving behind the faint scent of heavenly ether.

Anger and frustration caused Sam's wings to extend momentarily, and fiery light flashed and sizzled around his white head. Blast and double blast! At once he realized that he had deliberately provoked this confrontation, and it had not been a good idea. The direct clash with Angelo was long overdue, yes, but he should never, never have permitted it to occur in front of Brett.

Instantly his wings vanished and his jeans and sweater reappeared. He dropped to his knees beside her and rubbed her cold hand between his own. "Brett?"

She was sprawled across the chair, as limp as an old robe, staring at him. Her mouth opened and closed, but no sound emerged.

"I'm sorry that happened in front of you," he said earnestly. "I apologize."

"Sam, you had wings!" Her lips formed the words, but still there was no sound. "And there was a strange light in here. And the plant leaves were moving as if . . ."

"I know." He rubbed her hands more vigorously, angry with himself. "I'm sorry about the wings. It was instinctive, I didn't think about it. If I had, I'd have—" What would he have done? Warned her? Confronted Angelo without wings, placing himself at a disadvantage?

"There were fiery gold sparks coming out of your hair!" She pulled one hand from his and made a stirring motion in the air above her head. "My God, Sam! I never in my life saw anything like it."

"I don't know what to say. Blast!" He shoved a hand through his hair, furious at himself. "I'm sorry I frightened you."

Gradually a little color returned to her cheeks. She managed to sit up a little straighter. But her eyes were still wide and darkly round, fixed on him with a strange awed expression. "That was amazing! You looked . . . magnificent!"

"Really?" He stopped rubbing her hands and searched her expression. Her eyes were glowing. "I was afraid I'd frightened you."

"Well, you did," she admitted, a little strength returning to her voice. "But you were fabulous, too. I've never seen anything like that in my entire life! I swear, Sam. You looked enormous! And you looked like a warrior, like you could wade through an army and conquer it single-handedly!"

Magnificent. Fabulous. A conquering warrior. Suddenly Sam didn't regret the incident quite as much as he had a minute ago. And it seemed appropriate to put his arms around her and hold her. As a gesture of comfort.

"What happened to cause that?" she asked, speaking against his shoulder. "You know, the wings and the fiery sparks."

He liked the way she felt in his arms, and the lemony scent of her hair near his nose. Her softness and the desirable warmth of her skin and body stirred him on a level that he'd believed he had left behind long, long ago. It occurred to Sam that he had some apologies to make. In the past he had assumed a superior stance toward those angels who formed attachments to mortal women. Now he began to understand how such relationships happened.

An angel could conduct himself professionally for centuries, then along came a woman with a particular combination of scents and coloring, of expressions and glances, and something opened inside and reached out. Something chemical or cellular, something mysterious and wonderful and unexplainable, something still connected to the earthly plane. And the angel tumbled from the heights and fell among the mortals. The simple act of holding her made Sam happier than he had felt in hundreds of years.

Until he recalled Angelo.

Gently and with deep regret, he eased Brett away from his body. "We have to leave."

"Sam, can't you tell me what happened?"

"Later."

She gazed into his steady eyes, then nodded and rose to her feet, testing the strength in her legs with an apologetic smile before she walked to the door, then wobbled down the staircase.

Dash and Kiel were waiting below with sober expressions. They sat on chairs facing the balcony, and it was obvious they had overheard everything.

"Courageous, but futile, pal," Dash commented sadly. His lips pressed in a sympathetic line.

"We're going to miss you, Sam," Kiel added, looking at the floor. "Send us an E-mail from the Fifth Choir."

Sam gave them a weak smile and a thumbs-up sign, then followed Brett to the car. The temperature had fallen, and it was dark outside. The street lamps had come on, and in the glow, Sam noticed paper pilgrims and a turkey cutout pasted on the door across the street.

It occurred to him that he had never celebrated Thanksgiving Day and he never would. He would never sit in a grandstand watching Fourth of July fireworks, would never erect an evergreen tree and hang lights on it or share in the silliness of Santa Claus.

Suddenly he missed these things he had never done and would never do. He felt their loss as an ache deep inside.

Neither he nor Brett spoke until they were out of the city and speeding along the highway, halfway to Roxborough. Then Brett twisted on the seat and looked at him. "Sam, I've been patient as long as I can. Something important happened back there. What was it?"

Before he could tell her about the new rules and regulations and about Angelo's thunderous appearance, he had to control a fresh onslaught of anger at the system. By the time he finished explaining, they were parked in front of the safe house in the pines.

Brett didn't question why he had taken her to the office if doing so was against the rules, and for that he was grateful. But she did ask in a hushed tone what would happen to him for committing the infraction.

He drummed his fingers on the steering wheel and gazed at the porch lights shining through the windshield. He couldn't tell her about the dreaded Fifth Choir. He didn't know anything about it. For sure, though, the rumors were dire enough to make his skin prickle.

But not dire enough to alter his convictions.

He shook his head. "I don't know. It doesn't matter."

She touched his arm. "Of course it matters."

Her caring made his chest tighten, and he reached to gently stroke her cheek, marveling at the softness of her skin. "That's my problem. We're supposed to be working on your problem."

Briefly she closed her eyes and leaned her cheek against his palm. "Oh, Sam. There are moments when I feel as if I've stepped into a different realm of reality, a place I didn't know existed. Part of this place is frightening, and part of it," she said softly, raising her eyes, "is wonderful."

Gently, he lifted her chin and gazed into her beautiful, glistening eyes. "Some things remain the same, even in alternate realities." If he let himself dwell on her words and the look in her eyes, he would do something they might both regret. He wouldn't be able to help himself. "We still have to eat," he said, forcing a smile. "Why don't you relax in a hot tub while I fix dinner."

She stared at him, then burst into laughter. "You sound like my mother used to. If you're upset, eat. You are definitely a man after my own heart. And I'm getting the idea that you like to cook."

This time it was easier to smile. "As a matter of fact, I do. Cooking and eating are two of the mortal pleasures I've fallen prey to. You remember the temptations I mentioned."

A few more temptations sprang to both their minds, and they gazed into each other's eyes for a long speculative moment before they pulled apart self-consciously and stepped out of the car.

"It feels like coming home," Brett murmured as they entered the house. "I wish this really was my home."

Sam helped her out of her parka, purposefully torturing himself by letting his fingers brush the nape of her neck. Tiny shocks of lightning ran up his fingertips. He hung her parka and his jacket side by side in the hall closet.

"I think I'll check my phone messages before I run a tub," Brett said, stepping away from him. Her throat was pink and her hands trembled slightly. Sam noticed and dared to hope the blush and the tremble had something to do with him.

"I'll fix us a drink. What would you like?" he asked.

"After a day like today? I think scotch and water."

Going into the kitchen, Sam poured them both a stiff drink, recognizing the task as an evening ritual that occurred in mortal homes all over the globe. For this moment he could pretend they were an ordinary couple, home after a day in the world, eager to relax and share a drink together. These simple pleasures, the warm comfort of togetherness, were why some angels felt a twinge of envy toward mortals. Sam understood it now.

And he suddenly understood that he had been lonely for a very long time.

When Sam carried their drinks into the living room, he found Brett sitting on the end of the sofa, bent forward, her white face cradled in one hand. Mutely, she extended the phone to him.

Puzzled, Sam pressed the receiver to his ear, then stiffened as a raspy voice grated against his ear.

"If you try to publish that manuscript, I'll kill you, you murdering bitch. You have no right to meddle in people's private affairs! If you want to live, then mail all copies of that slanderous piece of garbage to Box 2580, Littleton, Colorado. And do it tomorrow! If you don't...well, you've been warned."

The next message began, a cheery hello from one of Brett's friends, but Sam hung up the phone. He sat on the sofa beside her and curved her stiff fingers around the scotch and water, which she accepted with a nod of gratitude.

"Was the message dated?"

Brett nodded. "It came in this morning."

"I intended to ask about your manuscript earlier, then let myself get sidetracked."

"It didn't seem important until now." She leaned back on the sofa and rested her head on Sam's shoulder, gazing at the darkness outside the windows. "The man on the phone...he must be the person who vandalized my apartment."

"Searching for your manuscript."

"Which I took to the cabin to work on."

"Is it a novel?"

Brett shook her head. A deep sigh lifted her breast and she took a sip of her drink. "I don't know exactly what it is, but it isn't fiction. After five years of living with a cosmetic surgeon, I picked up a lot of information about cosmetic surgery." She turned troubled eyes toward Sam. "Today, we tend to take cosmetic surgery for granted. It's easy to overlook the very real risks involved. In fact, clients often brush aside warnings as if they don't really apply. But operations *do* go wrong. Sometimes terribly wrong."

"You're writing an exposé?"

"Partly," she admitted with a nod. "Partly it's a warning, and partly it's the study of a growing industry. You know, who the clients are, who the doctors are, what happens in the operating room, what to expect afterward, and what can go wrong. The book is a little bit of everything, a hodgepodge." She frowned. "Which is a problem. If I were going to continue with it, the focus should be narrowed. But I don't know if I want to finish it or try to find a publisher. That's one of the decisions I'd hoped to make while I was at the cabin."

Sam rubbed her shoulder, enjoying the warmth of her body curved against his. "Who knows that you're writing this book?"

"Billie, of course. She was very helpful, actually, telling me about various clients, about operations that didn't turn out as well as expected." She thought a minute. "Paul knew. He wasn't happy about it, but I don't think he expected I'd finish the book or do anything with it. Obviously Billie or Paul mentioned it to Alan Barkley, which means that Bob Pritchard knows, too. A couple of women friends are aware that I'm trying to write a book, but they don't know the subject matter."

"Could one of the patients at the clinic know?"

Brett fell silent, thinking about the question. "I suppose it's possible," she said finally. "A patient could have been in one of the private waiting rooms while I was talking to Billie in the reception area. If the door was open a crack, he might have overheard our conversation. Or maybe Paul or Billie mentioned the book to a client for some reason. Or— and this would be a stretch but not impossible—maybe a patient was sitting nearby when Billie and I had lunch and overheard us discussing material for the book. We usually went to Maud's, which is near the clinic."

Sam nodded thoughtfully. "Do you recall the name of any patient who might object to being mentioned in your book to the extent that he would threaten to kill you if you proceed with the project?"

"I'm not using real names. But I've been thinking about that as we've been talking, and the answer is no." She lifted her head to look at him, and he felt the warm flow of her breath on his chin. "People seek cosmetic surgery for all sorts of reasons," she continued. She glanced at his mouth, then lowered her head. "Maybe one of the clinic's patients had surgery to disguise his appearance, and now fears exposure. Or maybe he had surgery and the operation went awry, and now he's disfigured and fears ridicule if he's mentioned in the book. Or maybe he's a public figure and has some kind of stake in letting everyone believe that he was born with the perfect nose or a flawless jawline." She shrugged helplessly. "The man on the phone could be anyone, and he could be upset for any number of reasons."

The man on the phone was not merely upset, Sam thought. He was violent and dangerous. And he wasn't just anyone. He had probably been a patient at Thatcher's clinic, and somehow he had learned about Brett's proposed book. This man had gone to her condominium and had torn it apart.

"Exactly how many cosmetic operations did the Thatcher clinic botch?" Sam asked.

"Considering the number of operations they perform, not many go wrong. A very small percentage, in fact. And it isn't always the fault of the surgeon. Smoking interferes with healing, but some patients lie about quitting. Some of them end up with ugly scars because of it. And some patients don't follow post-op instructions. Others insist on proceeding even though they've been informed their skin is the wrong type or consistency or texture to adapt to the procedure they insist on having.'' She paused. ''And sometimes, things just go bad for no discernible reason.''

''Maybe because the surgeon is drunk?''

Her eyebrows lifted. ''You're referring to Alan Barkley. He may have a drinking problem outside the clinic, Sam, but I've never heard a whisper that he ever operated while under the influence of alcohol.''

''But he might have.''

Brett frowned. ''I suppose he might have . . . but I just can't believe that he would.''

''What if Paul discovered that Barkley had botched an operation because he had been drinking? And what if Paul threatened to report Barkley to the authorities and support the patient in a lawsuit?''

''There were problems among the partners,'' Brett said uneasily. ''If something like you suggest actually happened, I can see Paul threatening Alan.''

''What would Barkley do to protect his reputation and his livelihood?''

Brett's body tightened. ''Alan would be desperate.''

They looked into each other's eyes. The look began with the recognition that there were new possibilities to explore. And ended in an acute awareness of each other. Sam felt a sudden tension draw his thighs and stomach. His pulse and his breath quickened. The muscles in his arms grew taut with the desire to pull her against his chest. He burned with a deep need to kiss her and touch her.

''Sam?'' she whispered, wetting her lips.

He closed his eyes and suppressed a groan. If he kissed her now, he would be taking gross advantage. Brett Thatcher was a woman undergoing enormous stress and upset. As would anyone who had gone through all that she had in the last few days. She was extremely fragile and vulnerable right now. Moreover, she looked on Sam as her warrior hero, her champion in her present difficulties. Only a cad—or an angel willing to throw his ethics to the wind— would take advantage of such a situation.

Battling disappointment and frustration, he gently eased away from her, both pleased and saddened by the flash of dismay that flickered across her face.

"I think we should eat something, then you need to rest," he suggested in a thick voice. "I'll have dinner on the table by the time you finish your bath."

The image of Brett relaxing in a scented tub made his senses reel. It required great willpower to move toward the kitchen instead of following her into the master bathroom. Angelo, he thought grimly, would have been proud of his control.

When she returned to the kitchen, she was wearing a white terry robe, she had a towel wrapped around her hair, and she smelled faintly of roses.

"I apologize for not dressing," she said as she sat down at the table, "but I suddenly ran out of energy. If you hadn't gone to so much trouble, I would have skipped dinner and gone directly to bed."

Smiling at her yawn, Sam served stuffed pork chops, potatoes au gratin and green beans amandine. In white terry, her face scrubbed clean of makeup, she looked sexy and adorable. He suspected he would never grow tired of looking at this woman.

"Do you ever sleep?" she inquired, trying to swallow another yawn.

The question amused him. "Angels don't require sleep."

"Always on the job, huh?" She smiled at him. "Your dinner is very good, by the way. Excellent. If you ever turn in your wings, you could get a job as a chef."

Sam laughed. "Once an angel, always an angel. There's no such thing as turning in our wings."

She put down her fork and gazed at him. "That was really... amazing, you know. I'll never forget the way you looked." Frowning, she searched for words. "You were frightening, but beautiful, too. An angel warrior. Awesome in the best sense of that word. But beautiful. That's the word that keeps forming in my mind." A violent blush bloomed on her cheeks, and she shook her head with a helpless gesture. "I know men don't like to be described as beautiful, but that's how you looked to me."

He laughed again, but he was absurdly flattered and pleased. If the lights had been off, he suspected his glow of pleasure would have lit the kitchen.

"Do you know how lovely you are?" he asked softly, admiring the pink in her cheeks. In his opinion, when Brett Thatcher smiled, she rivaled any angel's radiance.

"Sam," she whispered, gazing helplessly across the table. "Something is happening between us. I sense your resistance, but I know I'm not imagining an attraction. I'm not sure how I feel about it."

"You're not imagining anything," he said gruffly. "And I don't know how I feel about what's happening, either." He hesitated, then said the rest. "The resistance you're sensing is my effort not to take advantage of a stressful situation."

She nodded as if she had guessed as much. "It *is* a stressful time. I'm meeting you at the worst moment in my life. But there are other problems. You're from heaven, I'm from earth. We're geographically incompatible." A lopsided smile curved her lips. "I'm not even sure that we're the same species. Besides which, you're not supposed to consort with mortals, and until a few days ago, I'm not sure I even believed in angels, let alone ever hoped to actually meet one. I swear, you don't. You're magic, I'm not. And once we solve Paul's murder, I suspect you'll have to leave. Is that right?''

Sam thought about Angelo and the looming threat of punishment. And he cursed himself that he hadn't led a blameless existence.

Brett spread her hands and shook her head. "Whatever's happening between us...it doesn't seem that it can go anywhere.''

"Right now you need some rest," Sam said, concerned by the circles beneath her eyes. "We'll talk about this tomorrow, after we've both had some time to think about it.''

"What is there to think about?" Tears glistened in her eyes. "You're an angel, Sam. We're sitting here in an invisible house, and once we solve the case, you're going to leave. It's all crazy." Jumping up, she ran out of the kitchen.

After a few minutes of staring at her empty chair, Sam went into the living room and sat on the sofa, staring into the flames crackling in the fireplace. He didn't move until he sensed that she had finally fallen into a restless sleep. A deep sigh lifted his chest. Sitting here like a love-wounded teen wasn't going to solve anything. Wishing for a solution wasn't going to make it happen.

What he needed right now was something to combat the loneliness that pierced him whenever he thought about leaving her. The odd thing was that he hadn't recognized how achingly lonely he felt. He hadn't put a label to the hollowness inside his chest. It struck him as ironic that he hadn't known he was missing anything until he found the thing he was lacking. Brett.

Dropping forward, he rubbed his jaw hard. This kind of thinking wasn't doing anything to help her.

Stiffening his resolve, he flashed instantly to the dark and deserted Thatcher clinic. After giving himself a minute to adjust to an abrupt change of surroundings, he began a thorough search of the patient files, compiling a list of male patients. His list would form the starting point toward finding the cretin who had threatened Brett.

But his thoughts remained firmly lodged at the Roxborough house, focused on a mortal woman who made his heart pound and his blood sing, a woman who was forbidden to him.

It was only his belief that one of the patients listed in these files had threatened to kill her that kept him from returning to Brett's side. The person who had vandalized Brett's apartment and threatened her might be the same person who had murdered Paul Thatcher.

And he might be planning to kill again.

Chapter Eight

After breakfast, Brett carried her second cup of coffee out onto the back deck and inhaled a scented breath of pine and spruce. Leaning her elbows on the deck railing, she examined the animal tracks left in the melting snow, noticing they veered around the house. Apparently the safe house was not invisible to deer and rabbits.

"It's going to be a beautiful day," she commented as Sam joined her on the deck. Because the conversation last night had placed a sense of awkwardness between them, she lifted her face toward the distant snowcapped mountains instead of looking at him as she wanted to.

On the one hand, their slight discomfort increased an already tense awareness of each other. On the other hand, Brett decided the awkwardness might be a good thing. The distance it created gave them both a chance to slow down and reevaluate their deepening attraction.

She wasn't sure how she felt. Thinking about falling for Sam frightened her. She could see nothing ahead but heartache. Turning her coffee cup between her hands, she studied the bright sky without really seeing it.

On the other hand, how often did a man like Sam come along? Not often: Sam was unique. Maybe, just this once, this one special time, she should just relax and let whatever was going to happen, happen. And deal with the consequences—and the inevitable heartbreak—later.

But throwing her fate to the winds wasn't an option for the other things going on in her life. Brett was desperate to evade the man who had threatened her on the phone, and she was frightened that she still might be arrested for Paul's murder.

"How many names did you come up with?" she asked, referring to the roster of male patients Sam had assembled.

"About thirty." He leaned on the railing beside her, his muscular shoulder brushing hers. "I also stopped by your condo. I'm certain no one has been there since we left it."

She hadn't had a minute to think about the mess they had left behind in her condominium, or to consider the time and effort it would require to restore her home to some kind of order. The condo seemed like a relic from a life and a world that existed in a different reality, one that Brett no longer felt connected to. She was sharing Sam's world now.

Sam gazed into his coffee cup. "I also returned to my office and tried to dig up some information about the Sansmith Development company. It's a holding company. The principals are buried beneath layers of corporate obfuscation. It's going to require some time to discover who's involved."

"Was Angelo still at the office?" Brett asked quietly, finally letting herself look at him. Today Sam wore a cable-knit sweater as light as his hair, and dark slacks and boots. It occurred to her that despite his warrior tendencies, there was a genuine sweetness about this man. It manifested in his automatic good manners, in the way his caring didn't waver, and in the compassion that warmed his blue eyes. This was not to say that he was a gentle man, although he could be gentle. It was more that his aggressiveness was tempered by flashes of an empathetic nature. It occurred to Brett that Sam would be appalled to learn that she thought he was sweet. Thinking of his reaction made her smile.

"Angelo was at the office, but there was no further unpleasantness. That will come later, after we solve the case."

Brett nodded, gazing at a thick stand of pines. "What's on our agenda for today?"

"I thought we'd pay a visit to Paul's first wife."

Brett made a face. "I'm not fond of Barbara, but I can't believe that she's a killer."

Sam's smile caused her heart to roll over in her chest. "You don't think any of the suspects could have done it."

"Sam, what do you think I should do about my manuscript?"

"What do you want to do?"

"The truth? I doubt I'll ever finish writing it or submit it for publication." Brett released a sigh and pushed at a wave of dark hair. "Maybe writing about cosmetic surgery was a way of working out my frustrations after the divorce." She hesitated, and her chin lifted. "But I don't want to give it to whoever vandalized my apartment. I don't want to knuckle under to threats."

"Good."

"I don't want someone out there trying to kill me, either." A shudder tickled up her spine. "So I wrote him a note, telling him that I intend to drop the writing project. We can mail it on the way to Barbara's house. Whatever he's afraid I'll expose—it won't happen, and I need to tell him that. I hope that will be enough. I hope he'll believe me."

Sam dropped an arm around her shoulders and gave her a quick hug. "No one is going to harm you, Brett."

"I'm not abandoning the book project because of this jerk," she said a little defensively. "I've thought about it, and the reason I'm giving it up is because, frankly, the book isn't very good. I'm not a writer. I'd like to see someone write a behind-the-scenes book about cosmetic surgery, but I've reached the conclusion that I'm not that person.''

It felt so safe and good to stand within the circle of his arms. But there was more than mere comfort. The instant Sam touched her, an electric thrill shot through Brett's body. She felt alternately hot and cold, shaky and steady. She wanted him to kiss her, thought about it every time she looked at him. But she understood their relationship would irrevocably change if he did. She wanted him, wanted to know him with her body as well as her mind, but even thinking about advancing their attraction to the next step raised the specter of the future. And that was a void she shrank from.

Closing her eyes, she inhaled the clean, outdoorsy fragrance of his skin, and her mind reeled with confusion.

Sam cleared his throat as they stepped apart, the sound deep and gruff. ''All right, here's how I see it. We need to check out the fight Paul had with the antique dealer, we need to learn more about the male patients, and we need to pay a visit to Barbara Thatcher.''

''Let's begin with Barbara, and get that one over with,'' Brett said, swallowing the desire to kiss him, trying not to notice the shape of his lips or the muscular length of his body. ''Bring some junk food, my friend. There's no way I'm going to get through an interview with Barbara without nibbling.''

They couldn't be together without looking at each other. Brett watched the sunshine gleaming in his light hair, defining the clean sweep of his nose and jaw, then she hurried inside to get her parka while Sam returned to the kitchen to find a box of cheese crackers.

They drove into town without speaking, occasionally sneaking speculative glances at each other. By now Brett knew the Mercedes would drive itself if need be, but she also knew that Sam enjoyed operating the car himself. She couldn't be sure if he focused his attention on the road because he was actually driving or if he only pretended that his mind was on the road. Maybe the only thing he could think about was the only thing she could think about— what would happen between them? Where was their unique relationship leading?

While Brett was mailing her letter at the Littleton Post Office, Sam asked the clerk who had rented Box 2580. Brett joined him at the counter in time to hear the clerk say, "Even if I had the time to look it up, I'm not permitted to give out that information. Sorry, pal."

They stepped out of the line in front of the counter. "He probably didn't rent the postal box in his own name, anyway," Brett decided.

After thinking a minute, Sam walked along the walls of postal boxes until he found number 2580. He extended a hand and the door to the box clicked open. After giving Brett a grin, he reached inside and withdrew a catalog and an advertisement.

"Both addressed to occupant," he murmured, disappointed.

"The angel magic always gets to me," Brett muttered, rattled. She glanced over her shoulder to see if anyone had noticed the postal box open by itself. And it occurred to her how truly unobservant most people were, including herself. As little as a week ago, she wouldn't have noticed Sam's razzle-dazzle. All the postal boxes could have popped open, and she would have figured someone had flipped a master switch of some kind. Like most people, she would have invented an acceptable explanation to account for that which could not be understood.

Taking her elbow, Sam led her out of the post office. "I'll bip in here occasionally and try to get a glimpse of whoever rented this box."

"You do that," Brett said with an amused smile.

In the car, he handed her the list of male clients he'd compiled at the clinic. "Take a look at this roster and see if you recognize any of the names."

"Sorry," Brett said after studying the list. "I've never heard of any of these men. None of the names rings a bell."

Thirty minutes later, Sam eased the Mercedes to the curb of a twisting street in Alpine South, a well-kept suburb. Snowmen stood melting in many of the yards, and Brett noticed basketball hoops above several garage doors. Her gaze was drawn to three bundled preschoolers playing with a sled a few doors from Barbara Thatcher's house.

"So you like children, Sam?"

He was watching the small preschoolers, too, a quizzical expression in his eyes. "They fascinate me. I know very little about children, actually. It's been centuries since I've spent any time around them."

"What is it that fascinates you?"

"Knowing there's an adult hidden inside them, a large person they will grow into." When he saw Brett's expression, he laughed. "Angels, regardless of age or size, don't grow. And we don't change much. Mortal children seem unique in that regard."

Brett tilted her head, watching him curiously. "The thing I want most in the world is children. A family of my own. That's what I'll regret most about my life if it never happens. Do you regret not having children when you were, you know, on the earthly plane?"

"When I was a mortal," he said in a quiet voice, "I didn't think about having children." A slight shrug lifted his shoulders. "Having children seemed a given, something everyone did. There seemed plenty of time…and then suddenly, it was too late. My time ran out."

Brett nodded, watching the children with moist eyes. She had always believed that she had plenty of time, too. Yet here she was, almost thirty, and she hadn't begun the life she wanted.

"I've watched mortals with their children, and I've heard them describe loving their children in terms no angel can fully understand, because most of us have never had children and will never experience that kind of love." When Brett's eyebrows lifted, he added, "There are many different kinds of love. But the love between parent and child must rank near the top of the list as the purest and most unselfish."

"Yes!" Brett breathed, looking at him with a shining expression. Taking his hand, she sat quietly, watching the brightly clad preschoolers tumble around the sled, bubbling with laughter.

"Well," Sam said finally. "Shall we go to work?"

Brett drew a breath then made herself look toward Barbara Thatcher's house. Barbara had chosen a Tudor with crosshatched windows and varying rooflines. Hers was the only house on the block with a hedge blocking access to the front yard.

"How shall we handle this?" Brett asked. She dreaded seeing Paul's first wife. Past encounters had been icily civil, two glaciers grinding past each other.

"I think she's more likely to open up if she doesn't know a stranger is present," Sam said, following Brett's gaze to Barbara's front door.

"I doubt she'll open up at all," Brett said, "but I'll give it a try." She ate a handful of cheese crackers to bolster her determination, then reluctantly opened the car door. "Wives and ex-wives seldom have anything pleasant to say to each other."

And this visit was no exception.

"You!" Barbara said, surprise turning to annoyance when she opened the front door. Her carefully penciled eyebrows crashed together. "What are *you* doing here?"

"I'd like to talk to you," Brett lied. She wished she were anywhere else other than standing on Barbara's doorstep.

Barbara hesitated, making no effort to conceal the battle going on between an inclination to slam the door in Brett's face and her curiosity as to why Brett had come.

Since Brett had last seen her, Barbara had cut her dark hair in a youthful, bouncy style and she had removed any hint of gray. Since she had the same nose as Brett, thanks to Paul, Brett experienced an uneasy feeling that she was observing an older version of herself when she looked at Barbara Thatcher. She hoped she wouldn't be as bitter and unhappy when she was Barbara's age.

Brett drew a breath. "May I come in?"

Barbara scowled and looked Brett up and down, guessing her weight, criticizing her makeup, dismissing her casual hairstyle, all without a word. Grudgingly, she opened the door wider and stepped back.

"I tried to phone you Saturday night," Brett said, improvising on the spot. "I guess you were out."

It was a shot in the dark, but she noticed that Barbara's eyes widened before she turned aside and gripped her hands together. Maybe it meant something; maybe it didn't. But she noticed that Barbara didn't deny that she'd been out, nor did she mention where she might have been.

"What do you want?" Barbara led the way to an elegantly furnished, formal living room. She waved a hand at a chair that seemed too delicate to bear a person's weight. Gingerly, Brett seated herself.

From this position, she had a clear line of sight into Barbara's study, where she saw Sam standing beside a Queen Anne desk. He was turning the pages of Barbara's appointment book.

Brett tried to ignore the fact that she could see Sam—Barbara obviously could not see him. Reaching inside, she summoned a pleasant smile. "Where were you Saturday night? As I said, I tried to phone you."

"Where I go and what I do is none of your business," Barbara replied, her face stony. "I repeat—what do you want? Why did you come here?"

Mind racing, Brett tried to think what to say. What struck her as significant was that it appeared that Barbara did not want to explain where she was at the time of Paul's murder.

"What kind of car do you drive?"

Barbara blinked, and finally sat on the edge of the designer sofa facing Brett's chair. "I drive a Chrysler. Why on earth would you ask?"

The car that had sped past Brett in the blizzard had been a large, heavy car. "What color is it?"

Barbara's frown deepened until she realized she was frowning. Then she pressed her fingertips to her forehead, smoothing out the line between her eyes. "It's white. I'm going to give you three minutes to state your business, then I want you to leave."

The car that had passed her that night had been a dark color. Brett was beginning to think that Sam was right. The car she had seen must have been Paul's.

"I'm worried about Paul." Groping, Brett let the words come as they may, ad-libbing as she went along. "Did you know he's been selling his antiques and his paintings?"

Barbara turned toward the windows overlooking the back yard and a pool covered for the winter. "I guess it's no secret that Paul is having financial problems," she said finally. "I told him not to get involved with those people. I told him they were unscrupulous, just a bunch of crooks."

From the corner of her eye, Brett saw Sam's head come up. "Stay on this subject," he called. "See if you can find out if she's referring to Sansmith Development."

His voice startled Brett, and she darted a quick look at Barbara. But Barbara had heard nothing.

She swung angry eyes back to Brett. "And then here you come, trying to take him to the cleaners! Everybody and his brother is trying to drive Paul into bankruptcy!"

"That isn't true." Brett leaned forward in her chair. She indicated the beautiful room they were sitting in. "I can't afford to live like you do, and I don't drive a big new car. My divorce settlement is minuscule compared to yours. Even when everything is settled, I'll have to find a job. I only asked Paul for what he'd promised in our prenuptial agreement."

"Paul and I were married for a lot of years! A lot longer than you two were. He owed me a decent life-style and he knew it." She stared at Brett. "I told him right from the beginning that you were a mistake, that he'd regret marrying you! And he did."

Brett bit off a sharp retort. "I didn't come here to rehash old grievances." There was no way she would ever convince Barbara that she and Paul hadn't started seeing each other until his first divorce was final. "I came here because even though neither of us is married to Paul any longer, I think we still care about him." She couldn't read

Barbara's expression. "I'm wondering if there is some way we can help him get out from under this Sansmith thing."

Sam smiled and made a circle with his thumb and forefinger. "Good work. Smooth," he said approvingly.

Barbara's eyes flashed. "Sansmith is bleeding him dry!"

"Maybe if he consulted an attorney," Brett suggested cautiously, feeling her way.

"That's what I suggested. But Sansmith plays rough. They've threatened that if he hires an attorney, he'll regret it."

"Is Paul afraid of them?"

"With good reason, wouldn't you say? Of course he was afraid of them. These people can ruin lives."

"Was?" Brett asked quickly, picking up on the past tense.

Barbara's hands twitched. "Paul's close to paying them off. Once he's free of them—and you—he can get on with his life."

"The thing I don't understand is how Paul got involved with Sansmith in the first place," Brett said, sliding a look toward Sam. He was standing in the doorway of the study looking at Barbara's hands as she made a dismissive gesture.

"That's because you never really knew Paul, did you. You thought you did, but you didn't."

Brett strained to hold a neutral expression on her lips. "Maybe I didn't. Why don't you tell me."

"Paul was always interested in get-rich-quick schemes. A tip on a hot stock, a new way to beat the IRS, anything that promised a quick and easy profit. We used to argue about it." She shrugged. "He was easy pickings for Sansmith."

"I'm sure Paul confided in you," Brett said between her teeth. "Exactly how did the Sansmith deal work?"

"Oh, it was slick, all right. It had sucker written all over it," Barbara said bitterly. "They persuaded Paul to invest five million dollars in a strip of land running along the shore in Costa Rica. They said they were going to build a luxury hotel and a golf course, big-ticket houses, you name it. Whatever the sucker wanted to hear. All Paul had to do was put up fifty thousand in cash, and they would carry him for the balance of the five million. Such a deal." She shook her head angrily.

"But things went sour?"

"What a surprise. Of course things went sour. Somehow the costs went through the roof. And one day Sansmith called Paul's loan. Suddenly he owed those crooks the rest of the money. Five million damned dollars, with no guarantee that costs wouldn't continue to rise or that he wouldn't lose everything in the end."

"Couldn't he get out of the deal?"

Barbara's stare lengthened. "You don't know anything about the Sansmith people, do you. These boys play rough. They are not nice folks. They have Paul's name on a contract, and they want their money. Period."

Brett considered the information. "Then the whole thing was nothing but a scam from the start?"

"Of course it was. But would Paul listen to me? No. He was going to make a fortune!"

Brett spoke into an abrupt silence. "It sounds like you've been seeing quite a lot of Paul."

Barbara stiffened, suddenly aware that she had done most of the talking. Her eyes narrowed. "For your information, Paul and I are considering a reconciliation. Now that he's finally gotten rid of you, we're discussing the possibility of getting back together. We never stopped loving each other."

"Really?" Brett's eyebrows lifted. Where did Billie Place fit into this picture? Did Barbara know that Paul had been living with Billie?

Her surprise angered Barbara. "Almost from the first moment Paul admitted that our divorce had been a mistake. He would have come back to me if you hadn't gotten in the way. Once he settles this Sansmith thing and works out a settlement with you, we'll get back together. You'll see."

Brett stared. "Barbara, when is the last time you visited my cabin?"

"*Your* cabin! Paul and I bought that cabin as a romantic getaway for ourselves!" Barbara sprang to her feet. "If I'd known earlier that he gave it to you, I'd...I'd have..."

"You'd have done what?" Brett asked, silently rising to her feet.

"Get out. Right now. You and I have nothing more to say to each other."

"When were you at the cabin last?" Brett insisted, amazed at her temerity.

"I haven't been there in years! I mean it, this interview is over. Get out of my house!"

"About us helping Paul...?"

"Paul and I don't need your help!" She stormed toward the front door. "You were always jealous of me. Now you're trying to muscle in where you don't belong. Well, you're not going to wreck my plans, not this time. If you try, I'll..."

"Stop threatening me," Brett said quietly, pausing beside the open door.

Barbara's beautiful face twisted into an ugly expression. "I'm warning you. Stay out of my way or you'll regret it for the rest of your life!" She shoved Brett outside and slammed the door.

By the time she walked back to the Mercedes, Sam was seated inside. Brett slid in beside him and clasped her hands tightly together. "That went about as I expected," she said with a heavy sigh. "I'm almost starting to get used to threats. Did you discover anything?"

Sam eased the car into the street, and they both looked at the yard where the preschoolers had been playing earlier. "Barbara apparently planned to have dinner with someone on Saturday night. But she didn't note the person's name or where they intended to meet. She erased the notation as if the dinner were canceled."

"I don't doubt that you can read a message that's been erased, but could the police read it if they have to?"

"I think so, yes."

"Maybe the dinner was canceled, and maybe it wasn't. Barbara didn't deny being out Saturday night."

"She was definitely seeing Paul. There are several notations in her appointment book that mention his name. She was seeing him infrequently, but they were meeting."

"I wonder how Billie Place felt about that?"

"That's assuming Billie knew. Maybe she didn't."

"I don't get it," Brett said, frowning through the windshield. "Paul was living with Billie, but talking reconciliation with Barbara."

"We only have Barbara's word that a reconciliation was a possibility," Sam reminded her. "Maybe Paul didn't see it that way."

"Where are we going now?"

"I thought we'd check out the antique dealer with whom Paul had the fight."

They wasted an hour driving across town, trying to find a parking place, and then wasted another thirty minutes talking to Mr. DeLasie. DeLasie remembered the incident with Paul and expounded on it at length, getting angry again as he talked.

"Dr. Thatcher insisted on thirty thousand dollars for the credenza, but it was only worth twenty, if that. Believe me, I offered top dollar! I told him to try someplace else if he thought he could get more. But he didn't get thirty thousand for that credenza, I'll bet the store on it!"

"How did the fight start?" Sam asked.

DeLasie shrugged. "Dr. Thatcher was spoiling for a confrontation when he came in here," he said in disgust. "He was upset before he entered the door, and he exploded when he found out he couldn't get the price he wanted. I just happened to be the person standing in front of him when he went ballistic." He shook his head and cast an unhappy glance around his showroom. Thin winter sunlight streamed through the front windows and shone on polished furnishings from another age. "He's lucky I didn't press charges."

"I think that's a dead end," Sam commented as they walked back to the car.

"Agreed. It seems to me that the Sansmith people are our best suspects. They must have been putting heavy pressure on Paul. He had a temper, but it just isn't like him to get into a fistfight."

"I suspect you want someone from Sansmith to be the murderer because he won't be someone you know," Sam suggested gently, opening the car door for her.

Brett reached for the cheese crackers immediately and ate a handful while Sam walked around the car, then slid inside.

"That's true," she admitted. "But you have to admit, the Sansmith group sounds like a ruthless bunch. If Paul was slow in paying off his note to them, or maybe if he told them to take a hike or something—which he was hot-headed enough to do—then maybe they killed him or paid someone to kill him."

Sam drove aimlessly while he considered her theory. "Would the Sansmith people know about your cabin in the mountains?"

"No," Brett answered, drawing the word out. "But of course Paul did. Maybe he took his killer there, not knowing what was about to happen."

"That theory doesn't wash for me. How does Sansmith get their money if Paul is dead?"

"If Paul signed a legitimate note, then the unpaid balance will have to be paid by his estate, won't it?"

Sam considered, then nodded. "But if Sansmith is as unscrupulous as it sounds, they won't want anything on record. I have a gut feeling that Sansmith won't file any lien against Thatcher's estate. My guess is they prefer to remain in the shadows. They'll write off the balance of Paul's note as a loss and just disappear."

"Until they find another sucker."

"Probably. But the principals are going to have some very uneasy moments after Paul's body is found. They have to know a few fingers are going to point their way." After a moment's thought, he added, "I can't accept that Sansmith would welcome any official attention. They wouldn't bring that kind of problem on themselves. For the Sansmith people to kill Paul just doesn't make sense to me."

Brett crossed her arms over her chest and considered his comments. "When you read about my case in the newspapers—before, you know, you jumped in to correct history—was there any mention of the Sansmith group?"

"Not that I recall."

Brett shifted on the seat. "Well, why wasn't there? Wouldn't the police have found the same page in Paul's apartment that we found? Wouldn't his bank account show checks written to Sansmith? And Barbara certainly knows about them and how threatening they are. Billie Place must know, too. Sansmith's name must have popped up here and there throughout the investigation. So why didn't the police follow up and track them down?"

"That's an excellent question."

"Are the principals so powerful that they can manipulate the police?"

"Maybe. Or maybe they didn't have to." Sam gave her a long look. "If you'll remember, you were found with Paul's body, the knife had your prints on it, Paul was going to meet 'B.' in Silverthorne, and everyone agreed you had a motive—money and hatred."

"I never hated Paul." Brett rubbed at the headache beginning behind her temples, then ate another handful of cheese crackers.

"Maybe the Sansmith involvement simply never came to light. Maybe the police focused on you and that was that."

"All this speculation is giving me a headache." She ate another handful of cheese crackers. "But let's talk about the knife. That's bothering me. I didn't touch it that night. How could the knife possibly have any prints on it?"

"Fingerprints can establish that a certain person was present at a scene," Sam explained. "But it can't determine when that person was present. The prints on the knife could be months old." He paused. "Of course, the police won't see it that way. They'll assume the prints are fresh."

"What about the killer's prints?"

"Whoever killed Paul was probably wearing gloves."

Brett nodded slowly. "It was a frigid night."

"Or maybe the killer was holding a towel or something when he stabbed Paul. In either case, only the original prints would appear on the knife, and those were yours."

Brett winced. The imagery rising in her mind was distressingly vivid. But they needed to talk about this. She thought hard, gripping the car seat near her thighs.

"In mystery novels, a knife is usually presented as an opportunistic weapon. It indicates impulse, not planning. Unfortunately, that seems to rule out the Sansmith people. If they sent someone to the mountains to kill Paul, it seems logical that the killer would have come prepared. He'd have a gun, wouldn't he? He wouldn't rely on a knife being nearby."

"Keep going," Sam said with a nod. "What you're saying makes sense."

"If we follow this line of reasoning, then Paul's murder was an impulsive act. Not planned." She frowned, staring into space, trying to work it out. "So, if it's impulsive, then the killer probably was not wearing gloves inside the cabin. Unless they walked inside and the murder happened within the next two minutes. But we don't know how long Paul and the killer were together in the cabin." Suddenly, Brett stiffened and sat up straight. Her eyes widened. "Wait a minute. Sam! I need a phone."

"Right now?"

"Yes!" Peering out the window, Brett spotted a 7-Eleven with a pay phone on the outside wall. "There!" she said, pointing. "Turn into that store."

"What are you thinking?" Sam asked as he wheeled the Mercedes into a vacant parking space.

"Greta Rawlings," Brett called over her shoulder as she threw open the car door. "It's possible that Greta can give us an idea if Paul and his killer were in the cabin for a while before he was killed." She sprinted to the phone, opening her purse to search for change.

In less than two minutes she had Greta Rawlings on the phone. "Mrs. Rawlings? This is Brett Thatcher."

"I was just thinking about you. I thought I'd come by and bring you an apple pie this afternoon," Mrs. Rawlings said in a soft voice. "I figure you could use some cheering up."

For a minute Brett didn't know what the woman was talking about, then she realized that Mrs. Rawlings thought she was still in Silverthorne, calling from the mountain cabin.

"Thank you," she said carefully, "but that isn't necessary. I'm on a diet." Guiltily she thought about the cheese crackers she was eating by the handful. "The reason I'm phoning is plain ole curiosity."

"I sort of expected you'd call."

"You did?" That was a surprise. "Well, I'm curious about a couple of items I noticed when I arrived at the cabin. Mrs. Rawlings, did you leave a bottle of champagne in the fridge?"

"Good heavens no." A chuckle sounded over the wire. "I've only been in a liquor store once in my life, and it sure wasn't to buy a bottle of champagne."

"What about the fireplace? Did you build a fire while you were working?" The embers had still been hot when Brett arrived at the cabin, glowing beneath a coating of ash.

"No, absolutely not. Build a fire in a client's house?" She sounded shocked by the idea. "No, ma'am. I clean the place top to bottom and then I'm gone. That's what I told the police, too. Sheriff Stone, he knows how thorough I am. Don't I clean his place every week? And him and the missus, they leave the place in a mess, I can tell you. Takes me four whole hours to clean their house and it's only—"

"Mrs. Rawlings," Brett interrupted. Suddenly, she couldn't catch a breath. Her chest felt as if a vise were closing around it, constricting her lungs. "Excuse me, but you've talked to the police?" Closing her eyes, she leaned her forehead against the brick wall of the 7-Eleven. Her heart was thudding so loudly that she feared she wouldn't hear Mrs. Rawlings's reply.

"They were here this morning. Course I expected 'em, since I'd heard the news about your husband last night on the radio. You poor thing. I knew the two of you wasn't getting along, but..."

"What did the news report say?" Brett wet her lips and repeated the question louder.

"Why, didn't you hear it?"

"I'm in Denver, Mrs. Rawlings. I haven't seen a newspaper or heard a news report in several days."

"Oh, my. Then you don't know." A silence opened. "I hate to be the one to tell you."

"Please, I... tell me what's happened."

"Well, I suppose if... Yesterday a hunter stumbled over Dr. Thatcher's body in the trees. Gave him quite a scare, I imagine." Her voice dropped almost to a whisper. "There was a knife sticking out of the doctor's back, big as you please. It was murder, all right." She hesitated a minute. "The sheriff asked me a lot of questions about you, Mrs. Thatcher."

"What kind of questions?" Brett whispered, holding her head.

"Oh, things like how often did you come up to the cabin, and did you and the doctor fight a lot, and did you mail me a check or did you arrive while I was still cleaning the place."

"I'm sorry, I forgot. I'll mail you a check immediately."

"They asked about the champagne, too, and some other groceries, but I told 'em the fridge was bare when I was there, that you always did your own shopping. And they wanted to know if I knew whether you and the doctor arrived at the cabin together, and then they asked if I saw either you or the doctor on Saturday before I left the cabin.''

''Did you see Paul?'' Brett felt like she could faint. She propped her back against the brick wall to hold herself upright.

''Oh, no. Didn't see a soul. Just did my work and went home before the storm hit.''

Brett didn't speak. Her mind was careening around in a dozen different directions, none of them focused.

''Mrs. Thatcher? I believe Sheriff Stone wants to talk to you.'' Mrs. Rawlings swallowed audibly. ''You might want to give him a call. Right away, probably.''

Brett nodded, forgetting that Mrs. Rawlings couldn't see her. Yes, she imagined Sheriff Stone did indeed want to talk to her. Probably wanted to slap on the handcuffs and drive her off to jail. ''Well,'' she said in a croaking voice, ''thanks for telling me. I'll be talking to you later.''

Hastily, she hung up the phone and sagged against the wall, pressing a hand to her forehead. She felt sick to her stomach.

It wasn't just her own peril that made her feel ill. It was also thinking about Paul again. Not the puzzle of his involvement with the Sansmith group, or the mystery of his relationship with Barbara and Billie, but thinking about him as she had last seen him. With the handle of a knife protruding from his back. The horror of it suddenly overwhelmed her, and she realized how hard she'd been fighting to keep that last image at bay.

When a teenager stepped up to the phone, Brett gazed at his leather and chains for a minute, then pushed from the wall and stumbled toward the Mercedes and slipped inside, falling into the passenger seat.

Sam materialized behind the steering wheel. "I checked the post office, but no luck. The guy hadn't been—" He stared at Brett's white face. "What happened?"

"Paul's body has been found." Her eyes widened until they ached. "The sheriff seems to think Paul and I went to the cabin together. It looks like I'm the primary suspect. Oh, Sam, it's just like you predicted. They think I killed him!"

Chapter Nine

"We knew this was coming," Sam reminded her gently. "It was only a matter of when."

He had hoped they would have more time before Paul's body was discovered. Now that the authorities knew of Thatcher's murder, Sam would have to race the clock to establish Brett's innocence. And time management was not his strong suit.

Mortals experienced time differently than angels. Mortals referred to time as passing slowly or swiftly, a concept Sam occasionally grasped when he was in a loophole. From his usual vantage, mortal time appeared to pass in an eye blink. Decades rolled by at a swift clip. But when he stepped into a loophole, time seemed to slow to a leisurely pace. It was easy to forget that earthly time was not leisurely. Events sped past.

The swift passage of mortal time accounted for Brett's caution that whatever was happening between them was happening very fast. But it didn't appear that way to Sam. To him, slowed by the mortal plane, their deepening attraction appeared to have ripened over a long period. Weeks and months, not days and hours.

To him, it had seemed as if they had endless time in which to explore each other and solve the mystery of Paul's murder. Now he realized they had probably wasted many hours. And that worried him.

"Mrs. Rawlings said the police want to talk to me," Brett reported in a low, dull voice. "I should check my phone messages at the condo." Her gaze swung toward the teenager walking away from the pay phone.

Sam placed a hand on her arm, feeling her tremble beneath his fingers. "Wait. Let's think this through." Her dark eyes looked enormous in an ashen face. "Are you ready for the police?"

"No," she whispered. "We don't have enough evidence to shake their belief that I killed Paul. We can point them toward Sansmith, but we don't know who the Sansmith people are." She rubbed her forehead. "And if you and I can come up with a half-dozen reasons why it probably wasn't the Sansmith thugs who killed Paul, so can the police. But right now that's all we've got."

"Then don't pick up your messages. Later, you can say you didn't know they were looking for you. And the truth is, you don't know for sure that they are."

She rolled her eyes toward the roof of the car, then looked at him again. "Come on, Sam. The police are going to beat a path to my door. When I don't respond to the messages they've probably left for me, they'll show up at the condo."

"And your neighbors will swear that you were home having a wild party on Saturday night."

She blinked and sat up. "That's right. I'd forgotten. But Sheriff Stone knows I was at the cabin."

Sam nodded around a frown. "Yes, but there will be some confusion. That will buy us a little extra time."

"To do what? We're no closer to finding this killer than when we started!"

He stroked his fingertips along the line of her jaw, thinking her skin was as soft and smooth as a drifting cloud. "That's not true, Brett. We've enlarged the suspect list. And your vandalized condo suggests that you're a target, too." He hesitated. "Did you erase the threatening call from your messages?"

"Damn! Yes, I did." She groaned and rubbed her forehead, then reached into the box of cheese crackers. "I'm an idiot."

"No," he said gently, "far from it. You're just not used to being in the middle of a murder case. I'm at fault here. I should have told you not to."

They both stiffened and stared straight ahead at the wall of the 7-Eleven as a squad car passed in the street behind them. Brett's hands shook in her lap, and she glanced over her shoulder with a frightened, apprehensive look, watching the cop car move up the ramp, then pull onto the Sixth Avenue freeway.

"Oh, God, Sam. I'm scared to death. I don't want to spend the rest of my life in prison. There are so many things I want to do, so many things I..."

"Shh." Leaning across the center console, Sam put his arms around her, holding her awkwardly, feeling the tremors that rippled through her body. "That isn't going to happen. We're going to solve this."

"How?" she said against his shoulder.

"I think we need to return to the clinic. Have another talk with Billie Place and the good doctors. Sansmith was putting enough pressure on Thatcher that he was starting to feel desperate. I think his fight with the antique dealer indicates the strain he was experiencing. How did Pritchard and Barkley react to Thatcher's stress? Did they exploit it in some way? Did Billie? These are things we can try to discover."

She eased back to look into his eyes. "Won't the police be watching the clinic?"

"Why would they?" He smoothed a wave of hair off of her forehead. It felt like fine, dark silk. "At this point, I imagine the investigation is concentrated on the cabin."

She was quiet a minute, studying his expression. Finally, she touched shaking fingers to his shoulder and leaned back in her seat. "Okay. We need to do something. I need to feel useful or I'm going to explode. Let's go."

Sam started the car, then looked at her in surprise when she suddenly laughed.

"I'm sorry," she said, shaking her head. "I just remembered an old camp fire song that I used to sing as a child." She cleared her throat and sang softly, "Oh, if I had the wings of an angel, over these prison walls I would fly..." Her voice trailed and died away.

Reaching, Sam caught her hand and squeezed it. "You aren't going to prison, Brett. Not if I can help it."

She gazed at him with large helpless eyes. "I wish you hadn't mentioned having had a few failures."

"We're not going to fail. Count on it."

He could feel her watching him as he drove, could feel waves of emotion emanating from her. "Sam? This is going to sound crazy, and I probably shouldn't say it. And you don't have to say anything back. But I think I'm falling in love with you."

He turned toward her in astonishment.

"I know it's fast, but everything feels speeded up, somehow." She made a helpless gesture with her hands. "As if we have so little time that emotions are compressed until nothing but the pure essence remains, and what's left is powerful stuff."

A burst of joy shot through his system, and his radiance lit the car. Abandoning the Mercedes to its own devices, he turned to her and reached for her hand. "I wouldn't have said anything if you hadn't." Her words lifted the stopper that had bottled his emotions, and gave him the freedom to speak. "I love you, too. I love you, Brett. You have to know that. Tell me you feel it."

"I do," she whispered, touching shaking fingertips to her heart, "in here." She stared at him with large, luminous eyes that shone with love and made him feel ten feet tall. "Sam, if I wasn't so frightened and miserable, this would be one of the happiest moments of my life." She managed a wobbly smile.

"You hang on to that feeling," he said in a thick voice. "Things could get rough." His hand tightened around hers, and he gazed deeply into her sparkling eyes. "Just remember that I love you."

Saying it aloud amazed him, and it relieved some of the tightness in his chest. He loved her. He had fallen victim to the mightiest of mortal temptations and pitfalls. He had fallen head over heels in love with a mortal woman. And he didn't care that he had finally succumbed. Loving Brett Thatcher felt right and good and wonderful. He loved being with her, loved her smile in the morning, loved the sensual way her eyelids drooped when she was sleepy. He loved the look of her and the scent of her, loved the shape of her capable hands and the curve of her inviting lips. He loved who she was and what she was.

"I love you," he said again, marveling that this could have happened to him. Sparks and bright light flashed around his head when he thought about her loving him, too. What had he done to deserve this? It must have been something wonderfully good.

"Oh, Sam. We've just complicated everything by about a thousandfold, haven't we?" she asked as he peeled out of the 7-Eleven parking lot.

Sam didn't care. "Say it again," he requested eagerly.

She laughed softly. "I love you."

Had there ever been three more wonderful words? He felt like breaking into song, felt like sprouting wings and looping a few figure eights across the heavens. Knowing she loved him was the most glorious feeling he had ever experienced. He laughed out loud with joy and struck the steering wheel with his fist. "She loves me!"

"Yes, she does," Brett said, smiling. "But, Sam?"

"Yes?" He grinned at her, happily, tenderly. He wished he had his favorite sword from the old days, and a dragon to slay and lay at her feet.

"Ah, you're driving like a maniac. And you're fizzing again. She tilted her head and studied his hair. "Can those sparks set the car on fire?"

"If they do, we'll put out the flames." He could no more have stopped the flashing and sparking and fizzing than he could have stopped the earth from spinning. This was the happiest day he could remember.

Brett smiled and laughed, and tucked her feet up on the seat beneath her. "At least slow down."

That he could do.

WHILE THEY DROVE to the clinic, Brett told him more about her conversation with Greta Rawlings.

"This means that Paul, at least, was at the cabin long enough to build a fire in the fireplace, and turn down the spread in the master bedroom." The last item puzzled her. "He must have intended to spend the night." Which seemed odd. Since giving her the cabin had been one of the few things in the divorce settlement that Paul had not disputed, it seemed strange that he would behave as if he still owned it.

"The killer must have been with him from the first," Sam reminded her, "since Paul's car was not at the cabin. They must have driven there together. After Paul's murder, the killer drove his car away."

"I'm convinced I must have passed the murderer on the road," Brett agreed. She could have kicked herself for not noticing more about that car.

"The bottle of champagne in the fridge . . . it suggests a celebration of some kind."

Brett ate some cheese crackers, trying to focus her mind on the discussion and not on Sam's mouth. "Maybe Paul was making his last payment to Sansmith. That would certainly be something to celebrate."

"Or maybe he had agreed to sell his interest in the clinic to Barkley and Pritchard? We know he needed money. But suppose he changed his mind, and one of them killed him in the middle of an argument."

"Maybe it was Billie Place. Maybe they went to the cabin for a romantic weekend—hence the fire, the turned-down spread and the champagne—but Paul told her that he planned to reconcile with Barbara and Billie killed him in a moment of rage?"

"Or maybe it was someone we don't know about yet."

"Maybe it was Colonel Mustard in the library with the candlestick," Brett said, hearing an edge of despair in her voice. The possibilities swirled in her mind, making her feel wild inside.

"What? Who?" Sam asked with a frown.

"Never mind. I'm getting a little hysterical." Brett rubbed her forehead and the building headache behind it. "That's a lot of possibilities and a lot of maybes, but no hard evidence."

"The evidence is there. All we have to do is find it."

"How does the guy who vandalized my condo fit into all of this? Could he have killed Paul?"

"He seems more focused on you." Braking for a stoplight, Sam tapped his fingers against the steering wheel, thinking. "He couldn't have killed Paul. He was trashing your condo that night. Considering the weather and the distance involved, I don't think he could have driven eighty miles in a blizzard, killed Paul, then driven eighty miles back in time to vandalize your place while your neighbors were still awake."

A long sigh lifted Brett's chest. "You're suggesting the vandalism and phone threat are not connected to Paul's murder."

"I think the intruder is connected to Paul only in that your manuscript deals with the cosmetic surgery performed at Paul's clinic. And the intruder is probably one of the men on my list."

Brett nodded as they pulled into the underground parking lot beneath the clinic. "Once we're finished here, let's try the post office again. See if he's checked the box." She consulted her wristwatch, then looked toward the elevators. "It's almost twelve-thirty. That's when Billie Place usually leaves for lunch." A grim look came into her eyes.

"Do you think she'll talk to you?"

"She has to. We need to know where Billie was Saturday night, and we need the names of the Sansmith principals."

Sam parked the Mercedes near the elevator doors and switched off the engine. He stretched and dropped an arm across the back of the seats, his fingertips lightly stroking Brett's shoulders. His touch sent a delicious warmth through her body.

"I'm so glad you're here," she said in a low voice. "I don't know how I'd get through this without you."

In some other history, the history without Sam, she hadn't gotten through it. She had been arrested almost immediately and charged with Paul's murder. In that history, her life had changed forever, had veered down a prison path that didn't include children or a husband or a career. Lowering her head, Brett pressed the heels of her palms against her eyelids.

When Sam had first told her about alternate histories and what hers might have been, it had been almost impossible to believe that anyone could think she was capable of murder. Now she saw how it could have happened.

Perhaps the police theorized that she had invited Paul to the cabin, perhaps to discuss the disputed settlement, or maybe—considering the champagne and invitingly opened spread—to discuss a reconciliation. "Dinner with B. at Silverthorne"—the authorities would assume the B. stood for Brett.

They would decide that she had met him for dinner somewhere, then she had driven him to the cabin, where the tension between them exploded and she killed him, leaving her prints on the knife. Afterward, she had dragged his body into the pines behind the cabin. Falling snow had filled in her tracks. The prosecutor's case opened in front of her eyes.

"Oh, God."

It would be a small mystery as to why she had told Sheriff Stone that she'd discovered Paul's body and then pretended to be amazed when his body was missing. But they would either ignore that puzzling incident or invent some reason to explain her strange behavior.

Brett could see it all, could see herself behind bars.

"There she is," Sam commented, watching the elevators open into the parking lot. Billie stood inside, wearing a dark suit and large sunglasses, gripping her purse in both hands.

"I'll handle this," Brett said.

She slid out of the car and walked swiftly toward the elevators. When Billie saw her, she stiffened, then turned, but the elevator door had closed behind her. She spun toward the parking lot and lifted her head as Brett came up to her.

"Paul's dead! And the police are looking for you!" Billie said between her teeth.

"I have to talk to you."

"Didn't you hear what I said? Paul's dead!"

Brett had just begun to frame a reply when a shot rang out, almost deafening in the enclosed concrete lot. Both women turned their heads to stare in astonishment at a hole gouged out of the wall behind them.

"That was a bullet!" Brett said, shocked.

The second shot passed so close that Brett's hair stirred. Frantically, Billie hit the elevator buttons and cursed when the doors didn't open. Then both women dropped into frightened crouches. It didn't help much. They were clear targets with no barrier between them and the hidden shooter.

"We're sitting ducks," Billie gasped.

In the back of Brett's mind she registered the sound of squealing tires, then another shot. A third bullet chunked into the wall beside the elevator. She didn't think her luck would hold much longer. The next shot would tear through her parka and sweater.

The Mercedes wheeled up beside them and Sam shouted, "Get in!"

The car doors flew open and Brett and Billie dived inside. Sam floored the gas pedal and the Mercedes flew up the ramp and outside into the street. He took the corner on two wheels, sped into a side street, then jumped out of the car in a flash of furious light, and vanished into thin air.

Billie Place pulled herself off the floor of the back seat a split second after Sam did his disappearing act. She had lost her dark glasses, and her eyes were wide and terrified. She gripped the seat back on the driver's side and stared at Brett.

"My God! My God!" she whispered in a croaking voice. "He was trying to kill me!"

Gasping, Brett placed a hand over her pounding heart and tried to catch a deep breath. She pushed back her hair and breathed deeply. "Kill *you?*" The words penetrated slowly. Billie thought someone had tried to kill *her*. Brett had been positive that *she* was the target.

Billie fell backward against the back seat and fanned her face furiously with one hand. "If that man hadn't rescued us when he did— Where did he go?"

"His name is Sam. And my guess is he took off after whoever shot at us."

Billie let out a breath she didn't know she'd been holding. "I'd be dead right now." She fumbled in her purse, hands shaking violently, and withdrew a crumpled pack of cigarettes. "I'm sorry, but I never needed a cigarette so badly in my life!"

Brett watched her struggle to hold a lighter steady enough to light the cigarette.

Billie rolled down the back window and exhaled a cloud of smoke with a sigh. "Paul didn't know I smoked," she said, answering Brett's unspoken question.

"Who's trying to kill you?" Brett was amazed that she possessed the presence of mind to take advantage of Billie's mistake. At least she thought it was a mistake. Her own hands were still shaking, and her heartbeat had not yet returned to a normal pace.

"The same person who killed Paul," Billie said impatiently, as if it should have been obvious. Tears welled beneath her lashes. "I really did love him. I've loved him for years. I would have done anything to keep him." She wiped her eyes. "The bastards killed him!"

The smoke from Billie's cigarette smelled good, reminding Brett of the days when she too had smoked. She considered asking for one of Billie's cigarettes, struggled with the thought a minute, then decided against it. She didn't need to add smoking to the list of her troubles.

"Who do you think killed Paul?"

Billie looked down at her lap, took a long drag on her cigarette, then exhaled out the window before she answered. "I guess it will all come out in the investigation."

"If you know who killed Paul, Billie, I beg you...please tell me!"

Billie raised her head and looked into Brett's eyes. "It was either those Sansmith bastards, or Barkley or Pritchard."

Brett tried not to let her disappointment show. For a minute she had believed that Billie had the answer.

"I know Paul refused to sell Alan and Bob his interest in the clinic, but that doesn't seem like enough of a motive to—"

Billie waved the cigarette with another gesture of impatience. "You don't understand. Paul was in deep with the Sansmith people. When this mess started, he owed them five million dollars. He sold just about everything of value that he owned to repay them, but it wasn't enough. He was still about a million short. They were getting impatient for their money." She closed her eyes. "And believe me, those guys know how to apply pressure. The threats were terrifying."

"I thought we were talking about Dr. Barkley and Dr. Pritchard," Brett said, frowning.

"I'm getting to them. Paul was desperate. He didn't have enough antiques or paintings left to sell, certainly not a million dollars' worth." She drew a deep, shaky breath. "So he started embezzling money from the clinic."

"Paul?" Brett stared, then shook her head sadly. "I'm sorry to hear that," she said finally.

"I showed him how to do it," Billie whispered.

"But somehow Barkley and Pritchard found out."

Billie nodded with an expression of disgust. "Paul got sloppy. He didn't have time to take a little here and there and cover his tracks. He pocketed everything he could get his hands on. Of course, Alan and Bob found out." She flipped her cigarette out of the window. "They were furious. Threats were made, a lot of ugly things said." She spread her hands. "They told Paul if he didn't repay the stolen money immediately, the clinic might go under. There would be a big scandal, reputations would be ruined, everyone would suffer."

"What kind of threats?"

"Alan Barkley said he'd kill Paul if Paul didn't return every nickel he'd stolen from the clinic." Billie nodded, tears filling her eyes again. "I didn't believe him. I figured it was just one of those stupid things people say when they're angry and out of control. But..." She shrugged. "Paul's dead, isn't he?"

"When did this confrontation happen?"

Billie thought a moment. "Early last week. Monday, I think. I'd have to check my calendar to be sure."

Brett considered Billie's story. It had the ring of truth. She could visualize the events happening as Billie claimed. Brett had never considered Paul as the type of man who would embezzle from his own clinic, but desperate people were driven to desperate acts. In the right circumstances, with a vise closing around him . . .

"But why would Barkley or Pritchard want to kill you?" she asked, frowning.

"Isn't it obvious? I was there. I heard them threaten Paul! What do you suppose the police will think when they hear that Alan Barkley threatened to kill Paul less than a week before he turns up dead? And Bob Pritchard made threats that were almost as bad. They'll both be suspects, in trouble up to their handsome eyebrows. Talk about a scandal! The clinic will be finished for sure." A shudder convulsed Billie's shoulders. "I'm not going back there. No way. They aren't getting a second chance to kill me!"

"Didn't you say it could also be one of the Sansmith people?"

"Maybe. But I'm not taking any chances."

"Can you tell me the names of the Sansmith people? Who was Paul dealing with?"

Billie shook her head. "I never met any of them. When they left a message, no names were ever mentioned. And Paul just referred to them as 'those Sansmith bastards.'" She hesitated. "I was curious . . . but these are people it's safer not to know much about."

Billie had said she wasn't going to take any chances, and Brett realized she shouldn't, either. She shouldn't believe everything Billie said. It could all be lies. "Tell me, where were you last Saturday night, Billie?"

"You still think that I might have killed Paul?" Sadness or a near approximation darkened her eyes. "I told you, I loved him."

The two women looked at each other across the seat backs. "Barbara claims she and Paul were discussing a reconciliation."

"That's a lie! Barbara's living in a dream world. She wanted a reconciliation, but Paul never did."

"Barbara saw Paul frequently," Brett said, watching for a reaction.

"Because he was trying to borrow money from her to help pay off the Sansmith people! I'm sure he was cordial—he was trying to borrow money, after all—but, believe me, Paul had no romantic interest in Barbara. That ended years ago."

Billie stared out the car window at the passing traffic, letting a silence build. "He didn't love me," she admitted suddenly, angrily. "He let me move in with him because he was afraid I'd tell Barkley and Pritchard about the embezzlement. I thought I could make him love me, and if I'd had more time, I would have." Her chin rose defensively.

Brett gazed at her with a flicker of sadness. So that's how Billie had insinuated herself into Paul's life, with subtle threats that she might tell Barkley and Pritchard about the embezzled money. Paul's foolish investment with the Sansmith people had ended by affecting every area of his life.

"Where were you Saturday night?" she repeated.

"I was at Paul's place, alone." Billie's expression dared Brett to call her a liar.

"But you knew he was going to Silverthorne."

Billie stared at her. "He went there to meet you. To try to buy more time on the divorce settlement. That's my guess."

Which circled them back to square one. Brett sighed, trying to absorb everything she had learned. She gazed at Billie, wishing she could read the woman's mind. Regardless of Billie's claims, it wouldn't have worked with her and Paul, and on some level Billie must have known that.

"If Barbara made it a condition of the loan that she and Paul remarry, he might have been considering it," she said softly, watching Billie's face. "Paul was desperate." Suddenly Barbara's insistence that a reconciliation was in the offing made more sense.

Billie flared and crimson pulsed in her cheeks. "Before I'd have let Barbara have him, I would have—" She bit off the words.

"You would have done what?" Brett asked in a quiet voice.

Before Billie could answer, Sam pulled open the car door and slid behind the wheel. He struck the dashboard with his fist.

"Blast! The shooter was gone by the time I returned to the parking lot," he said in a voice heavy with frustration.

"Sam, this is Billie Place." Brett nodded toward the back seat. "Billie, this is... ah, Sam Angel. My friend and attorney."

"Pleased to meet you," Billie said automatically, staring at Sam. A faint glowing aura pulsed around his head. Billie blinked, frowned, then apparently decided she was imagining things. "You know," she said slowly, shifting her stare to Brett, "something occurs to me... where were *you* when Paul was killed? And why are you so sure he was killed on Saturday night? None of the news reports have mentioned when he actually died. In fact, I'm not sure anyone knows yet. It's odd that you seem to know."

Brett glanced at Sam as he directed the Mercedes into traffic, then she drew a deep breath and told Billie her story, omitting the part about Sam being an angel.

"You found his body?" Billie's eyes widened. "What do you mean, he disappeared?"

Brett was stuck with that part of the tale, there was nothing she could do about it. "I put his body on the porch, but when I took the sheriff outside... Paul was gone." She didn't risk a glance at Sam, but she could see the muscles swelling on his shoulders. This part of the story would always be a mystery.

"Bodies don't just disappear!"

"Paul's did," Brett repeated stubbornly.

"So," Billie said after a minute. "You were the last person to see Paul alive. Very interesting. This puts a different slant on things."

"Paul was dead when I arrived at the cabin. That's the truth."

"I'd say you're going to have a hard time proving it," Billie announced with a gleam of satisfaction. Her voice sank to a purr. "Rather a lucky break for the killer, isn't it?" Leaning forward, she tapped Sam's shoulder. "Let me off near the next bus stop, will you?" She studied Brett's troubled expression. "Are you going to tell the police about the embezzlement?"

Brett almost felt sorry for her. "It's going to come out, you have to know that. Maybe there's some way you can downplay your role." She glanced out the windshield, saw the bus stop on the next block. "Would you take a quick look at this list and tell us if any of these men would have a reason to object if it were known they'd had cosmetic surgery?"

The abrupt change of subject sent Billie Place's eyebrows soaring. "Medical records are confidential."

Brett nodded, extending the list of male clients over the seat back. "I'm not asking for medical information." They both ignored the fact that Billie had given her confidential medical information in the past. "All I'm asking is your opinion. Do you think anyone on this list would be furious if he thought his case would appear in a book? Even under a disguised name?"

"That damned book of yours! I'm so sick of hearing about it." But she took the list and ran a long acrylic fingernail down the names. She thrust the page back at Brett. "I'll tell you this much. Every guy on that list had minor surgery. Ears pinned back, moles removed, a hair implant, something like that. I suppose they might be a little embarrassed if they thought the news about their hair implant, for instance, was going to appear as public information, but I can't imagine any of them getting into a lather about it."

"Odd," Brett murmured, frowning at the list of names. "You're absolutely positive that none of these men had something major done? Something that might alter his appearance?"

"I'm positive," Billie said firmly, losing interest.

"One last thing. I trusted you not to tell Barkley and Pritchard about my book," Brett said as Sam braked in front of a bus stop. "Did you tell anyone else? Any clients?"

"I might have." Billie's chin came up. "So what?"

"Who did you tell? Billie, please. This is important."

She reached for the door handle and her eyes narrowed. "I never liked you. You never appreciated Paul or the life he gave you. You were always whining about how your house was too big, and you didn't like a live-in housekeeper, and you wanted a lot of snotty little kids but Paul wouldn't see things your way. A pretty face and a great body landed you a dream life, but you were too dumb to appreciate it." Disgust wrinkled her expression. "I don't know what the hell you wanted!"

"What do you want, Billie?"

"It doesn't matter," she snapped, her eyes filling with tears. "Now that Paul's dead, I'll never have it." Opening the car door, she slid outside and slammed the door behind her.

"I thought I knew her, but I never did," Brett said finally. She stiffened her spine and sat up straighter. "This has been a wild day."

Sam drove to the nearest parking space, an opening in front of a small restaurant. He cut the engine, then turned to examine her face. "Are you all right?" he asked softly. "You'll never know how crazy I felt when I heard those shots!"

"The truth?" Brett pulled a hand through her hair, then briefly closed her eyes. "I don't know. Every day I think things can't get worse. But they do. Now someone's shooting at me. Billie thought she was the target, but you and I know someone is trying to kill me."

Fury sent sparks shooting from his head, and the burst of light that filled the car was so bright that Brett had to shield her eyes.

"I should never have let you walk off alone!"

Brett touched his arm. "It wasn't your fault, Sam." Before he could argue, she repeated everything Billie had related.

"Interesting," Sam said after he'd heard it all. "Paul was embezzling money from his partners at the clinic, and Billie was helping him do it."

"I don't know if I believe that Billie loved Paul, but I do believe she planned to marry him, even if she had to use blackmail to do it. She wanted the life she thought Paul could give her." Brett shook her head. "I don't think Billie would have killed the golden goose. If Billie was inclined to kill anyone, it would probably have been Barbara. If we believe Billie's story, then Barbara was probably dangling her bank account in front of Paul, hoping to exchange it for a reconciliation."

"I wouldn't count Billie out just yet. She might have decided if she couldn't have Paul, then no one else would, either." He thought a moment. "And the stakes just went up for Doctors Barkley and Pritchard. Paul wouldn't sell out to them, plus he was systematically looting the till. I'd say Barkley and Pritchard have motive written all over them."

"Poor Paul," Brett said softly, turning her face to the side window. "He must have been absolutely frantic, and getting more desperate every day. Everywhere he turned, someone was twisting the screws on him. Even me. Now I understand why he fought the settlement. He couldn't pay me because he needed every nickel to pay Sansmith or repay his partners."

Sam let his fingers play along her shoulder blades. "From the sound of it, you aren't going to receive any settlement. Or the five million dollar buyout from Paul's partners. When he died, Paul was nearly bankrupt, and it sounds like the clinic is very close to closing up shop."

Brett shook her head. "That's the least of my worries. I didn't know about the five million in the first place, so that's not a real loss. As for the settlement..." She thought about her old Buick, "It didn't amount to that much, anyway. I'll get by without it." After a pause, she straightened her shoulders and met Sam's steady, concerned gaze. He had the most beautiful eyes she had ever seen, warm and deep and compassionate. "What do we do now?"

"We should return to the clinic and talk to Barkley and Pritchard. Are you up to it?"

"Frankly, no." A long sigh lifted and collapsed her chest. "I've had enough of playing detective for one day."

A frown appeared, then swiftly disappeared on Sam's brow. "What would you prefer to do?"

"It's going to sound cowardly."

"Brett," he said, taking her hand, "you're entitled. Someone tried to kill you. Taking a time-out sounds like a good idea." Something flickered at the back of his mind, reminding him of his earlier thoughts about wasting time. Then he looked into the distress darkening Brett's eyes, and the thought faded.

"If I could do anything I wanted to do right now, I'd return to the house, put some soothing music on the CD player, and I'd relax in a hot tub full of bubbles, and I'd try to put all of this out of my mind for a little while."

"It sounds good so far." Sam smiled. "And afterward?"

"Afterward," she continued, returning his smile, "it would be nice to go somewhere candlelit and romantic for dinner, nice to pretend that the police aren't searching for me, and some crazy person isn't trying to kill me. It would be wonderful if we could just put everything on hold for a few hours and pretend that none of this is happening. I'd like to spend an evening with you that didn't revolve around the mess I'm in."

Sam's eyebrows rose in an expression of delight. "A date?"

"Yes. Could we have a date, Sam? Like ordinary men and women?"

He gazed at her, and the light filling the car altered to a softer, warmer color. "I think we can manage that," he said in a gruff voice.

Her suggestion utterly captivated him. Sam had never been on a date before.

Chapter Ten

The manual that explained mortal customs was frustratingly unclear regarding practical decisions involved with dating. The manual offered no clue as to what constituted an ideal date. Or if dinner was a date or only a prelude to a date. And Sam couldn't find any information on who decided where to go, the man or the woman or the couple together. How and when the date ended also was dishearteningly vague.

Standing in the kitchen, he reread the definition of dating, and the purpose, then, frowning, he studied a page of illustrations, trying to glean what scant information he could.

After having read everything available, he shut the manual with a slam and raked his fingers through his hair. "Blast!"

A date seemed important to Brett, and it was becoming important to him, too. He didn't want to botch it.

In a state of growing agitation, he decided to consign his anxieties to the back of his mind and focus his thoughts elsewhere in the hope that his subconscious would process the dating information if he gave it a chance.

Flashing over to the Littleton Post Office, he checked Box 2580, hoping for some action. Brett's letter had appeared within the box, but it hadn't been picked up. That was good. Sam wanted to be here when it was. To that end, he flashed to the post office every time he had a spare moment.

Next, he paid a quick visit to Brett's vandalized condo, ignoring the mess. The message light blinked on her answering machine, and when he checked the counter on the machine he saw that she had eight messages waiting. Some would be from friends who had learned of Paul's murder. At least one, probably more, would be from the police. He stared at the answering machine and felt a pressure building inside his chest. The case was heating up.

On a hunch, he next appeared in Paul's house near the Denver Country Club. It didn't surprise him to discover that Billie Place had moved out. Her clothing was gone, but she had overlooked the monogrammed silk robe hanging next to Paul's in the bathroom. It would be enough to point the police in the right direction.

A more sobering discovery was finding that the ledger of payments to Sansmith had vanished. Carefully, Sam went through every document in Paul Thatcher's desk. There was nothing whatsoever that related to Sansmith Development. No ledger, no canceled checks, no contract, no scribbled slip of paper, no mention of them in Paul's address or appointment book, nothing.

When he inspected Paul's checkbook, examining the stubs, Sam found that every check stub that might have recorded a check written to Sansmith had been carefully altered. The stubs now noted checks written to 8dnzmeth. The police could search from now until kingdom come for a company or a bank account in the name of 8dnzmeth, and they would find nothing.

A momentary flash of admiration tightened Sam's expression. The Sansmith people were good. The alterations were performed so skillfully, that unless an observer were specifically looking for an alteration he would never spot it. Sam wasn't sure the authorities would spot the alterations even if they were looking.

Now he understood why no mention of Sansmith had appeared in the original version of Brett's arrest, trial and subsequent conviction. The police might have turned up a lot of smoke about Sansmith, but there would have been no evidence to prove there had ever been a fire. There would be no evidence to actually link Paul Thatcher to a shadowy group called Sansmith.

In that alternate history—as in this one—Sansmith had effectively vanished.

Sam didn't think the Sansmith thugs had killed their cash cow, but if they had, his job had just become a thousand-fold more difficult.

Worrying that unpleasant thought in his mind, he appeared outside the Thatcher clinic. He thrust his hands in his pockets and looked up, studying the light shining out of Dr. Alan Barkley's office window. The good doctor was working late. Deciding it was worth a closer look, he flashed into Barkley's office.

Alan Barkley paced across the carpet in front of his desk, pausing frequently to consult his gold wristwatch or to glance at the newspapers spread across his desk. The headlines of the evening edition expanded on the report of Paul Thatcher's murder. Grainy photos of Paul and the clinic occupied a prominent space.

Sam checked his own watch and frowned. His date was scheduled to commence in about three minutes if he was reading the time correctly.

"Where the hell have you been?"

Alan Barkley's angry question brought Sam's head up. He watched Bob Pritchard enter the office and throw off a topcoat, then walk directly to a panel hidden in Barkley's bookshelf. He opened the panel and poured a full glass of bourbon before he answered.

"I've spent the last three hours nose to nose with the president of Litton's Bank, trying to negotiate a loan to keep this place afloat," Pritchard snapped.

"What was the verdict?"

"None yet," Pritchard answered, draining half the glass of bourbon. "But it doesn't look promising."

Barkley waved a hand toward the newspapers scattered across his desk. "We could be in a hell of a lot of trouble!"

"You've got that right. Paul's murder isn't helping our chances for a loan."

"That's not the only thing I'm talking about, and you know it."

Chewing his lip, Sam frowned down at his wristwatch. In about thirty seconds he would be late.

A battle erupted in his mind. On one side was an urge to remain with Barkley and Pritchard in the hope that he would learn something important versus the urge not to disappoint Brett.

A melting feeling poured through his body. It was no contest.

Twenty seconds later he rang the doorbell to the safe house. Standing on the porch, experiencing an uncharacteristic nervousness, he swallowed hard and adjusted the knot of his tie. When Brett opened the door and he saw what she was wearing, he released a silent sigh of relief. He'd been correct to don a suit instead of remaining in his jeans and sweater.

She smiled. "I was wondering where you went."

"You look fantastic!" he whispered, staring.

She had dressed her dark hair into an upsweep, allowing silky tendrils to drift around her cheeks and the nape of her neck. The soft glow of pearls gleamed at her earlobes and throat.

"Do you like the dress?" she asked almost shyly, turning for his inspection.

"Yes!"

"You don't think it's too tight? All those cheese crackers..."

A tawny skirt floated out from her knees when she spun around. The color blended a shimmering swirl of gold and caramel, like her eyes. The filmy material reminded Sam of purest gossamer. He glanced at her strappy sandals, then returned his stare to the top of the dress. It molded her breasts like a second skin, and bared perfect milky shoulders. She was so beautiful that she took his breath away, leaving him speechless for a moment.

"Here," he said hoarsely, thrusting forward a bouquet of roses and a heart-shaped box of chocolates. He'd seen both in one of the illustrations in the manual. "These are for you."

"Thank you." Dropping long lashes, she leaned to the roses and inhaled. "Lovely. I'll put them in some water, then we can go."

"Ah, where would you like to go?" He followed her into the kitchen, watching her hem caress the back of her knees. This was the first time he had seen her legs. Suddenly he understood the fuss mortal men made over women's legs. Brett's legs were beautifully shaped, slender at the ankle, and rising toward...

He gave his head a shake.

"Did you make dinner reservations?" she asked, arranging the roses in a vase.

He held his breath for a moment. Blast! He hadn't known he was supposed to make reservations. "What's your favorite restaurant?" he asked, hedging.

"Le Chat?" she inquired, her face brightening. "Is that where we're going?"

"I knew you'd like it," he said, thankful that he could perform small miracles. Instantly, a reservation for Mr. Sam Angel appeared on Le Chat's list.

Almost at once he discovered there were nuances to dating that he hadn't expected. A date required certain ritualistic behavior that he identified as the date unfolded.

Whereas Brett had previously exhibited very independent behavior, tonight she seemed to expect that he would help her on with her coat, which he did, and that he would open the car door for her, which he also did. These were acts he had been informed that the modern mortal woman rejected as almost insulting. But he began to get the hang of it. On a date, old-fashioned manners prevailed.

After parking the car in the lot in front of Le Chat's, he opened her car door, assisted her outside, then offered his arm. He liked having her close enough to inhale the heady scent of her perfume and the unique fragrance that was hers alone. What was less pleasant was the fear that he would do something wrong, something undatelike.

Treating Brett as if she were made of porcelain, he escorted her inside the restaurant, inquiring if she was warm enough, comfortable enough, cautioning her to watch her step.

The maître d' smiled and inquired if they had a reservation, then checked his book before he smiled again and led them to a table overlooking a spotlit, snowy garden. The maître d' and Sam bumped shoulders as they both attempted to seat Brett. Sam's combative glare sent the man scurrying away with an expression of alarm. In this instance, Sam didn't care what the date rules were, he didn't want another man performing this small service for *his* date.

After they ordered drinks, Brett dazzled him with a candlelit smile. "Where did you go while I was in the tub?"

For a moment he couldn't answer, paralyzed by the imagined vision of Brett in her bath. He tasted his martini, then related where he had been. It required a great effort of will to keep his gaze focused above her neck.

Brett's face sobered. "You left Barkley and Pritchard just when the conversation was starting to get interesting?"

"I didn't want to be late for our date."

"Oh, Sam," she said softly after a full minute of silence. "How can I be feeling like this when we've known each other for so short a time?"

"It doesn't feel like a short time to me," he said, watching the candlelight gleam in her hair. Reaching across the table, he took her hand in his. She had small, capable hands, the nails short and buffed to a soft sheen.

"I've only known you a few days," she said in a wondering voice, gazing into his eyes. "But I feel as if I've known you forever. We've been through so much that it seems like we've been together always. Nothing like this has ever happened to me before."

"Me, either," he said with a smile.

"When I think about it, it doesn't seem possible that I could be in love with a man I've known for so short a time and with whom I haven't even..." A becoming flush of pink brightened her cheeks. "But I am." Happiness and helplessness glowed in her eyes. Her feelings bewildered her but she accepted them.

"I love you," Sam said simply. The joy of loving her had filled the hollow space behind his chest. For the first time in centuries he didn't ache with the pain of loneliness. As if the weight of his loneliness had anchored him to the ground, he now felt free and buoyant with an effervescent lightness.

They looked at each other and laughed at nothing, laughed at their own happiness, laughed because the joy of the moment could not be contained.

Totally absorbed in themselves and the power of wonder and discovery, they held hands across the table, gazing at each other with happy, self-conscious smiles.

"Sam...what happens when this is all over?" Brett finally asked in a tremulous voice. "You'll have to leave, won't you?"

This was the dark edge to his happiness. "I don't know. Maybe something can be worked out."

Her face lit in a radiant smile. "Would Angelo let you stay?"

Angelo. Instantly, Sam crashed into reality. He was in trouble with Angelo. Angelo would not be predisposed to grant him any favors. "I shouldn't have provoked him," he murmured, frowning down at their clasped hands. "Blast!"

Brett turned her lovely face toward the window and gazed out at the fairy-tale play of light against snow, but not before he noticed a shine of moisture in her eyes.

"It's all right," she whispered. "I'll take whatever time with you that I can get and be thankful for it, no matter how brief it turns out to be."

The first course arrived then. After their waiter left, Sam searched his mind for a cheerful topic. "How did you decide to become a nurse?"

He'd made the right decision. Brett's expression tilted upward again as she told him about her nursing career, made him laugh with anecdotes about patients she had tended and doctors she had dealt with.

"You miss nursing, don't you," he asked when dessert crepes had been served.

"Yes," she said simply. "I think that's one decision I've made. When this is all over, I plan to return to nursing." After drawing a deep breath, she gazed into his eyes. "Can you tell me about some of your previous cases?"

He wasn't permitted to speak about previous clients or cases to mortals. But what was one more infraction when he was already in so much trouble? And how could he refuse her anything? Over after-dinner drinks, Sam related some of his more interesting assignments. Sheepishly, he admitted his difficulties abiding by the new rules and regs. "I think I've mentioned this problem before. Now you see the extent of the difficulties."

"That last thug you mentioned, I can see why you had to pound him. He deserved it, and he would have gotten away otherwise." Endearingly, she came down firmly on Sam's side.

He grinned. "I'm afraid Angelo didn't see it that way. In fact, I'm about this far—" he held his thumb and forefinger an inch apart "—from being dismissed from the Avengers and sent to the Fifth Choir."

"What's the Fifth Choir?"

He frowned and shrugged uncomfortably. The Fifth Choir was nothing to joke about. "It's where erring angels are sent for rehabilitation or punishment."

"You're not a bad angel," she said flatly, reaching to press his hand. "Where is this Fifth Choir, and what do they do to you there?"

"I don't know the answer to either question. None of us do. All I can tell you is that no angel returns from the Fifth Choir."

"They kill you there?" Her eyes widened and she gasped.

He laughed and shook his head. "No. That kind of mayhem doesn't exist in heaven."

At least he hoped not. At the back of his mind Sam suspected that he was going to discover the answers once this case was concluded. Angelo didn't make idle threats, and Angelo had reached the end of his patience. Sam suspected he was destined for the dread Fifth Choir. But when he looked into Brett's shining eyes, he didn't care. If he couldn't stay with her, then it didn't much matter where Angelo sent him.

"Mayhem," Brett repeated. His remark turned her thoughts to Paul Thatcher. She sighed and touched her fingertips to her forehead. "I'd hoped we wouldn't have to talk about my case tonight, but that really isn't possible, is it," she said with an apologetic shrug. The golden reflection of candlelight caressed her bare shoulders and cast an intriguing shadow along the line of her cleavage. "Maybe we should discuss what do to next."

Right now Sam preferred talking about more personal subjects, would have liked to explore their deepening feelings for each other. But the case was why he was here. And time was flying by.

He released her hand and eased backward in his chair, wishing the restaurant permitted smoking and he could light his pipe. "We need to speak to Doctors Barkley and Pritchard. And we need to nail the bastard who's threatening you and taking wild shots at you. And there's something—" frowning, he studied the lights shining on the snow outside "—there's something I've overlooked, something small but important that I can't quite remember...."

"Like what?"

"I wish I could tell you, but . . ." The information hovered tantalizingly just out of reach, somewhere on the periphery of his mind. "It will come to me eventually," he said, trusting in past experience.

Brett gazed at him across the table, studying him with soft eyes as if she were committing his features to memory. "Thank you for tonight, Sam. This was wonderful." She glanced toward a tiny dance floor and a three-piece combo that played romantic music suitable for dining or slow dancing. "Do you dance?"

It devastated him to admit that he had never danced.

When Brett noticed the emotional flashes sparking near the surface of his hair, she laughed and pushed back her chair. "It's all right. I didn't want to dance, anyway."

"Blast! I'm sorry." Upset, he rose hastily to help her out of her chair. The manual had not mentioned anything about dancing being a requirement for a date. He felt like he'd let her down and maybe ruined everything.

"Really, it's not important."

When he helped her with her coat near the restaurant door, his fingers brushed her bare shoulders and for an instant he could not move. All of history's great love stories flashed through his memory, and he finally understood them. Yes, a man would go to war to reclaim his Helen. Motivated by love, a man would level mountains and drain oceans. A man would challenge heaven if need be. And he would learn how to dance before the next date. If there was one.

"I was naive to think we could pretend we were just ordinary people," Brett said, taking his arm as they walked to the car. She ducked her head. "Or to think we could get through an evening without discussing the case." She lifted her head. "Could we stop by the Littleton Post Office and see if . . ."

He nodded. Maybe they'd be lucky this time.

A police siren howled in the distance, and they both froze beside the Mercedes. When the sound receded, they gazed into each other's eyes for a minute, then climbed into the car.

Sam didn't know how much time they had left, but instinct told him it wasn't much.

AT THIS LATE HOUR there were only two cars parked in front of the post office. Sam stiffened the instant he switched off the ignition, and he gripped the steering wheel tightly.

"He's inside," he announced abruptly. He sensed the same furious, darkly focused presence he had felt outside Paul Thatcher's home. This time the presence was nearer, stronger. Now he also picked up a sour undertone of fear and despair.

"The killer?" Brett gasped, her eyes widening.

Sam hesitated and frowned. "I don't think this man is a killer," he said, as surprised by the answer as she was. "But he's the person who vandalized your condo and the man who shot at you." He touched her hand. "Wait here."

Instantly he appeared inside the nearly deserted post office. He waited until a woman left, absorbed by the mail in her hand, then it was just him and the man standing before Box 2580, reading Brett's letter.

And Brett. She burst inside the post office in a swirl of cold air, looked around with a wild glance, then stood stock-still, staring at the man holding her letter.

"Mr. Slivowitz!" she blurted, then lifted a hand to her lips.

"You know that man?" Sam asked.

"We've never met, but yes, I know who he is."

Karl Slivowitz's head jerked up and he focused on Brett. Shock rounded the eyes behind his spectacles, then anger and hatred. His shoulders rolled back in a combative gesture, and his body went rigid.

Sam's muscles swelled in a reflex action, but he couldn't bring himself to view Karl Slivowitz as a threat. The man had to be seventy years old at least. He was an inch shorter than Brett, and when he straightened, he automatically reached for the cane resting against the wall of post office boxes and leaned on it heavily. Still, this was the creature who had badly frightened Brett, and Sam wanted to pound him.

"I don't believe what you say in this letter," Slivowitz said furiously, waving the pages covered with Brett's handwriting. "I want something better than your word, I want that manuscript. I want to destroy that slanderous piece of garbage myself!"

"Mr. Slivowitz...you vandalized my home. You killed my fish. And you shot at me. You tried to *kill* me!"

A flush of color darkened the old man's face. He glanced at Sam. "It's true. I shot at her. But I wasn't trying to kill her." For an instant the old man looked appalled at what he was saying, at what he had done. "I only wanted to frighten her. So arrest me. But you should arrest her, too." He pointed a bony finger that shook with anger and despair. "She intends to kill my wife!"

Brett moved backward a step. "That isn't true! I don't even know your wife! I've heard of her, of course, but I've never met her! Certainly I have no reason to wish her any harm."

"Which makes it even worse!" the old man cried, shaking. "You're killing a stranger. Sylvia has never done any harm to you or to anyone!"

Sam stepped forward and raised a hand. "Would someone explain what is going on here?" When they both spoke
at once, he pulled to his full height. "Stop! One at a time."

"Please," Mr. Slivowitz said, placing a hand over his
heart. "These have been terrible days. I must sit down."

Brett whirled, looking around, then she upended a
wastebasket, spilling out junk mail and advertising flyers,
and carried the wastebasket to Mr. Slivowitz's side. "Here.
Sit on this." She studied the bluish tint of his lips. "Are you
all right?"

Sam watched her in amazement. This man had admitted
vandalizing her apartment and shooting at her. But she was
trying to help him, was worried about him. Sam sighed and
narrowed a watchful gaze on Slivowitz in case the old man
was healthier and stronger than he looked. He had, after
all, found the strength to pull the mattress off of Brett's bed
and overturn heavy furniture.

Slivowitz blotted his forehead with a handkerchief. "I'm
all right."

"I don't think so, Mr. Slivowitz. I think you should see
a doctor."

He gave her a despairing look. "I don't want your ad-
vice or your concern!"

Brett drew a long breath. "Mr. Slivowitz, the first thing
you should know is that I didn't mention Sylvia Bardo in
my manuscript. Plus, I swear to you that I'm not going to
finish writing the book. I intend to destroy it. It will never
be published. That's the truth. You and your wife have
nothing to fear."

The fight and fury had drained out of the old man, leaving only despair. "She's a proud woman, my Sylvia," he
said, speaking in a low voice. He glanced up at Sam. "Sylvia doesn't look a day over fifty. She tells interviewers that
she has never had cosmetic surgery." He shook his head

sadly. "It will kill her to be labeled a liar, or to have any-one know..." His voice trailed and he closed his eyes. "Learning about your manuscript has sent her to bed in fear. She looks like an old woman now, thanks to you. She'll die, Mrs. Thatcher, if you tell the world that Sylvia Bardo is seventy-three years old and has had several com-plete face-lifts." His eyes blinked open, filling with fury. "Do you understand? You will kill her!"

"No, Mr. Slivowitz," Brett said softly, sympathy dark-ening her gaze. "I won't harm your wife." She turned to Sam. "Sylvia Bardo was a young film star during World War Two."

"Her photograph was in every GI's locker!" Karl Sli-vowitz interrupted proudly. "You never saw a more beau-tiful woman in your life. She was every man's dream. She still gets fan letters."

"She never made it big like some of the others from that era," Brett continued.

"That's not true!" Slivowitz insisted sharply. "Sylvia was as big as Lana Turner, bigger than Hedy Lamarr!"

"But every GI who had her pinup adored her." Brett glanced at the old man's flaming face. "If I remember cor-rectly, Sylvia Bardo had one big film right after the war, then she did a few minor roles and dropped out of sight."

"Again, lies!" the old man protested hotly. "Sylvia was a big star! She quit the business at the top of her career!"

Brett leaned against the wall of post office boxes, watching Karl Slivowitz defend his adored wife while she continued speaking to Sam in a low voice.

"Every few years or so, someone remembers Sylvia Bardo and interviews her. Until about ten years ago, she was a celebrity in Denver. Then she began to curtail her appearances because she didn't like the way she looked."

Karl Slivowitz tried to rise from the upturned wastebasket but failed. He stared at Brett. "Your husband wouldn't do another face-lift for her!"

"Her skin has lost its elasticity, Mr. Slivowitz. Another face-lift would have left her looking as if she were wearing a mask." The glance Brett cast Sam told him that Sylvia Bardo already wore her skin like a mask.

"Sylvia is more beautiful than you will ever be, young lady!" Slivowitz hissed.

Brett continued speaking as if she hadn't heard him. "Karl is Sylvia's fourth husband, but theirs is a true love story. He was one of those GIs who had Sylvia's photo pinned in his locker. If the interviews I've read are true, he fell in love with her then but didn't meet her until they were both middle-aged." She looked at the old man. "They've been together ever since."

Slivowitz closed his eyes and swayed atop the wastebasket. "She is as beautiful today as the day I first gazed at her picture."

"You came within a hair's width of killing Mrs. Thatcher," Sam said between clenched teeth. His accusation jerked both Brett and Slivowitz from their absorption with Sylvia's story. They both stared at him. "You tore Mrs. Thatcher's home apart and you threatened to kill her. You almost did."

The old man lifted his head defiantly. "I only meant to frighten Mrs. Thatcher." He gave her a challenging look. "But I'll do whatever I must to protect Sylvia."

"Would you kill Paul Thatcher?" Sam snapped.

Genuine shock flared in Slivowitz's eyes. "Me? I was not sorry to read that he's dead," he said slowly. "He wouldn't do as Sylvia asked. But no, I didn't kill him." Light flashed off his spectacles as he slid a glance toward Brett. "I regret it if I frightened you, Mrs. Thatcher—"

"If?" Brett asked incredulously. "You *did* frighten me. You scared me to death! That's what you intended!"

"It was necessary. I can't allow you to brand my Sylvia as a liar or tell anyone that she's had cosmetic surgery. That kind of exposure would kill her." He looked down at the floor and sighed. "I didn't mean those shots to come so close. I'm not as good a shot as I once was."

"How did you learn of my manuscript, Mr. Slivowitz?"

"Two weeks ago I went to the clinic to beg your husband to reconsider and give Sylvia another face-lift. I overheard Miss Place telling Dr. Barkley about your book. I mentioned it to Sylvia before I realized you would of course exploit her name by including her in your exposé. Sylvia saw at once that you would use her celebrity to sell books. She became distraught, and—" he shrugged "—I promised her that the book would never be published."

"Why didn't you just make an appointment and speak to Mrs. Thatcher?" Sam demanded. He didn't need to glance at the sadness in Brett's eyes to know that using Sylvia's name had never occurred to her. Moreover, Sylvia Bardo's name would have gone unrecognized by most readers; the world had forgotten yesterday's pinup girl. But neither Sylvia nor her husband could admit it.

The old man straightened proudly. "Sylvia's name would have made Mrs. Thatcher's book a success. She would never have agreed to omit Sylvia's name!"

Brett went to Slivowitz and knelt beside him, covering his shaking hands with her own. She looked into his eyes. "Mr. Slivowitz, go home and tell your wife that you have succeeded. The book will never be published. I give you my solemn word on this. By this time tomorrow the manuscript will be nothing but ashes. The world will remember Sylvia Bardo as she is, beautiful and youthful."

For a long moment they held each other's gaze, then Slivowitz closed his eyes and his shoulders slumped. "Thank you," he whispered.

Brett stood and looked at Sam. "It's over," she said softly. She walked past Sam and out the door of the post office.

Sam studied Karl Slivowitz for a long moment. "Whatever you feel for Sylvia Bardo is only a fraction of what I feel for Brett Thatcher," Sam said between his teeth. He didn't share Brett's sympathy for this old man. "If you *ever* threaten her again, if you ever even *think* about shooting at her again…" His hands clenched and tiny flashes of light sparked around his head.

For the first time Slivowitz looked frightened. "Who are you?" he whispered, staring at the light fizzing around Sam's hair.

Sam swelled in size. Luminous wings sprouted from his shoulder blades and soared over his head. The radiance of his anger and protectiveness filled the post office with a blinding light. He showed himself to Karl Slivowitz in his full and terrible angelic magnificence, gripping a flaming sword before his robe. "I am vengeance," he stated in a deep voice that boomed off the walls.

The manifestation was theatrical, impressive, and it worked every time. The terrified man would have had a heart attack if Sam had advanced a single step toward him. When Sam was absolutely certain that he had made his point, he thrust the tip of his fiery sword toward the high ceiling and vanished.

"You don't need to worry about Karl Slivowitz," he said, appearing behind the steering wheel of the Mercedes, dressed in his suit and tie. "He won't bother you again."

Brett, who had not seen his flaming display, shook her head sadly. "That poor old man. He's dying, you know."

"That poor old man is filled with hate."

"He loves his wife."

"It's a sick love. As shaky as his hands are, it's a miracle that he didn't kill you." Sam reached for the ignition.

She shook her head again, the motion stirring the loose tendrils around her cheeks and the nape of her neck. "Leave him alone, Sam. He's an old man. He was desperate to protect his wife. I think he believes me now, about the manuscript. And you've assured me that I've seen the last of him...."

Sam agreed that Karl Slivowitz would not be a problem in the future, but everything that made Sam what he was shouted that Slivowitz should be punished for what he had done. It was difficult to allow this injustice to go unpunished even to please Brett.

They didn't speak again until he stopped the car in front of the safe house. "Look," he said, turning on the car seat to face her in the light shining from the porch, "I'm sorry our date ended on an upsetting incident."

He didn't need instructions to recognize the date had concluded. He felt the difference in their moods.

"Me, too," Brett agreed, trying to smile. "But I'm glad we know the answers to at least a few of the puzzles." Closing her eyes, she let her head drop wearily to the back of the seat. "I was hoping that if we found whoever shot at Billie and me, we'd find Paul's killer. I know that wasn't realistic, but I hoped we'd find *all* the answers, and I'd be off the hook."

She sat up abruptly and stared at him with stricken eyes. "I mean... Oh, Sam. Part of me wants this nightmare to end. I don't want to freeze inside every time I hear or see a patrol car. I want whoever killed Paul to be caught and punished. But part of me wants to stop time right here so you and I..."

"I know," he interrupted, taking her hand. He wanted the pleasure of rescuing her from the threat of unjust imprisonment, wanted the joy of being her conquering warrior, but he didn't want the case to end.

"Suddenly I feel very tired and very discouraged," Brett whispered. "Very confused."

"A good night's sleep will help." Sliding out of his seat, trying to swallow his own disappointment, Sam walked around the car and opened the door for her. He knew from the manual that there were several ways a date could end, ranging from a handshake to the joy of sharing the same bed. He also knew he was not the type to take advantage of a vulnerable moment.

Taking her arm, he helped her across a patch of ice and up the steps of the porch. Pausing beneath the porch light, he placed a finger beneath her chin and tilted her face up toward his.

"Good night, Brett," he said in a husky voice.

"Sam?" she said softly, peering deeply into his eyes. "Please kiss me."

Gently, he folded her into his arms, holding her carefully as if he might damage her if he crushed her against him as he longed to do. Drawing a breath, he pressed his lips to her forehead.

She melted against his body, and he felt the soft, human weight of her, felt her connection to the earth and her own mortality. She was flesh and bone, passion and life, not a manifestation as he was. She vibrated with life and forces and energies that Sam could no longer fully understand. He could only observe and envy her free will and the ability to make her own choices. He envied the full range of qualities that made her so gloriously human.

He held her another long moment, burying his face in her hair, then he vanished. If he had remained another instant, the heat and weight of her body, the yielding of her limbs and the fragrance of her, would have caused him to behave very badly.

It wasn't until he'd popped up in front of the Logan Street Avenging Angel headquarters that he realized she had been asking him to kiss her on the lips.

"Blast!" He was an idiot. He'd been trying so hard to consider her sensibilities, trying so hard not to violate any dating rules, that he had entirely misunderstood what she was actually wanting and feeling. "Blast!" he said again, striking a fist against his forehead.

Brooding, angry at himself, he glanced up at the light shining from the window of Angelo's office.

Why not? He might as well discover what his chances were.

Striding forward, he opened the door, walked through the deserted main room and up the staircase. He knocked at the door to Angelo's office, then stepped inside.

Angelo leaned back from his master computer, folded his hands on his desktop and considered Sam with a hint of sympathy. "No," he said softly but firmly. He knew why Sam had come.

"Why not?" Sam demanded angrily. "Other Avengers have fallen in love with mortal women. You've allowed them to—"

"This is your last case, Samuel."

Despair flooded his being. "I love her."

Angelo's beautiful eyes softened, but his expression didn't. "I'm sorry, Samuel. I've discussed your case with . . ." He twirled a finger toward the ceiling. "You've broken one rule too many. When this case wraps up, you're being sent to the Fifth Choir."

Sam stared. "There's no reprieve?"

Angelo looked at him and tapped a file that was six inches thick. "Samuel, you've had dozens of reprieves already."

"Then there's no possibility that I can stay with her?" he asked in an anguished whisper.

Angelo's gaze was genuinely sympathetic, but his reply was like a dagger to Sam's heart.

"None."

Chapter Eleven

Sam bought the morning newspaper, and Brett read it over breakfast, nervously eating several pieces of toast as she read that the police sought her for questioning in regard to Paul's murder. The article didn't say that she had fled, but a whiff of that suggestion wafted through the piece.

Biting her lip, she raised her eyes from the headlines. "This article says the police are following several leads, but it doesn't mention any suspects. Except me, by implication. I'm the only person they're looking for."

Sam stood before the kitchen window, hands in his jeans pockets, gazing outside. "By now, they've talked to a lot of people. You're simply the only person they can't find."

"Sam?" She spoke to the back of his white blond head, calmed by the sight of him. "I'm going to have to turn myself in, aren't I?"

He turned to face her and nodded reluctantly. "I'd say we have today and tomorrow. If the police haven't talked to you by late tomorrow . . . well, it's going to become clear that you're avoiding questioning."

Brett's stomach tightened, and she felt her face turn pale. Two days wasn't much time. It didn't seem like enough time to solve Paul's murder, and more important, it was no time at all for her and Sam. "I've been thinking about us. Maybe Angelo—"

He shook his head, gazing at her with those beautiful blue eyes so filled with compassion and love and now pain. "I spoke to Angelo last night," he said in a low voice. "The instant this case wraps up, I'm being sent to the Fifth Choir. There's no hope for a reprieve."

Brett's hands flew to her mouth. "Oh, no. Sam, I'm so sorry! Maybe if I spoke to Angelo, if I told him—"

"No." They stared at each other across the sunny kitchen. Brett could hear the clock in the living room, ticking off their remaining minutes together. She heard her heart cracking into little pieces.

"It isn't fair," she finally whispered, tears brimming in her eyes.

How could she have fallen head over heels in love with a man she had known for only a few days? A man she hadn't even kissed? How was such a thing possible? And yet, she loved him. Sam was the heart of her heart, the man she had yearned for, waited for, and despaired of ever finding. She had always told herself that she would recognize this man when she found him, and she had.

Standing, she moved forward blindly, walking into his arms.

"Oh, Sam!"

He held her so tightly that she felt the emotion trembling through his body, then he smoothed back her hair. "It wouldn't have worked, sweet Brett." Lifting her face, he brushed a toast crumb from the corner of her lips. "More than anything, you want children. I couldn't have given them to you." He tried to smile, tried to sound like his words weren't wounding them both. But Brett saw the agitated flashes sparking around his head and knew his anguish plunged as deeply as hers. "I couldn't have supported you, mine isn't a paying job."

"I plan to return to nursing. I could have supported—"

He placed a gentle finger across her lips. "It can't happen, Brett. Even if we could work out the problems, I'm going to be sent away."

"Isn't there anything we can do? Anything at all?"

"No," he answered quietly. The finality and the sadness in his tone made her feel like weeping. "You and I . . . we have no future together."

They held each other tightly, clinging to their discovery of each other and dreading their approaching loss. And in that moment, standing in an invisible kitchen, held in the embrace of an angel, Brett understood she would never love another man as she loved Sam. For him she would have given up her deep yearning for children. For him she would have abandoned a social life or a career or whatever was necessary to live her life with this special angel.

"I wish to heaven that I knew what was going to happen to you," she murmured against his chest, swallowing tears. "I can't stand it to think that you're going to suffer."

He held her closely, resting his cheek on top of her hair. "I don't know that I will. I don't know anything about the Fifth Choir. Maybe it's not punishment as much as it's just . . . different."

She lifted a tear-stained face. "Do you really believe that?"

He kissed her then, his lips as light against hers as the brush of a butterfly's wings, a lightning flash of heat and sweetness and wonderment, then gone. Brett gazed at him, her heart in her eyes, and she touched her fingertips to her lips.

Suddenly she understood there would be no passionate kisses for them, no physical relationship. She saw in his sad eyes that he would not allow that. He would permit their doomed relationship to progress no further than this. She perceived that he would do that for her, because Brett had to live in the mortal world, and he didn't want to damage her future by creating a memory with which no mortal man could compete.

"We can be together. It doesn't matter," she said, her whisper a plea.

"Yes, it does," he answered in a voice so filled with pain that it hurt to hear. He touched her face. "Someday, my beloved, you will have the children you long for. And your children deserve a father who is loved by their mother."

"Sam!" Her fingers dug into his shoulders. "I'll *never* forget you! I'll *never* love another man!"

He crushed her in his arms, and spoke near her ear. "Listen to me. It will destroy me if I must think of you living the rest of your life alone." He fell silent a moment, collecting himself. "You were born to be a mother, Brett. There will be another man."

"No!" She burrowed closer to his body.

"Not someone to love instead of me," he said thickly, "but someone to love alongside of me. For I will always be with you in spirit, loving you and your children and the man who makes you happy."

They held each other while Brett wept until no more tears could come.

BRETT POWDERED HER reddened eyelids in the visor mirror above the windshield. After she tucked her compact into her purse, she and Sam held hands over the center console. Occasionally they gazed at each other with bittersweet glances blending love and the impending pain of loss.

"Do you think Billie Place left town?" Brett asked as they approached the clinic's underground parking lot. She had to think about something other than losing him or she would go crazy.

"Billie moved out of Thatcher's house," Sam replied, guiding the car into a parking space. "I checked last night. But she's still in the Denver area. Someone tipped the police to her new address and suggested that she had some interesting information about the people involved in the Thatcher case."

"You?" Brett asked with a smile.

He smiled. "Could be." After he told her what he had discovered regarding the disappearance of the Sansmith papers from Paul's records, they walked toward the elevators, pausing to examine the bullet holes gouged out by Slivowitz's wild shots. Sam pressed the button to call the elevator. "If the police haven't yet discovered that Alan Barkley threatened to kill Thatcher or that Bob Pritchard made threats equally as damaging, I suspect Miss Billie Place will give them an earful."

"Will she? Or will she be too afraid of implicating herself in Paul's embezzlement? Or fear getting crossways with the Sansmith thugs? They may have disappeared from the investigation, but they're still out there."

Sam shook his head. "Sansmith moved quickly to eradicate any evidence that might lead to them. My sense is that Sansmith has cut their losses and you won't hear anything about them again. I think we were right to figure they weren't involved with Paul's murder."

"Maybe Billie hasn't figured that out."

"When I located her, she was seething with resentment. She's lost a good job, lost a man she saw as a ticket to a cushy life. She's angry enough about getting shot at that I think she'll tell the police everything she knows and let the chips fall where they may."

"Good. I hope so!"

"The police won't find anything helpful about San-smith, but they'll find plenty to work on with Barkley and Pritchard."

They stepped into the elevator and emerged two minutes later in the reception room. A bright-eyed young woman smiled up at them from Billie Place's desk. "May I help you?"

"We have an appointment with Dr. Alan Barkley," Sam said pleasantly. "Sam Angel, attorney, and Mrs. Brett Thatcher."

"Really?" The young woman's gaze flicked to the door of one of the private waiting rooms, then she checked the appointment book in front of her. "Oh. Here are your names," she said, sounding puzzled.

Brett suppressed a smile. The appearance of their names in the receptionist's book wasn't the only thing that had changed in the last two minutes. During the ride in the elevator, Sam's attire had altered from jeans and a comfortable sweater to a very lawyerly suit.

"Your nine-thirty appointment is here," the receptionist announced cheerfully, opening the door to Alan Barkley's office. "Mrs. Thatcher and her attorney, Mr. Angel."

Alan Barkley looked up from his desk, and his face clamped into a scowl. "Well. You didn't waste any time, did you." Reaching, he jabbed a button on his intercom system and leaned to the speaker. "Pritchard? You better come in here. Brett is in my office with her attorney. I'm sure they're here to discuss how much of our clinic Brett owns and how we plan to buy her out."

Bob Pritchard burst through the door as Brett and Sam were seating themselves in front of Alan Barkley's desk. Pritchard looked as if he hadn't slept in a while. He shook hands with Sam and nodded to Brett. "The police want to talk to you."

"I know," Brett answered uneasily. It was making her nervous that so many people had warned her that the police were looking for her.

"Two detectives appeared at my door at seven this morning," Pritchard said unhappily. He shot a glance toward Alan Barkley, then turned back to Brett and Sam. "I don't know how much you know about what's been happening here at the clinic, but we've had several near-violent confrontations with Paul. Some unfortunate things were said, some threats were made—"

"Which Billie Place repeated to the police," Barkley interrupted angrily. "Now Pritchard and I are suspects in Paul's murder. It's outrageous."

Pritchard's eyes narrowed. "You *did* threaten him, Alan."

"I lost my temper." Alan ran a hand over his head and looked at Brett and Sam. "Thatcher cleaned out the clinic's bank accounts. He hasn't made a mortgage payment in six months, and we're about to lose the building. MedCo repossessed our monitors yesterday, and if we don't come up with an outrageous sum by Friday, we'll lose the rest of our equipment, too! Unfortunately, Pritchard and I are tapped out. Wouldn't *you* be angry? Wouldn't *you* threaten the son of a bitch who destroyed years of hard work?" He turned an angry face toward his bookcases and the panel that hid his liquor cabinet. "Thatcher stole every cent this clinic has taken in for the last six months, plus everything that was in our reserve accounts. Before this is over we'll lose everything, not to mention the scandal."

Sam tapped his fingers on the arms of his chair, his expression thoughtful. "Just how angry are you, Dr. Barkley?"

"I didn't kill him if that's what you're implying. But I applaud whoever did!"

"Where were you last Saturday night, Alan?" Brett inquired softly.

"Unfortunately, I don't have an alibi," he snapped. "Like I told the police, I didn't know I'd need one."

Pritchard stood up and moved to the window. "I was at a black-tie fund-raiser. A hundred people will verify that." He glanced at Brett over his shoulder. "And where were you when the deed was being done?"

"Mrs. Thatcher will speak to the police when the time comes," Sam said smoothly. "Perhaps we should discuss the fact that Mrs. Thatcher has inherited forty percent of this clinic from her ex-husband. I believe there is a key-man buyout policy?"

"Not anymore there isn't," Alan Barkley said bitterly. "Thatcher didn't pay the premiums. The policies lapsed months ago." He stared at Brett. "So if you came here hoping to get five million dollars for your forty percent, it isn't going to happen."

Pritchard agreed. "Right now our stock in the clinic isn't worth spit. The scandal of Paul's murder is going to drive away future clients. You wouldn't believe the cancellations we've already had! And unless the three of us can come up with a hundred thousand plus change and do it immediately, the bottom line is we're going to lose the building and have to close up shop!"

Brett blinked and leaned forward. "If you're including me— "

"I said the *three* of us. That certainly does include you."

"I don't have any money to speak of." She cast an anxious glance from Pritchard to Barkley. "I'm sorry. I really can't help you."

Alan Barkley leaned his elbows on his desk and dropped his head in his hands. "Maybe the best thing is just to let the clinic fold. Go somewhere else and start over." He lifted his head and gave Brett and Sam a defiant stare. "I hope you aren't planning on inheriting anything from that bastard. I have a blizzard of bills I intend to submit to whoever probates Thatcher's estate. As near as I can figure, he embezzled about a million dollars from us!"

Sam stood. "Have either of you been to Mrs. Thatcher's mountain cabin outside Silverthorne?"

The abrupt change of subject silenced them both.

Finally Alan Barkley waved his hand in an irritated gesture. "I've never been there."

"I stayed at the cabin once with Paul for a weekend skiing trip. It must have been five or six years ago," Pritchard said, frowning.

Sam helped Brett to her feet. "Then your fingerprints won't be in the cabin," he said pleasantly.

"That's right!" Bob Pritchard agreed with a look of relief.

Alan Barkley didn't appear as happy. He watched Sam and Brett leave his office without speaking a word.

"ALAN BARKLEY IS SHAPING up as a strong suspect," Brett decided when they were back in the car, driving out of the clinic's parking lot. "He hated Paul, that's obvious, and he doesn't have an alibi for Saturday night."

"Did you notice his hands?" Sam asked idly, braking for a red light.

"His hands? No, what about them?"

"The nails are trimmed very short."

Brett lifted an eyebrow. "Most doctors trim their nails short. Am I missing something? Where are you going with this?"

"I'm not sure," he answered, frowning. "But there's something about hands, something at the edge of my mind that I can't quite remember.... Blast! It's been bothering me for several days."

Brett reached for the box of cheese crackers she'd left in the car and munched a handful.

"Your question about fingerprints worries me to death. *My* fingerprints are all over the cabin! And on the knife," she ended dismally. "No wonder the police are looking for me."

He took her hand out of the cracker box and gave it a reassuring squeeze. "You heard what Pritchard said. The police didn't waste any time following up Billie Place's information. By now they know there are a lot of B.'s whom the notation in Paul's appointment book could refer to. You're a suspect, Brett—we always knew you would be— but there are others, too."

"Thanks to you," she said softly. "If it wasn't for you, Sam, I'd be in jail right now and the police wouldn't be looking at anyone else. Wait!" Reaching, she turned up the news on the radio.

They listened in silence as a news reporter announced that Paul Thatcher's car had been located, and it had been ascertained that he had dined at Medra's Restaurant the night he was murdered.

"When questioned about the person accompanying Dr. Thatcher, restaurant employees offered conflicting statements: a dark-haired woman and a middle-aged man. But employees agreed Dr. Thatcher and his guest left the restaurant between seven and seven-thirty that evening as the restaurant closed at eight due to the blizzard. In other breaking news..."

"What time did you arrive at the cabin?" Sam drove aimlessly, thinking.

"I wasn't watching the clock," Brett said, reaching into the cracker box. "Let's see ... I left my condominium a little after five o'clock. Ordinarily the drive would take about an hour and a half, but the weather was terrible that night. I remember there was a long wait on this side of the tunnel while snowplow crews cleared a snow slide off the highway." She tried to remember. "I stopped at the Silverthorne City Market to pick up some groceries before I went on to the cabin.... I think by the time I arrived it was between seven-thirty and eight. I must have missed witnessing the murder by mere minutes!" Closing her eyes, she rubbed her temples.

"Whatever happened between Paul and his killer happened quickly."

"I wonder whose fingerprints are on that champagne bottle?" Brett thought about that question. "I told the sheriff that I'd stopped for supplies...and Mrs. Rawlings confirmed that the police believe all the groceries in the cabin, including the champagne, belong to me." Excitement lit her eyes. "Sam! Do you know what this means? The killer's prints must be on the champagne bottle!"

"Unless Thatcher bought the champagne," Sam reminded her. "And didn't you tell me that you handled the bottle, too?"

"That's true," Brett admitted with a sigh. But hope died hard. "Still, the killer's prints *might* be there. Along with mine and Paul's. Damn!"

Sam gave her a thoughtful look. "Are you up to a visit to the crime scene?"

Frankly, she didn't like to think about going back there. "Why?" Brett asked, hedging.

"There's something at the scene that I'm overlooking. Maybe if we see it again..."

Brett hesitated. "Silverthorne is a very small town, Sam. I don't know a lot of people there, but I do know a few. If someone recognizes me as we drive through...well, you know what will happen. Sheriff Stone will be after me like a flash.''

He smiled at her. ''You're an angel in my eyes, but if you were an angel in fact, we wouldn't have to drive. We could just appear at the cabin without having to drive through town.''

''How does one get to be an angel?'' Brett asked quietly.

Suddenly the conversation was deadly serious and a little frightening.

Sam gazed deeply into her caramel eyes, then the Mercedes pulled into a side street and stopped. Sam reached for her, gripping her shoulders. The warmth of his hands, the radiance of who he was, spread through her body.

''Don't even think about it, Brett. Believe me, that isn't the answer.''

''Maybe it is,'' she said, gazing into his eyes. Her thoughts scared her, revealing a love and a desperation the depth of which she had never before experienced.

Anger darkened Sam's eyes. ''Suicide is absolutely forbidden, and rightly so.'' He stared at her, then pulled her into his arms, holding her so tightly that the console between them pressed hard against Brett's body. ''My darling Brett. Someday, years from now, I'll find you if it's possible and if you still want me to. I swear this to you.'' He held her away from him so he could gaze into her eyes. ''But don't think about joining the heavenly choir prematurely.'' He wiped a tear from the corner of her eye and tried to smile. ''Newcomers don't go to the Fifth Choir. If you popped up before your time we wouldn't have a chance of finding each other. Okay? Promise me you won't do anything foolish.''

"Oh, Sam." She pressed her head against his chest, inhaling the clean, good scent of him. "I feel like it's almost over, and I can't stand losing you. It hurts."

"I know," he said gruffly, stroking her hair. "I know."

DURING THE DRIVE into the mountains and to Silverthorne, they talked about anything and everything, cramming questions and answers into a tumbling conversation that contained an undercurrent of desperation. Both were aware of precious minutes ticking away. Both sensed that events had taken on a life of their own and were accelerating toward a conclusion. There was so much to say, so many questions to ask, and not enough time.

When they drove through Silverthorne, Brett resisted an impulse to sink down below the dashboard and hide. It seemed to her that every car was driven by someone who seemed excessively curious about the occupants of the Mercedes, someone who recognized her and who would stop at the first pay phone to call Sheriff Stone.

"How long will you be able to stay?" she asked Sam in a whisper. "At what point will you have to leave?"

He turned off the highway onto the dirt road that led to the cabin. Relieved, Brett sat up a little straighter now that they were the only car on the road.

"As soon as it's clear that you're exonerated, I'll have to go," Sam answered. Sorrow clouded his gaze. "It isn't a matter of choice, Brett. Angelo is watching, and his powers are stronger than mine. He'll exert a force that I won't be able to resist."

She gripped her hands together in her lap and dropped her head. "How soon after that will he send you to the Fifth Choir?" She couldn't stop worrying.

"I don't know, but I imagine it will happen immediately." He touched her clasped hands. "Time isn't the same for us as it is for mortals. What is immediate for me may be months in your perception of time. Maybe years." He shrugged as if it didn't matter.

Brett nodded and peered out the windshield with dulled eyes.

"There's my old car," she said without much interest.

The snow had melted off the roof of the Buick, but the tires were still mired in mud and snow.

"I'd planned to use part of Paul's settlement to buy a new Subaru." The faint smile that curved her lips didn't reach her eyes. "But considering the enormity of Paul's debts, there isn't going to be a settlement. Which is okay. A new car is a good motivation to return to nursing immediately."

Sam parked and they stepped out of the Mercedes, eyeing the yellow tape that surrounded the cabin, identifying it as a crime scene.

Sunlight sparkled on the snowdrifts rolling back toward the pines and spruce. Crusts of ice had formed in the shadows, but it was a pleasant forty degrees in the sun. Water dripped off picturesque icicles melting along the cabin's gables.

"I always loved it here," Brett commented softly. "It's so quiet and so beautiful. So hard to believe that a murder occurred here."

"Do you want to come inside, or would you prefer to remain out here?"

She hesitated. "Are we allowed to cross the tape? Won't we leave footprints that will tell the sheriff someone violated the barrier?"

"I'll carry you. I don't leave footprints, remember?"

She really didn't want to enter the cabin, but she didn't want to waste a minute of the time she had left with Sam by being apart from him. Nodding, she lifted her arms and he swung her against his chest as if she weighed nothing. For a moment he held her in his arms, cradling her against his body and looking into her eyes.

"I love you."

"I know," she whispered. "I love you, too."

Before he sailed over the tape, Brett noticed through her tears that the Mercedes had vanished.

"There's no sense telling anyone who drives by that someone is here," Sam explained when she asked.

She thought about his answer after Sam set her on her feet on the cabin's porch. He vanished for a minute, then opened the door for her from the inside.

It amazed her how easily human beings adjusted to the most incredible things. A week ago Brett would have scoffed at the idea of material items vanishing into thin air. Now she merely nodded as if to say of course the Mercedes could disappear in the blink of an eye. A week ago she would have thought anyone who claimed to have seen an angel must be hallucinating. And now she was in love with one. And it didn't seem weird or strange or bizarre or even particularly unusual. Just heartbreakingly sad and hopeless. The best and the most painful thing that had ever happened to her.

They walked into the living room and stood close together, looking around. The curtains were drawn and it was dim inside, cold enough that Brett could see a hint of vapor when she spoke.

"The police have dusted for prints."

Dark graphite dust, the residue of the fingerprint crew, coated several surfaces, and the furniture was disarranged. But all in all, the police had treated the cabin with consideration.

Brett rounded the room divider and walked into the kitchen, half dreading to find a chalked outline on the floor. But of course, there was none. Paul's body had been discovered in the woods. She drew a breath and opened the refrigerator door, getting graphite on her fingers.

"My groceries are still here," she noticed, peering inside the fridge. "And there's the champagne bottle. There's no graphite on it." Which meant she had guessed correctly. The police believed the champagne was hers. They had not checked the glass bottle surface for prints.

"Don't get your hopes up," Sam said from directly behind her. "Paul might have bought the champagne, remember? The killer may not have touched it at all."

She turned and looked up at him, feeling the solid warmth of his body close to hers. She wanted to hold him, wanted to convince him that he was wrong about his decision to restrain the passion between them. She wanted him to make love to her, wanted to make love to him, longed to have that memory to cherish and lean on after he left her.

Instead, she held her voice to a level tone and asked, "Have you remembered whatever it was that was bothering you?"

He scanned the kitchen, then the frown smoothed out on his brow. "Yes," he said softly. "Now I know who killed Paul Thatcher."

Brett's eyes widened, and she stared up at him. "Who? And how do you know?"

"I should have remembered sooner." He gazed into her eyes and added softly. "I guess I didn't want to remember, didn't want the case to be solved."

Brett gripped his arm. "Sam, what are you talking about?"

"A broken fingernail. There was a tip of a fingernail on the kitchen floor. It's not there now. Detectives must have bagged it for evidence."

There had been no mention of a broken fingernail in the original version of Brett's trial. If the police had noticed it at all, either they had felt it was not significant, or they had suppressed or ignored this piece of evidence. It would be different this time. This time the police had conducted a very different investigation.

"Well, it wasn't mine," Brett said.

"I know." In the first version, the police had not run any tests on the scrap of nail. If they had, they would have discovered the DNA in the tip of fingernail did not match Brett's DNA profile.

"I see where this is leading!" Brett's caramel eyes sparkled. "And it works, Sam! Greta Rawlings will testify that she cleaned the cabin thoroughly. That means the nail was broken *after* Mrs. Rawlings cleaned here. The broken nail places the killer in the kitchen between the time Mrs. Rawlings left and the time I arrived. And if the killer's prints are also on the champagne bottle... Sam, we've got him!" She stared up at him. "Who is it? Who killed Paul?"

Raising his head, Sam frowned at the curtained window, listening. "A car is turning in the driveway."

They stared at each other.

Then Sam took her arm and drew her into the bedroom hallway and out of sight.

Brett held her breath and waited to see who would cross the yellow tape and open the door.

Sam already knew who would step into the cabin.

Chapter Twelve

The front door opened and closed. The sound of snow boots walking across wood planks moved quickly through the living room toward the kitchen.

Brett glanced at Sam, saw him nod, then she peeked out of the corridor and gasped. "Barbara!"

Barbara Thatcher jumped, then whirled to face Sam and Brett as they stepped out of the corridor. "What are you doing here?"

"Since Brett owns this cabin, a better question might be what are *you* doing here?" Sam inquired, stepping further into the living room.

A glance at her hands revealed the same long nails he had noticed when he and Brett called on Barbara at her home. At least one of them had to be a false nail like those Billie Place wore. If Barbara hadn't repaired the nail, Sam knew the broken piece on the kitchen floor would have matched the torn nail on Barbara's right hand.

The broken bit of fingernail had been niggling at his mind all along. Billie Place wore false nails; the broken tip couldn't have been hers. The doctors did not wear polish, of course, nor did Brett. But Barbara did.

To confirm his evidence, he performed a tiny miracle and restored Barbara's fingernails to the state they would have been in shortly after Paul's murder.

Barbara didn't look down at her hands. Had she done so, she would have noticed her fingernail polish had altered from pink to the scarlet shade she had worn on Saturday night. And she would have noticed the ragged, torn fingernail on the second-to-last finger of her right hand.

"Oh, Barbara," Brett said softly, sadly. "You killed Paul, didn't you?"

Barbara tossed back a wave of short dark hair and smoothed a hand down the front of her parka. "Of course not. I came here— "

"And crossed a police barrier," Sam reminded her, warning that her reason for entering the cabin needed to be strong.

Her cheeks colored and she lifted her chin. "I came to see if I'd left a set of Christmas dishes up here."

Brett stared then rolled her eyes. "Oh, come on. After all these years? You're only now missing a set of dishes that you had when you were married to Paul?" She shook her head. "Why did you do it? What did Paul say or do that made you furious enough to kill him?"

"How dare you! Paul and I are in love. We're considering a reconciliation." For an instant she looked confused, as if she had briefly blocked out that Paul was dead. "If someone hadn't killed him, we'd be together now!" Her eyes flicked toward the kitchen and her mouth tightened.

"You told Brett that you hadn't been to this cabin in years, and I suspect you told the police the same lie," Sam said, watching her. "Then you started worrying about your broken fingernail. Isn't that correct? And maybe you started worrying about leaving prints on a certain champagne bottle. So you came here today to retrieve the champagne and the broken nail tip if you could find it.''

"That's nonsense!" she snapped. But Sam recognized the sudden panic in her eyes and understood he had scored a hit. Brett had been right about the champagne bottle. Barbara Thatcher's prints were on it.

Brett caught the look, too. "Oh, Barbara," she said again. A mixture of sorrow and accusation drew her expression. "What happened that night? Did Paul insult you? Did he reject you out of hand?"

"Just shut up!" Barbara hissed, crimson flooding her face.

Sam saw it all as if he were watching it happen.

"You created a romantic fantasy," he said slowly, working it out aloud. "Or maybe you tried to re-create an evening that had happened long ago. You convinced Paul to meet you for dinner in Silverthorne."

Brett saw where he was going, and picked up the story, speaking softly. "You bought champagne, made a fire as soon as you arrived here, or maybe you asked Paul to make the fire. And you turned down the spread in the master bedroom because you hoped the evening would end romantically, in bed."

Barbara covered her ears. "Stop it, shut up!"

"You were in the kitchen when things came to a head," Sam continued, speaking quietly, watching the scene unfold in his mind. "Maybe you offered to pay Paul's debts if the two of you remarried. But Paul rejected your offer. Maybe he wanted your money, but not you. Maybe he phrased his rejections cruelly. However it happened, your romantic evening collapsed, and so did your hope for a reconciliation." He studied the fury twisting her face. "Did you have a dish towel in your hand when you picked up the knife? Was it the towel that snapped off the tip of your fingernail? Is that why your prints are not on the knife? Or was it a scarf?''

"I won't listen to any more of this!" Grabbing the shoulder strap of her purse, Barbara jerked her purse forward, tore at the flap, then withdrew a pistol. She pointed the shaking barrel at Sam and Brett.

Brett blinked hard, then covered her eyes. The gesture told Sam that she had resisted the truth, had wanted to believe they were wrong to accuse Barbara.

"Put the gun away, Mrs. Thatcher."

"Who the hell are you, anyway?"

"Just put down the gun." Sam drew a breath. "Right now Greta Rawlings is telling Sheriff Stone that she saw Brett drive through Silverthorne, headed toward the cabin. The sheriff is going to arrive here in about ten minutes."

Barbara stared at him. "You can't possibly know that."

"I do know it. The sheriff just hung up his telephone. He's picking up his car keys."

Her stare lengthened. "Even if you're right, which you aren't, it doesn't matter. In ten minutes both of you will be dead."

Brett stiffened. "You can't possibly believe that you can kill two more people and get away with it. How would you explain two dead bodies?"

"I won't need to. I'll just drive away like I did before." She shrugged.

"There's something I should mention," Sam said in a pleasant voice. "Everything we're saying is being recorded." A nod at the kitchen counter produced a tape machine. Another nod imprinted everything that had been said since Barbara entered the cabin.

"Thank you for pointing that out," she said with a thin smile. "I'll remember to take the machine and the tape with me when I leave."

Sam glanced at the pistol in her hand, then looked at her face. "Mrs. Thatcher, don't make this any worse for yourself than it already is. I promise you, Sheriff Stone is on his way here right now."

She dismissed Sam as if she believed he were speaking nonsense, and shifted her stare to Brett. "I'm more clever than you ever gave me credit for. I'll tell the sheriff that I followed you to the cabin. I'll tell them I accused you of murdering Paul. You're their top suspect, anyway. They'll believe that you attacked me and I had to defend myself." She waved the pistol threateningly. "How fortunate that I happened to bring my pistol to protect myself." A nasty smile of triumph distorted her lips.

"The police won't believe you," Brett whispered.

"Won't they? They know you were here Saturday night, the newspaper articles said so." She smiled again. "*My* fingerprints are not on the knife. No one saw *me* in this cabin. And *I* don't have a motive. Paul and I were discussing a reconciliation, remember? Oh, yes, the police will believe you murdered Paul and then tried to kill me. I had to protect myself from you and your friend here. Afterward, I stumbled to the kitchen, looking for something to drink to calm myself. I touched the champagne bottle to move it. That's why my prints are on the bottle if they should check."

"And the broken fingernail?" Sam inquired, watching her. "In case you're interested, it looks like the police found it and bagged it for evidence. DNA tests will place you at the cabin."

She shrugged. "But DNA tests won't show when I was here. In fact, it may not be a problem at all. I doubt they'll even test the piece of nail. They'll assume it came from her."

"They will test it, Barbara," Brett said firmly. "And the sheriff knows that piece of fingernail fell on the kitchen floor between the time Mrs. Rawlings cleaned the cabin and the time the sheriff bagged it for evidence. He'll know you lied. You were here."

"That's easy to explain. Mrs. Rawlings could have overlooked the nail tip when she cleaned. I'll tell them I forgot that I was here a few weeks ago at Paul's invitation. It was a romantic tryst. Which is why you killed him, by the way," she said to Brett with an icy, satisfied smile. "The police will believe me when I tell them that when you learned Paul and I borrowed your cabin to plan our remarriage you flew into a jealous rage and killed him."

"Is that why you insisted on meeting Paul in Silverthorne? So you could come to the cabin after dinner and revive romantic memories? Did you think it was doubly sweet to seduce Paul in my cabin?"

Barbara bared her teeth, and the gun shook in her hand. "You bet I did!"

Sorrow and pity filled Brett's eyes. "Oh, Barbara. I was never a threat to you. I never really loved Paul, and I doubt that he ever really loved me."

"Liar! If it wasn't for you, Paul and I would never have divorced!"

"If you'd be honest with yourself, you'd know that isn't true."

Sam spoke before Barbara could answer. "Barbara, the police will know the broken fingernail belongs to you, and they will know it got here very recently. Look at your right hand."

When she glanced down and saw the scarlet polish that she knew she had removed, when she saw the ragged fingernail that would match the scrap found on the cabin's kitchen floor, Barbara stared in astonishment, then started to tremble.

"This isn't possible," she whispered. But her confusion lasted only a minute. When she raised her head, her expression had hardened. "This is all your fault!" she screamed at Brett. "Paul and I were happy until you came along. You stole him and you ruined my life. You turned him into a money-grubbing, cruel man!"

Her teeth clenched, her arm steadied and she fired at Brett point blank.

Sam reacted instantly. He speeded time for himself and Brett and pulled her out of the path of the bullet.

The shock on Brett's pale face was profound. "Oh, God, Sam, she's really going to kill us!"

"It won't happen. Look." He directed her attention to the bullet that seemed to be traveling at a snail's pace.

Brett's lips opened, and she extended a hand as if to pluck the bullet out of the air. "If I wasn't seeing this..." she whispered, shocked. She stared at the bullet, and her fingers hovered above it, then she glanced at Barbara's seemingly frozen form and her arm dropped. "I'd be dead if you weren't an angel. How is this happening? Barbara and the bullet are moving in slow motion. That isn't possible."

There was no explanation that would make sense to her. "The sheriff will be here in less than five minutes," he said as Barbara fired again. Again, sidestepping the second bullet was child's play. Barbara fired wildly, terrified and confused that she could no longer see or hear them.

"The sheriff won't believe her story, will he?" Brett asked anxiously, her hand on Sam's sleeve. But her head was turned, watching Barbara as if she believed time would suddenly right itself and they would be in mortal danger.

"There isn't a chance the sheriff will believe her." He nodded at the tape recorder gently whirring on the kitchen counter.

The recorder and Barbara's own words would place her at the scene; the champagne bottle and the fingernail chip would prove it. And when the restaurant employees saw Barbara Thatcher in a lineup, they would remember that it was she who had dined with Paul Thatcher the night of the blizzard. Whatever alibi Barbara had concocted for Saturday night wouldn't hold up to scrutiny. Piece by piece, the police would assemble enough evidence to convict her.

All that remained was to concentrate Sheriff Stone's focus and point him toward realizing Barbara Thatcher was capable and cold-blooded enough to commit murder. What was needed was something to nudge the sheriff to immediate action. Sam knew how to catch the sheriff's attention.

He counted the shots, then slowed his time and Brett's to normal speed. When he and Brett came into focus, Barbara stared at them through terrified eyes. Panicked, she fired again.

Calmly and deliberately, Sam stepped in front of Brett and staggered slightly as the bullet tore into his shoulder. Although he was prepared, and there was no pain, the forceful impact momentarily dazed him.

Above the ringing explosion, he heard Brett's scream.

Then a Brett-shaped blur flew past him, fists flying. For an instant Sam believed time was still distorted, because it seemed as if the next events unfolded in ultraslow motion.

He watched Brett's fist come back, then move forward and connect with Barbara Thatcher's jaw. Barbara's head jerked and so did the gun.

That's when he discovered to his horror that he had miscounted the number of bullets fired. The sound of the last shot seemed louder, more shockingly explosive than any of the others. Above the ringing in his ears, he heard his own scream as Brett floated backward in slow motion, doubling at the waist before her body crumpled to the floor.

Time sped up then and Barbara ran to Brett's body, firing the empty pistol again and again at Brett's chest. Her face twisted with hatred.

Without a thought for rules and regulations, Sam leaped forward and backhanded Barbara Thatcher, putting some muscle behind the blow. She flew backward, striking her head against the wall, then she slumped to the floor unconscious. But Sam wasn't watching.

He dropped to his knees beside Brett and stared in horror as a spot of crimson appeared on her sweater near her heart. The spot grew like a scarlet blossom unfurling bright petals.

"Oh, God! Blast!" He rubbed her hand, and now he heard the siren atop the sheriff's approaching squad car. With a thought he added an ambulance that would arrive minutes behind the sheriff, who was sliding into the cabin's driveway now. Another thought flung open the cabin door.

When he was absolutely certain that he had pointed the police toward the evidence they needed to put Barbara away for the rest of her life, he cupped Brett's cheek in his shaking palm and leaned over her.

"I'm so sorry, darling. Angels have never been good at counting, I thought... blast! This is my fault! Blast! The medics will be here in less than two minutes. You'll be all right!"

But this was the loophole where anything could happen. And Sam's bag of miracles did not include healing mortal wounds. The decision between life and death was made by powers far higher than his.

Frantic, Sam watched the blood spreading across her chest, then he looked into her white face and prayed as he had never prayed before.

"Don't leave me, Sam." Her voice was nearly inaudible. Her lovely caramel eyes, huge in her snowy face, fastened on him, begging him, loving him. "Help me die with grace."

"I'm here, darling."

But already he felt the tug of Angelo's power, calling him back to headquarters.

"Please, not now," he pleaded, flinging a silent appeal across the mountains toward the Logan Street office. "I beg you, not now. She needs me. Give me time to help her. Let me stay long enough to know that she'll survive!"

Angelo's impatient voice whispered in his mind. "You've done your job, Samuel. It's over now. Barbara will be convicted of Paul Thatcher's murder. The injustice done to Brett has been overturned and put right. Your assignment has concluded."

Sam's shoulder suddenly felt hot, and it tingled. When he glanced down, all signs of Barbara's shot had vanished. As he watched, the threads of his sleeve knit together over the bullet hole, as his flesh was doing beneath the material. Within the span of a heartbeat, he was looking at unmarked cloth. No hint of blood remained. There was no sign that he had been shot.

"Your noble gesture wasn't required," Angelo explained, his voice deep inside Sam's mind. "Certainly we don't want you to play such a role that you'd be asked to testify in court. I expect you here within the hour. And, Sam, backhanding a mortal woman, even a murderess, is not going to look good on your report. Be prepared to surrender your sword and sash."

An hour. That's all he had. He stared down at Brett's beautiful, pale face with despair filling his eyes.

She gripped his hand as the bloody blossom slowly widened across her chest. "I love you, Sam."

"Hang on, darling. The ambulance is almost here."

The words hadn't left his lips before the sheriff burst into the cabin. Sheriff Stone skidded to a halt on the hardwood floor, taking in the scene. The medics from the ambulance rushed up the porch, a step behind him.

"Over here!" Sam shouted. "She's been shot."

Two white-coated medics shoved him aside and bent over Brett.

"What about that one?" Sheriff Stone demanded, nodding toward Barbara, who was coming to, moaning and holding her head.

"The first Mrs. Thatcher," Sam said bitterly. "You're going to find that she murdered Paul Thatcher and came within a fraction of an inch of killing the second Mrs. Thatcher."

The sheriff bent and lifted Barbara's gun off the floor by the tip of the barrel. "I need a statement from you," he said to Sam. "I want to know what happened here."

"Sorry," Sam called over his shoulder, dashing to follow the medics who were wheeling Brett out the door. "I'm going with her. You'll get your statement later." Almost as an afterthought, he jabbed a finger toward the still-recording tape player. Then he was out the door and racing across the yard toward the ambulance.

The strong, persistent tug of Angelo's power announced that the sheriff would get no statement from Sam Angel. Sam's disappearance would become another mystery in a case that would be riddled with unsolved mysteries. There would be no explanation to answer how Paul's body had moved from the back porch of the cabin to the woods

where it was found. Barbara's eventual story of shooting
Brett would contain wild assertions that Brett and Sam had
vanished into thin air for a brief period. She would insist
that she had shot Sam, but Sheriff Stone would swear that
Sam Angel had not been wounded when the sheriff arrived
on the scene minutes later. No trace of Sam's Mercedes
would ever be found, the sheriff would not be able to explain what happened to the car Greta Rawlings had seen in
Silverthorne, or how Sam and Brett had reached the cabin.

This glimpse of the future appeared in Sam's mind, then
was pushed aside by his panicked anxiety for Brett. He
climbed into the ambulance behind her and knelt at her
side, taking her limp hand between his.

"Hang on, darling," he urged as the ambulance shot out
of the driveway, siren wailing.

"Don't leave me," she whispered, the effort to speak
causing her pain. "Stay with me to the end. Please."

"Don't try to talk." His anxiety was so great that he
could hardly speak himself. "Think the words—I'll hear
them."

"Am I dying, Sam?"

"No, darling, no." But he didn't know if she was or not.
As pale and weak as she looked, it was very possible that
she was dying. And he could do nothing. Impotence and
fury rose to choke him. What good was he, what good were
the miracles he'd been blessed with, if he could not save the
woman he loved?

"Barbara?" She drew on a dwindling reservoir of
strength. *"What will happen to her?"*

"She'll be convicted on circumstantial evidence." He saw
the conclusion as it would appear on Angelo's master
computer. Barbara Thatcher would not receive the death
penalty, but she would spend most of the rest of her life in

prison. When he tried to see Brett's future, he drew a frustrating and frightening blank.

"Please," he prayed silently. "Don't let her die."

"I love you, Sam. I'll find you." She struggled to smile. *"There must be a map to the Fifth Choir."*

"When the time comes, I'll be waiting for you, darling. I'll be there for you." But not now. Now was too soon. She had a life in front of her; and he was being sent to angel Siberia.

Whatever it took, whatever sacrifices or compromises he had to make to redeem himself and secure his release from the Fifth Choir, he swore he would do. He would move heaven and earth to be there to welcome her into his arms when she made the transition.

"Just don't let it be now," he prayed. "Let her live a full life and have the children she longs for. I beg you. Don't save her from a life in prison, then give her no life to replace it. That is not justice. She deserves better than that. Please."

For the remainder of the forty minute trip to the hospital in Vail, he murmured assurances aloud to Brett and implored the higher powers in his mind, demanding, pleading. Then, as each sensed their time together drawing to a close, they spoke quickly and desperately of their love for each other, spoke of what might have been, and made heartfelt promises they each knew they could not keep.

When they were five minutes from the hospital, Sam glanced down at his hand holding hers and saw that his mortal flesh was fading, beginning to shimmer faintly and lose substance.

"No," he whispered.

"You're flashing," Brett said, framing inaudible words with her lips. "Oh, Sam. There's a halo forming around your head." Her eyes softened with tears. "So beautiful."

Angelo was pulling him back, drawing him out of the loophole. Sam's frantic efforts to fight were futile. And the emotional battle was causing him to flash and fizz like a fireworks display.

Bending over her, he kissed her, bathing her beloved face in the radiance of the light sparking around his head. His passion for this woman, a passion that would never know fulfillment, burst over them in an explosion of radiant light, nearly blinding them both. He restrained his yearning to crush her in his arms and kissed her lightly and lingeringly, tenderly, anxious not to cause her more pain.

"I must leave you now," he said gruffly, fighting hard to hold his voice steady. "But you won't be alone, darling. Your guardian angel is near. Remember me, and know that I loved you with all my heart. Wherever I am, darling Brett, my spirit is with you, loving you, wanting only the best for you."

"No, Sam, no!" Ignoring her pain, blinded by tears, she rose on an elbow and reached for him.

"Get well, my darling. Find a man you can love and who loves you as you deserve. Fill your wonderful house with children."

He felt his mortal form leaving him, felt himself rising weightless. Frantic, desperate to touch her one more time, he reached for her but felt nothing. "I love you, Brett!"

"Sam? Sam! I love you! Where are you? Sam!"

He heard her voice calling in the distance, and then he was spun into a swirling vortex of light and wind.

As he tumbled out of the loophole, he struggled to breathe around the hole in his chest. She was gone. He wouldn't know if the ambulance reached the hospital in time to save her life. He would never know if she would ever hold an infant to her breast. Would never know if she would remember him or even think of him again.

Not knowing her fate was worse than anything Angelo could do to him.

Chapter Thirteen

Toward dawn the hospital was always dim and quiet. With her duties completed and her shift almost over, Brett finally sat down and relaxed for a moment. After making sure that everything was up to date and in good order for the next shift, she chanced to notice the date on the calendar beside her nameplate. It saddened her and gave her a jolt.

Exactly a year ago today Barbara Thatcher had shot and almost killed her, and Sam had vanished from her life as suddenly as he had come into it.

Leaning forward, she propped her elbows on the desk and pressed her palms against her eyelids. Sometimes she wondered if it had all been a dream. No. Sam had been real. As real as a heartbeat. As real as love.

After her recovery, and following the most dismal Christmas she had ever experienced, Brett had taken a refresher course to renew her nursing license. Then came Barbara Thatcher's trial, with all the publicity and her own emotional testimony. And always, she had memories of Sam, missing and wanting him; her pain was as great as if he had taken her heart with him when he vanished. Then came the legal mess caused by the bankruptcy of Paul's clinic. And finally, Brett had made herself accept that Sam was not coming back, had made herself return to the world. Two months ago she had accepted a nursing position at St. Mary's Hospital.

Slowly, she was putting her life back on track, but it was a life without Sam. And that meant she was half a person with half a heart. The best part of her was missing.

"Thatcher? Are you all right?"

Brett dropped her hands. "Just tired," she said to Elise Mowbry, who was rapidly becoming a good friend. "I'm glad our shift is almost over."

Everyone at the hospital seemed to know Brett's story. A whiff of notoriety followed her. Most people appeared vaguely sympathetic, but they kept their distance as if they really didn't want to become too involved with a woman whom murder had touched so closely. So far, only Elise had offered genuine overtures of friendship.

Elise handed Brett a cup of coffee, then took the chair next to her. "What do you think? Is today the day that room 520 finally becomes lucid?"

"Thanks for the coffee." Brett glanced down the dim corridor. "Martha's with him now. She said there was additional activity during the day shift and another episode right before we came on duty. He's been quiet tonight, though. Nothing's happened so far."

"Darn." Elise glanced at her wristwatch. "I wanted him to fully awake on our shift."

The man they were discussing, as they did every night, was Tom Arden, a pediatric specialist until his accident three months ago. Head down and deep in thought, Tom had been struck by a speeding car while crossing the street. The impact had broken nearly every bone in his body, most of which had healed during the time he'd been in a coma. Everyone agreed it was a miracle that Dr. Tom Arden had survived the accident; he was, in fact, a patient who had "died" on the operating table, but had been resuscitated. Slowly, he was beginning to emerge from his coma.

"Martha said he was awake for nearly an hour earlier today," Brett commented.

"But he isn't really awake," Elise reminded her absently. "They come out of it slowly. He won't remember these early waking periods when he's finally and totally lucid."

Tom Arden had captured Brett's imagination, partly due to her natural compassion, and partly because he looked so boyish and vulnerable, as if he were merely asleep. Also, he didn't have any family to worry about him, so she had unconsciously assumed that duty. And finally, she admired him for having chosen pediatrics as a specialty. As soon as there was an opening, Brett hoped to transfer upstairs to the pediatrics division. Perhaps she would run into Dr. Arden in the future.

Tom Arden was also an attractive man. Because she compared every man to Sam, she had noticed that Tom was not as classically handsome as Sam had been. But Brett found him appealing enough that she'd said a few things that had earned some teasing from Elise.

A sigh lifted her chest. Tonight, a year to the day that her angel had vanished, her thoughts were full of Sam.

She missed him every day of her life. Sam was a painful loss that Brett carried with her always. Every night she tossed and turned, tormenting herself with questions that could never be answered. Had Angelo sent Sam to the dread Fifth Choir? Was he suffering there? Did he ever think of her?

Occasionally she recalled what Sam had mentioned about time unfolding differently for angels, and she would look at the calendar and wonder if today was the day in earthly time that he faced an angel tribunal, or if he had been dispatched to the Fifth Choir minutes after leaving her.

And always she wondered if she would ever find him again as she longed to do, if they would be permitted to be together when her time for transition arrived.

So many questions, and no possibility of answers.

"Easy does it, Thatcher," Elise said, studying her over the rim of her coffee cup. "You're getting teary." She examined Brett's face, then said softly, "You have the largest, saddest eyes I've ever seen."

"Sorry." Brett turned aside and pressed a tissue beneath her lashes. After a minute, she turned the calendar away so she couldn't see the date.

"What you need is a new man," Elise commented, looking wise.

Brett shook her head. "There was a man...."

But how could she explain that she had fallen in love with an Avenging Angel? Who would believe that she could have experienced a love this profound, this life altering, in so short a time?

Elise started, her gaze swinging to the light board. "Room 520 is flashing!" Jumping up, she pressed the intercom. "Martha?"

Martha's voice sounded calm and steady. "Tom Arden is waking again. Phone Dr. Wayne, will you, Elise? He wanted to be present during the next episode."

Elise reached for the telephone, and Brett stood. They both knew from Martha's tone that Tom Arden was not yet lucid. He was still in a half-dreaming state.

"I think I'll just take a peek," Brett said over her shoulder. Walking rapidly down the corridor, passing silent rooms with sleeping patients inside, she strode toward room 520.

Martha Holmes was the senior floor nurse on this shift, and she didn't need Brett's assistance. But Brett experienced a compelling impulse to be present during one of Tom Arden's waking episodes.

Pausing outside his doorway, she stood in the darkened corridor and smiled with happiness. Tom Arden's fight to survive had been long and arduous. Everyone at St. Mary's was pulling for him. Elise had already begun to plan a celebration for the time when Dr. Arden was declared fully recovered.

"Where am I?" His voice was groggy, deep and raspy from disuse.

"There was an accident," Martha said in a soothing tone. She had explained this three times before and would explain it again as Tom moved ever closer to full consciousness. "But you're going to be all right," she added quickly, reassuringly.

"Not an accident. It was murder," he stated firmly. Then, in a confused voice, he said, "What is this tube going into my arm? Blast!"

Brett stiffened and her eyes widened. What had Arden said? Murder? Blast? Straining to hear, she edged closer to the door, her knees shaking. She placed a trembling hand against her chest, feeling her heartbeat accelerate.

"Don't be an idiot," she admonished herself. "A lot of people say blast." But she had met only one. Only one person in her life had ever used that mild expletive. And why on earth would this man emerge from a coma and mention murder?

"Try to remain calm, Dr. Arden, your doctor will arrive soon. He'll explain everything."

"Doctor?"

"Your name is Thomas Samuel Arden. You are a doctor. You specialize in children's chronic disease. You are thirty-two years old, unmarried, and you live in Denver, Colorado. You are in St. Mary's Hospital, and—"

"Is this the Fifth Choir?"

Martha paused. "This is the fifth floor, Doctor. Is that what you're asking?"

Brett sagged against the corridor wall. It wasn't possible. Tom Arden could not be her Samuel. Yet how could she explain the reference to the Fifth Choir?

"You'll regain your memory gradually, Dr. Arden, but the doctors are optimistic that there won't be any long-term loss. You probably won't remember the accident, and you won't remember this conversation, either, but you should be able—"

"Blast and double blast!"

His voice drew Brett into the doorway, where she stood, shaking and staring at him. He didn't look like Sam. His hair was not white blond and flowing, but dark and curly. His eyes were not the deep, compassionate blue that she remembered whenever she gazed at the sky. Tom Arden's eyes were a warm, dark brown, confused and slightly unfocused as he cast a bewildered look around the hospital room.

"Brett!"

Until he called her name she hadn't realized that she had moved into his room and now stood at the end of his bed. She gripped the footboard and stared at him, white-faced.

His face lit with such joy that Martha Holmes gasped in astonishment. Slapping at the tubes beneath his nostrils and hooked to his arm, he struggled to sit up, not taking his eyes off of Brett.

"How did you get here?" he asked. "Brett! Oh, God, Brett. I despaired that I would ever see you again!"

Martha Holmes looked at Brett's white face. "I didn't realize you knew Dr. Arden."

"Sam?" Brett whispered, her lips pale, her gaze riveted to his face. "Is that you, Sam?"

He was a ruggedly good-looking man, but she saw nothing of Sam's physical appearance in him. He was dark where Sam had been white and golden. Laugh lines radiated from his eyes, and his mouth was wider than Sam's. He needed a shave. But his voice was close to what she remembered, perhaps a little deeper, a little softer.

And yet . . .

And yet, she knew. She *knew* this was Sam. Paralyzed with joy, she stood at the end of his bed, staring at him, wanting it to be true.

"These blasted things!" Frustrated, he jerked at the tubes, pausing when Brett suddenly rushed to his side and placed a restraining hand on his. His hand was trembling, too.

"Don't. It's all right. Just lie back and rest."

He let his head fall to the pillow and gazed up at her with love and concern shining in his dark eyes. "Brett. Oh, my darling. Whatever did you do to get yourself sent to the Fifth Choir?"

Martha Holmes slowly rose from her chair beside the bed, looking from Tom Arden to Brett. "You should have told someone that you knew Dr. Arden!" she said in a low, sharp voice.

There was no answer Brett could make. She didn't know Tom Arden, had never met him. Yet he had called her by name.

How was that possible? How had a man she had never met been able to recognize her and call her name? Her mind raced, looking for answers.

Had Tom Arden truly died on the operating table? And then somehow, in some miraculous way, Sam had taken his place? Was the human realm the dreaded and unknown Fifth Choir that was an angel's "punishment"?

Tom Arden's doctor strode into the room, already reaching for his stethoscope. Martha Holmes caught Brett's arm and tugged her away from the bedside.

"You'll have to leave now," she said in a low voice, her eyes narrow with curiosity.

Dazed, Brett tried to see around her. "Please. Let me stay."

Smoothly, efficiently, Martha Holmes moved her into the corridor, then gently shut the door.

Bewildered, shaking with happiness and confusion, Brett waited in the hallway.

"How about some breakfast, Thatcher?" Elise asked, walking up to her, shaking the weariness out of her arms. "The next shift has arrived."

"You go ahead. I'm going to stay here awhile." Adrenaline whirled through her body, and she was as wound up as she had ever been. Incredibly, impossibly, Dr. Tom Arden was her Sam.

Elise studied her radiant face for a long moment and opened her mouth as if to ask something. Then she shrugged and changed her mind. "See you tonight."

Brett watched Elise walk away, but her mind was concentrated on trying to hear the low conversation on the other side of Tom Arden's door. Once she thought she heard him call her name, but she couldn't be certain. All she could do was wait. And hope.

"Angelo?" she whispered, wondering if he could hear her. "Tom Arden is Sam, isn't he? And this—" she spread her hands, indicating the hospital, the city, the world "—is the Fifth Choir, isn't it?"

Her heart leaped with the rightness of knowing the answer. The dreaded Fifth Choir from which no angel ever returned was the earthly realm teeming with temptations and triumphs, with justice and injustice, with joys and sorrows. Here one could find heaven or hell depending on one's choices. Here an angel could begin again along the long road to heaven.

The irony of it, the sheer justice of it, made Brett collapse against the corridor wall in dawning wonder. A marveling smile curved her lips. Where else would one send an erring angel but to an imperfect world?

All morning she waited in the corridor. The other nurses looked at her curiously as they went about their duties, but Brett didn't notice. Her heart and mind were in the room behind her.

FINALLY, IN MIDAFTERNOON, she was able to slip into Tom Arden's room. Snow slid down the windowpane. The machines monitoring his pulse and heart rate hummed quietly beside his bed. Brett stood beside him, studying his sleeping face in the wintery light.

Already Tom's face had begun to blend with Sam's in her mind. She couldn't decide if his jawline was fuller than Sam's had been, couldn't quite remember if Sam's mouth had been as sensual or as beautifully shaped. It seemed to her that many of the features she examined were the same as she remembered, but it could have been an effect of the uncertain light or even her imagination.

As she watched Tom and dared to lightly stroke his hand, he stirred, yawned and gradually awakened, gazing up at her from his pillow.

"You must be an angel," he whispered, staring at her. "Whoever you are, you're the most beautiful woman I've ever seen."

She smiled through a sharp bite of disappointment. "You don't recognize me?" she asked softly.

Sam's memories were fading. She understood that it had to happen, but she had hoped it wouldn't happen this soon. Please, not this soon.

Tom frowned, trying to concentrate. "I think we've met before, haven't we? I feel as if I know you...." Already he had forgotten that hours ago he had awakened with her name on his lips. A puzzled look darkened his warm eyes. "I know I sure *want* to know you. I feel as if I do. Your name...it's on the tip of my tongue, it's...it's...."

"Brett," she said softly, blinking at sudden tears. With every passing hour he would forget a little more of heaven and remember a little more of earth. She sat in the chair beside his bed and took his hand in hers, pressing it to her cheek.

"Brett, yes! But I think you'll always be Angel to me." He smiled, and his dark eyes examined her face as his fingers gently caressed her cheek. "This is going to sound...why do I know that you eat when you're nervous?"

"Because I do," she said, trying to smile through the tears glistening in her eyes. She lowered his hand, holding it between both of hers.

They regarded each other in the shaded light shining from his bedside lamp, studying each other's faces as if trying to recognize an old and dear friend.

"Angel, what I'm about to say is going to sound very strange." Tom rested on his pillow with his head turned toward her. His gaze caressed her face. "You and I are going to love each other, and one day we are going to be married, and we are going to have four children. I don't know how I know this, but I've never been more certain of anything in my life."

She laughed softly, and gently stroked the cheek of the man who was Sam but who was not Sam.

"I know it, too," she whispered, gazing into his loving, dark eyes. "And we're going to name our first son Sam."

He smiled at her. "Sam. Is there any special reason?"

"Oh, yes," she said softly. "I'll tell you all about it on our fiftieth anniversary."

He nodded, yawned and adjusted his head on the pillow. Before his eyes closed, he brought her hand to his chest and cradled it there. When he looked at her, Brett imagined a flash of blue in the depths of his eyes. "I know you, sweet Brett. I know about the bullet wound near your heart. I know about your sister and parents. I know how much you want a home and children. I can describe your house." He tightened his grip on her hand, and a look of confusion flickered in his gaze. The hint of blue faded. "I don't know how I know these things, but I do."

"I know that you make the best French toast in the world, and sometimes you smoke a pipe, and you think rules are made to be broken, and you can't dance."

"Right on every point." He laughed softly as his eyes closed. "I love you, Angel. Please be here when I wake up again."

Leaning, she kissed his forehead and watched him smile, then he fell asleep. Gently, she tried to withdraw her hand, but he held it close to his chest.

As the afternoon passed, Brett continued to sit beside him, watching the snow slip down the windowpanes and thinking about the future.

Dr. Tom Arden was no longer the same man he had been when he arrived at St. Mary's. And Samuel, her Avenging Angel, was no longer the same man she had known. By some miraculous intervention, the two were blending, perhaps combining the best qualities of each.

She looked at the man sleeping in the bed, and Sam's voice murmured in her memory. "Not someone to love instead of me, but someone to love alongside of me. For I will always be with you in spirit."

Her eyes filled with tears. "Goodbye, Sam," she whispered.

Tom stirred, moved his dark, curly head on the pillow, then his eyes opened and he smiled at her. "Hello, Angel," he said softly.

Brett gazed at the man with whom she would spend the rest of her life, and returned his smile. And suddenly the tears shining in her eyes were tears of happiness.

"Hello, Tom. Welcome back."

UNLOCK THE DOOR TO GREAT ROMANCE AT BRIDE'S BAY RESORT

Join Harlequin's new across-the-lines series, set in an exclusive hotel on an island off the coast of South Carolina.

Seven of your favorite authors will bring you exciting stories about fascinating heroes and heroines discovering love at Bride's Bay Resort.

Look for these fabulous stories coming to a store near you beginning in January 1996.

Harlequin American Romance #613 in January
Matchmaking Baby by Cathy Gillen Thacker

Harlequin Presents #1794 in February
Indiscretions by Robyn Donald

Harlequin Intrigue #362 in March
Love and Lies by Dawn Stewardson

Harlequin Romance #3404 in April
Make Believe Engagement by Day Leclaire

Harlequin Temptation #588 in May
Stranger in the Night by Roseanne Williams

Harlequin Superromance #695 in June
Married to a Stranger by Connie Bennett

Harlequin Historicals #324 in July
Dulcie's Gift by Ruth Langan

Visit Bride's Bay Resort each month wherever
Harlequin books are sold.

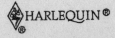

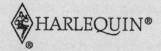

HARLEQUIN®

I N T R I G U E®

Into a world where danger lurks around
every corner, and there's a fine line between trust
and betrayal, comes a tall, dark and handsome man.

Intuition draws you to him...but instinct keeps you
away. Is he really one of those...

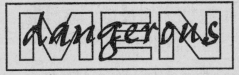

You made the dozen "Dangerous Men" from 1995 so
popular that there's a sextet of these sexy but
secretive men coming to you in 1996!

In March, look for:

**#361 LUCKY DEVIL
by Patricia Rosemoor**

**Take a walk on the wild side...with our
"DANGEROUS MEN"!**

Yo amo novelas con corazón!

Starting this March, Harlequin opens up to a whole new world of readers with two new romance lines in SPANISH!

Harlequin Deseo
- passionate, sensual and exciting stories

Harlequin Bianca
- romances that are fun, fresh and very contemporary

With four titles a month, each line will offer the same wonderfully romantic stories that you've come to love—now available in Spanish.

Look for them at selected retail outlets.

 HARLEQUIN ®